Let Me CALL YOU SWEETHEART

Let Me CALL YOU SWEETHEART

Jennifer Ann DuCharme

ReadersMagnet, LLC

Let Me Call You Sweetheart
Copyright © 2021 by Jennifer Ann DuCharme

Published in the United States of America
ISBN Paperback: 978-1-956780-82-6
ISBN eBook: 978-1-956780-79-6

All rights reserved. No part of this publication may be reproduced, stored in a retrieval system or transmitted in any way by any means, electronic, mechanical, photocopy, recording or otherwise without the prior permission of the author except as provided by USA copyright law.

The opinions expressed by the author are not necessarily those of ReadersMagnet, LLC.

ReadersMagnet, LLC

10620 Treena Street, Suite 230 | San Diego, California, 92131 USA
1.619. 354. 2643 | www.readersmagnet.com

Book design copyright © 2021 by ReadersMagnet, LLC. All rights reserved.
Cover design by Ericka Obando
Interior design by Mary Mae Romero

To my mom, who is no longer with us, for moving us around the country to instill the love of traveling.

To, my dad, my number #1 fan and to my supportive family.

I want to thank my wonderful friends, especially Lisa Johnson, Tammy Ford, Andrea Lamb, Christal Brice and Amanda DeNichols for your continuous support.

PROLOGUE

Water splashed on the panes of a six-story apartment complex situated on one of the crowded, narrow streets of Boston in the North End.

Lightning flashed across the darken sky, followed by thunder rumbling off in a distance causing the glass of the windows to rattle. It was offset by the strokes of a keyboard by its resident when the shrill of the phone aroused him from his work.

"Hello," the man barked into the receiver, evidently irritated for being disturbed.

"Hello Lopez," a course voice crackled over the line. "Is the storm bothering you? You seem a bit on edge."

"I haven't gotten much sleep lately," he explained, closing out his e-mail.

"Is your conscious bothering you?"

"Is there a reason for this unexpected call Saelac?" He ignored the last statement and got right to the point.

"We have a problem."

"Do we?" He took a sip of his coffee. "Did a client not get what he wanted?"

"This has nothing to do with a shipment," Saelac bit out. "It has to do with you."

"Did I not meet this month's quota," he said, flipping through the paper work on his desk. "You short a few million?"

"Don't get smart with me," Saelac snapped. "I just been notified of some disturbing news."

"Sorry to hear that." he drawled, in dead tone. "And that concerns me how? I'm just the middle man. I don't solve problems."

"No, you only make them." Saelac bit out. "Tell me who his Hayden Davis?"

Lopez didn't immediately respond. He lit a cigarette and placed it between his lips.

"Well Lopez. Who is he?"

"Just a client." Lopez answered, taking another draw of is cigarette and exhaling.

"Yes, a private client of yours," Saelac sneered. "From what I hear he's paying you well for *our* services." There was a brief pause. "You have been doing freelance work on the side, haven't you Lopez?"

"As the saying goes you don't put all your eggs into one basket. With the statistic's with the economy, a man like me has to plan for the future."

"I don't recall you being promoted to my position, nor was Davis put on the Payroll," Saelac sneered. "I'm the head of this operation and all transactions go through me, period. My great-grandfather didn't build this business with you in mind so you could branch off to build you a little nest egg to satisfy your champagne tastes for when you're old and grey."

"So, sue me," he challenged. "I'm a resourceful man who looks out for his own interests. You knew that when you approached me. You said I reminded you of you, that we shared the same drive and ambitions."

"That is where you are wrong." Saelac barked. "I didn't get to where I am today by making foolish decisions and being stupid. There is reason why we don't take on clientele who are a risk factor and can potentially jeopardize the organization. Davis is a perfect example. He's on the FBI's and CIA's radar which means so are you."

"Look there's always some government agency on our heels, threatening to expose us in some form or another. It comes with the territory. You know that as well as I do but I'll take care of them," Lopez reassured him. "Nothing will lead back to you. It never does."

"Again, that's where you're wrong, you imbecile! Your last business transaction with this Davis character has made you priority one," Saelac bit out. "The item you've obtain from him threatens National Security and is worth millions of dollars on the black market. They will do anything to get it back. Your stupidity has led them straight to *you* and it is only a matter of time before they uncover what other extra curriculum activities you are involved with. Do you know what will happen if that isn't rectified?"

Lopez knew exactly what would occur. If he did not end up six feet underground, he would end up in prison. He knew the risks, so did the big honcho. Like he stated there was always a threat of being put out of business, but the organization always came out untouched. The line of decedents since World War II has kept it flourishing and intact since its birth but that did not matter to Saelac. He was a paranoid old soul obsessed in preserving the dynasty the family had left behind. Lopez was tired of being the lanky and getting the crumbs on deals he brought to the table. It was why he branched out on his own and agreed to take on clientele that would be more beneficial to him and the organization.

"What would you like me to do?" Lopez asked, giving the situation much thought.

"I'm glad you asked."

Easing back, Lopez listened to the plan conjured up by Saelac, smiling to himself.

CHAPTER 1

Walking off the plane, Cheyenne Nicholas sighed in relief. She was glad to be on solid ground. She had been in the air for twelve hours, with a stopover at Heathrow airport in London.

She brushed off a few strands of ash blonde hair off her forehead and paused by a window to see the majestic snow-capped mountains of Austria in the distance. The sky was a deep blue and clear as crystal. There was not a cloud in sight. The land, what she could see of it, was lush and green. There were patches of wild flowers of every color nestled in the grassy hills. She smiled at the beauty of it. There was something graceful and simple about the scenery, even though the sense of it was overwhelming and rich in detail. She had to pinch herself to make sure was not dreaming.

Even though she traveled to many distant places outside the U.S. during her three-year employment as an international courier for *Insured Courier Services*, it felt unreal to her. She never dreamed she would visit the places she had always dreamed of going to. She owed it all to her love of languages. She had been fascinated by other cultures that she learned their languages in hope to bring their world into hers. Her appreciation was what got her the job at the locally owned based courier company in Boston. Her knowledge of languages made her a great asset and when she was not trotting over the globe, she was the office assistant to the vice-president of the company Rachel Sullivan.

Thinking about her boss brought her back to days earlier when she was called her into her office. Cheyenne had just returned from Canada on a routine job and was looking forward to the two-week's vacation, she had put in for. Little had she known her plans would be altered?

She walked towards her office and spotted Alan J. Royden, the founder of ICS and the president of the company.

Steven Alder stepping out of the boardroom with the partners. Like clockwork, Royden came in every Tuesday to meet with the heads to stay abreast with the company's interworking regardless if there was not anything to report. Royden had been at the helm since the company was erected but he had stepped down from the responsibilities of running it to enjoy the success it had reaped by becoming semi-retired. She figured it had to have been extremely hard for a man of his stature to hand over the reins to others while he enjoyed life.

Since he had no heir to groom to take his place, he had to diversify the power among those qualified. There were not many within the company that had the experience or skills to handle what he expected of them. He eventually had to hire outside the company, hiring Alder and her boss, which she knew, had to be difficult for him. These weekly visits she suspected was his way of telling people that he was still involved with the core of the company, not to forget who wrote the checks.

Upon entering Rachel Sullivan's office, Cheyenne took a seat as she normally did waiting for Rachel to tell her what she needed to say, give Cheyenne her orders and dismiss her. However, that morning her boss was silent, and quiet, which was unlike her. She usually came off straight forward and to the point.

As a woman in the business world especially at a high-level position you could not be chummy and friends with those under you. Her boss knew this and did not become personal, though she was pleasant, fair, and understanding. If she came off too shrewd and unapproachable, she would alienate herself from those she worked with. She needed to have good working relationships with the other employees to have things run smoothly. Nevertheless, she also had to be firm and decisive in dealing with how her department functioned.

Cheyenne settled into the maroon leather chair she had sat in and crossed her legs.

"You wanted to see me."

"Yes," her boss stated, closing a file on her desk. "I need to talk to you."

"About what?"

"Another courier job."

"But as of tomorrow, I'm on vacation," she reminded her.

"I'm aware of that Cheyenne and I wouldn't ask this of you if I had no choice," Her boss stiffly smiled, apologetically. "One of our biggest clients is merging with another steel corporation in Austria and there are important documents that they need to be signed by the parties involved in order for them to proceed. They cannot wait any longer. They need it done pronto."

"Can't you have Lawton do it?"

"Would I be sitting here asking you to go if he was available?"

She slumped into her chair. "I guess not."

"I know I'm asking a lot, but we're in a jam. I promise I will make it up to you when you get back."

"That's what you said last time and I'm still waiting on that promise," she said, crossing her arms.

"I clearly remember compensating you with a dinner show; Red Socks tickets and a bonus in your check."

"First of all, the dinner and tickets were fringe benefits we got from clients. And the bonus was for Christmas," she stated.

"Then I suppose we'll add this to the tab."

"But ma'am...."

"It's only a delay in your plans Cheyenne. As soon as you complete the job, you can go on your vacation."

"How long will I be in Austria," she asked relenting.

"A couple days or so. You will have to make a stop in San Antonio first and make a return trip on the way back. But that will only be a day or two, tops."

"Great," she said inwardly groaning.

"All the details are in this vanilla envelope." Her boss handed it to her. "Have a safe trip."

Her dismissal had been so final and quick that day, Cheyenne had almost thought she imagined it but here she was in the beautiful city of Vienna. She sighed thinking she should not complain. She was in Austria. She might never get another chance to visit the country so she might as well enjoy it. Sometimes you had to pick and choose. However, she really did not have a choice. Rachel wanted her to think she did but when it came down to it, she just politely manipulated her into it without having to order her to.

She stopped in front of the revolving platform where the luggage was dispersed. As hers came into view, she could see them taped up so they would not fall apart. To her luck, one of the trolley's that had been hauling the luggage to the plane in Houston had a mishap. It had made a sharp turn causing the luggage in the compartment to tumble out. They had been pinned underneath the wheels of a second trolley that followed it. The items that happened to meet this demise were hers and two other passengers.

Her trip had not started out well to begin with. Bad luck had become her middle name since she set foot in the cab to the airport. She had almost missed her flight to San Antonio because of an accident on the highway. A semi had skidded off the road into the medium blocking off lanes.

Her boarding ticket to Houston had mysteriously disappeared. In flight to Austria from London, they hit turbulence and her lunch fell into her lap. She never had such unfortunate luck. There had been minor inconveniences in the past but nothing major like the incidents that had occurred. She blamed her roommate Tamara for filling her head about superstitions before she left but Cheyenne was not the superstitious type. Things just happened and there was no rhyme or reason to them.

Humping off her bags off the loading deck, she headed out towards customs. There was a line a mile long yet it moved quickly.

After answering a few questions and giving the uniformed man behind the counter pertinent information on why she was in Austria, she made her way to the entrance of the airport.

She paused shortly to take out the confirmation slip of the hotel she was staying at so she could it convey to the cab driver. As she slipped it out, a young man, who looked like he belonged in a grudge band rudely rammed into her, knocking her clean off her feet without a word of an apology. She yelled after him but was ignored. Embarrassed she was sprawled out on the floor, she tried to stand up only to fall on her rear.

"Fraulein are you all right," a male voice asked in German, evidently concerned of her predicament.

"I think so," she replied, looking up at an elder gentleman in a dark tan suit, carrying a brief case. He had kind eyes and a stout disposition.

"Let me help you up." He extended out his hand. She grabbed it and pulled herself up.

"Are you sure you're okay," he asked, once again.

"I believe so. No broken bones," she replied, dusting off her stained blouse and trousers. "I will though have a nervous breakdown if anything else happens."

"It appears your suitcases need some special attention too," he pointed out, smiling wryly.

She glanced down to see them split apart and the contents of her purse scattered about.

"Why me," she groaned, kneeling down to gather her things.

"Let me be of service and see if lost and found has any traveling gear to spare."

"That's very kind of you but you don't have...."

"It would be my pleasure miss...."

"Nicholas," she replied. "Cheyenne Nicholas."

"What an attractive name," he complimented. "I'm Tretan Roderick."

They shook hands.

"Nice to meet you."

"Likewise, Ms. Nicholas," he responded. "I'll be right back."

She watched him walk off and thought it was nice of him to come to her aid. She did not know what this world was coming to. Little by little, the act of being civil was becoming extinct. Everyone was in a rush, having no patience or common courtesy. You open a door for a man or a woman and they just walk through not giving you the time of day. No one said thank you or was appreciative. Rudeness was taking its place. Yet this man seemed to have some decency and was not corrupted by the fast-paced world.

He returned carrying two, old, tethered cloth suitcases and set them down.

"I hope theses will do," he grinned, shrugging his shoulders helplessly, apologizing for the condition of them. "These were all they had that they could get their hands on."

"They'll do fine. I appreciate the trouble you went to obtain them for me."

"I'm glad I could help a maiden in distress." he smiled.

He bid her good-bye and she thanked him once again for his help. She hauled her bags to the nearest ladies' room and re-packed.

Thirty minutes later, she flagged down a cab and was on her way to her hotel. When the cab pulled up to the entrance of the Marriot, Cheyenne marveled at its modern exterior of tinted glass and steel bronze planks. Cheyenne thought she was looking at a giant green house than a hotel.

She did not know how right she was until she entered the Lobby. Her senses were flooded with greenery and captivating floral arrangements. Ivy hung down off each level outlining the floors. There were large round planters with an array of plants and trees. In the far left corner was a bar and in the center an open restaurant with a waterfall flowing over rocks.

She walked up to the reservation desk and checked in. The clerk's fingers danced over the computer and verified her room type. She had been expecting the usual standard room the company set up for her, but apparently, they were feeling gracious and upgraded her to a room with a view. Her boss must have had been felling guilty, she thought.

After taking care of the particulars, the clerk snapped his fingers and a bellboy was at her side, ready to be of service. He did not comment or raise an eyebrow at the condition of her bags, which she was grateful for.

Her room was a corner unit on the eighth floor. It was very spacious for a hotel room. It was furnished with non- scripted furniture. The color scheme was of neutral colors.

She tipped the bellboy and once he was gone, collapsed on the bed, exhausted. She kicked off her flats and stretched.

Closing her eyes, she thought of her brother, Shawn. She knew he would have been jealous that she was there. He had loved to ski and it had been his dream to go to Austria. She wished he were there. Her mother would say he was in spirit. She missed him terribly. He had been her best friend and he had been taken from her a few years back in a car accident. He was driving down from school over the holidays when he hit a patch of ice and lost control of his car. His loss had devastated her.

She touched the locket she wore that had his picture in it. She clicked it open and the tune *Let me call you Sweet heart* drifted out. She smiled. The song had been a favorite of their mothers. She used to play it on the piano when they were little. He gotten the necklace for their mother, but when he passed her mother gave it to her as a memento of him. She rarely took it off. There were so many nicks and scratches on it from wear. The song was even fading from its many debuts. It eventually would whine down and be no more. She dreaded that day. It would be like losing her brother again, corny as it sounded.

She stood up and went over to gaze out the window to see she had a panorama view of the inner city where the tower of St. Stephens could be seen. She sighed and said a prayer for her brother. In a way she felt what she was experiencing, he was too. It gave her comfort to believe that.

CHAPTER 2

The next morning Cheyenne awoke to the warm rays of the sun filtering in. She glanced at the clock to see it was a quarter to ten. She groaned. She was supposed to be at Krantz Steel Corporation by eleven to drop off the package. That gave her an hour and fifteen minutes to play with.

She rolled over, and sighed, thinking she would never get used to the time change matter how frequently she traveled. She suspected it was a state of mind. It was just time after all. If she could program herself to wake up one minute before her alarm went off, she could train herself to adapt to time zones.

She sat up and rolled the kinks out of her neck. She threw off the covers and proceeded to get out of bed when she caught a glimpse of a shadow lingering under the crack of her door, as if someone standing in front of it.

She eased out of bed to investigate when a white crisp envelope appeared. That is odd, she thought. Who would be leaving her notes? The hotel would just inform her of any important messages.

She picked it up and examined it. There was no writing on the envelope, but she turned it over and opened it anyway.

She withdrew the article inside and glanced over its contents queerly. She was not sure what she saw was some sort of joke but all that was written were a series of numbers in rows, spaced out like words in German. She did not know what to make of it but the more she stared at it, the more she realized the note had been written in some sort of code. Who would be sending her a coded message? The last time she saw something similar was in grade school when her friends would pass notes about boys they liked but they would encrypt them so if they fell in the hands of the teacher, they would not know what it said. She was tempted to yank the door open and look up and down the hall but she knew whoever slipped it under the door would be long gone.

Piqued in what it said, she went over to the table situated by the window. She grabbed the note pad provided and began to decipher the message.

After two failed attempts of trying figure out the numbering sequences to the German alphabet, she finally cracked it. Each of the numbers represented a letter. One represented A, and so on.

She did not quite understand the message but it read "*Priests hole, three o'clock at the tower of St. Steven.*" What that meant to her, she did not know. It sounded like prelude to a romantic rendezvous a lover might set up between him and his mistress. Since it had not been addressed to her, just slipped under her door, she had to have gotten it by mistake.

Annoyed that she spent so much time on it when she should have been in the shower, she balled up the note and threw it in the trash.

Forty minutes later, she was down in the lobby rushing to catch her cab when her phone alerted she had a text. She inwardly groaned. She didn't have to glance down at the screen to know it was from her supervisor / ex Gary Lopez. He had texted her several times since she left Boston which she chose to ignore because it had nothing to do with her job. It was personal in nature and she knew this one was as well.

Chey, Just checking in. I haven't heard from you since you left. Everything alright? Are you in Austria? Sullivan hasn't been in the office to concur. I hope you aren't dodging me love. You know how I hate that. Please call me when you get this. G.L.

She shook her head and rolled her eyes heavenward. She already confirmed her arrival with his department relaying only what they needed to know, but Gary appeared not to be satisfied with that. He had to know the specifics directly from her. God love him but he seemed to forget they weren't together anymore. Moreover, at times so did the office.

Not knowing if they were on or off, kept the gossip flowing around the water cooler. If their co-workers were not talking about the latest reality show or the world events they were trying to figure out if she and Gary were *together*. It did not take long for it to become obvious for he paid her more attention and favored her over the other couriers in his department. It made her working relations with them tense and uneasy. They tended to be resentful and frosty towards her.

Their indifference though did not stop them from talking about them and giving her knowing looks in passing. It used to infuriate her because Gary would fuel the fire by making crude remarks and hinting derogatory comments about her with other heads and employee's he hung out with off the job. She would hear bits and pieces of it as she passed through departments or when she was in the break room, when they did not know she was there in hearing distance. The ironic thing about it was there had not been anything going on between the sheets. He just piped in and told them what they wanted to hear to save face and be one of the guys.

Like any typical male, Gary wanted to take their relationship to the next level shortly after they started dating. She wanted to take things slow and not rush it. She was not like most modern woman whom could blow off the morality of it and separate the emotional from the physical. Her heart had to be fully invested first and it had not been. She had just started to get to know him and had not known really how she felt about him. In his mind, she was outdated and stifled by her *old fashion* ideals. He had told her the *Joan Clever* persona she emulated, died out with the fifties and that she needed to join the sexual revolution. He of course apologized after when she suggested they might as well break up since that if that is how he felt.

For a while, she thought things might work between them since he backed off, and tried to be satisfied in the generality of what couples do. She suspected he thought if he pacified her wishes he eventually get what he wanted but she refused to play that game.

Since his efforts did not lead them to bedroom, he became frustrated and annoyed. Her steadfast, unwillingness to explore that aspect of their relationship, had him looking for it elsewhere. Call it woman's intuition but she knew he did not stay chaste. She tried to give him the benefit of the doubt since she really had no proof, but it was obvious he did not want the same things out of the relationship as she did. Why he stayed with her as long as he did, she did not know. Maybe he thought he had the influence and talent to seduce her to his way of thinking, hoping his efforts would not be in vain. Whatever his reasonings were, she could not stay in the relationship since his concept of what he wanted out of it was carnal. She had no choice but to move on.

Her cab sat patiently at the curb as she emerged out. She gave the driver the address of Krantz Steel Corporation and settled back. The cab pulled up to a chalk white high rise in the business district of Vienna twenty minutes later. A receptionist sat behind a grey marble desk in the center of the lobby. There were two security guards causally walking around assessing the area. Cheyenne spotted only a handful of businessmen and women moving about the main floor, as she approached the receptionist desk. The pleasant young woman sitting behind it informed her, the executive offices were on the 12th floor.

She emerged off the elevator and headed down the corridor towards two tinted glazed doors that had the company's logo in gold stenciling. Underneath it, it read *The Executive Offices of Friedrich Lindbergh*.

Upon entering, her eyes were drawn to a welded steel sign mounted across the wall to her left. It was an impressive piece of work made out of scraps of steel and other metals she gathered were produced at Krantz. It appeared Lindbergh wanted to get across to those who tread through his doors that he took pride in what he did. The whole waiting emulated it. The furnishing's metal hardware in the tones of copper and silver were polished, giving the area an industrial feel. The tables were marble adorned with several articles of reading material. There was a glass sculpture of a high rise in the center of the coffee table. The crisp white walls had framed black and white photos of skyscrapers and other edifices in stages of production. As waiting areas went, Cheyenne thought it fit the mold of being for style rather than comfort.

She turned towards the receptionist to see the woman behind the stoic cold desk was just as uncommonly beautiful as the one down stairs.

It did not surprise her that she off set the decor. Some businesses still had the mentality that they had to have attractive secretaries on staff to appeal to the client, which did not make much sense to her. Clients would be interested in what Krantz produced, steel, not sex appeal, which the woman before her had in spades. She looked like she walked off Vogue magazine with her classic, chic looks. She had perfect skin and a model figure most women strived to have but never could achieve. She was dressed conservatively but her French cut tweed suit she wore accented her attributes. Cheyenne critically looked at herself then back at the receptionist.

There was no comparison. Her simple, no frills, gray pantsuit did nothing for her. But then again she did not dress to kill. She was just a courier delivering a package.

"May I help you," the receptionist addressed in German.

"Yes. I'm from ICS Corporation. I'm here…."

"To deliver a package right," the woman finished for her.

"Yes," showing her the item in question.

"Please sign here," the receptionist said, indicating to a sign in book situated on the edge of the desk.

Cheyenne grabbed a pen and proceeded to give her John Hancock when the woman commented, "You're early."

"Pardon?"

"Early," the woman repeated. "We weren't expecting you until…"

"Miss Hans, have you gotten hold of Nicolai Krestyanov," a deep, brisk voice announced startling them both.

Cheyenne turned to see a very striking man in a grey Italian suit standing in a doorway of an outer office that connected with the reception area. He had bluest eyes she had ever seen and hair as dark as a raven. It was such an arresting combination, that she could not help but stare.

Once the mesmerism wore off, she began to wonder if he was Lindbergh. He certainly had the air of authority in his corner and presumed in charge of things; though she was expecting him to be older, more distinguished like aged wine. Krantz was an established company that had been in business over twenty years. The man before her would have had to just graduate out of high school or started college when the company came into existence. Perhaps he was the son of the founder and took over when his father retired.

Cutting into her thoughts, Miss Hans's response brought her back to reality. "No sir. His secretary informed me he's out to lunch with a client."

"Did you try his cell?"

"Yes, but I got his service."

"Then I'll just have to crash his luncheon. Where is he dining?"

"His secretary didn't divulge that information." Miss Hans informed him.

"Then find out," he demanded.

He turned to leave but Miss Hans coughed indicating he was over looking something.

"What?"

"The courier from ICS is here," Miss Hans said, indicating to Cheyenne. It appeared that announcement caught him off guard for he did not immediately respond.

When he turned her way, she noticed his eyes cloud over and become dark, even though his other features stayed pleasant. It disturbed her. Why would her presence cause such an effect on him? It was as if her appearance was a turn off or a disappointment as if he was expecting someone else and got her instead. However, he did not want her to know that.

"Is there something wrong," she asked, feeling insulted by his prejudices.

He coughed then smiled, softening the lines around his eyes that had been more defined when he first appeared.

"No, not at all Miss......."

"Nicholas," she finished for him. "Are you Frederich Lindbergh?"

"No I'm not, I'm Vincent Dmitri. I am the acting laissez for Krantz and Hurst Industries," he answered, leaning against the door jam.

"You're negotiating the merger."

"Correct," he said. "And those documents you carry will get us one step closer to finalizing the deal, so I appreciate the effort of ICS has gone to, to get them to us."

He pushed off the doorframe and took a step toward her. His chest was eye level with hers and she had to lift her gaze to make eye contact. She swallowed. Lord he was tall, she thought. She felt very small and unimportant as she blinked stupidly up at him. He was so mesmerizing that she lost her train of thought. She wondered if she was the only woman to feel its effect. She doubted it. He screamed masculinity and appeal that they would have to be dead not to be captivated by him.

She noticed that he extended out his hand for her to hand over the package, and she found herself doing just that when her fuzzy brain was jolted back to reality by the sound of a phone ringing.

She blinked. "I'm sorry, but Mr. Lindbergh is the only one I'm authorized to give the package to."

"I assure you Miss Nicholas, he won't mind you giving it to me," he said stepping closer making their proximity more intimate.

She stepped back. "That maybe so but I need to hear it from him."

"I'm afraid he's not here to confirm," he said. "You'll have to take my word for it."

Ignoring that last statement, she asked, "When will he be in?"

"That's uncertain," Dmitri stated. "Lindbergh has been unexpectedly called out of town so it could be a few days or possibly a week."

"A week," she exclaimed.

"Look Miss Nicholas, why don't we discuss this in my office," He indicated to the one behind him. "We'll be more comfortable in there."

He stepped aside and she reluctantly went in, knowing there was not really anything else to discuss.

She sat in one of the empty commercial chairs, while he settled into his black leather desk chair.

Leaning forward, she said, "Mr. Dmitri..."

"Please call me Vincent."

"With all due respect I rather not. I'm here on business not a social call," she pointed out not knowing why she felt the needed to put him in his place.

"I'm aware of that, Miss Nicholas, but under the circumstances we don't have to be formal with each other," he stated, his voice calm and cool.

Her eyes narrowed in contempt, knowing he meant that as an insult because of her position at ICS as if she was some mere common servant. His blood was blue, hers not. She stood.

"Mr. Dmitri since Mr. Lindbergh has been indisposed I should take leave and call my boss on the next course of action."

"As I have mentioned Lindbergh has no problem with me receiving any parcel matter how sensitive or confidential it is in his absence," he said with authority. "I'm the one who is negotiating the terms and will be looking over those documents before the partners sign it."

"That maybe so but I still need verbal or written confirmation from Lindbergh stating as much."

He leaned back, "You don't trust me?"

"This has nothing to do with the fact if I do or don't trust you. It is company policy, plain and simple. Your name is not listed on the manifest as one of the authorized personnel."

She noticed that little detail irritated him. It was not her fault that her company had certain protocols they followed or that Lindbergh was the only one listed. It was certainly odd but that was the instructions. It was possible that there was a miscommunication or an error on the manifest, but she couldn't determine that until she spoke with Sullivan. Secondly, why they had not notified her boss that Lindbergh had been called out of town for whatever reason, she did not now. If they had, certain steps would have been made. It was the most logical and sensible thing to do. Lindbergh must have had to leave some sort of instructions on how to deal with problems that would develop in his absence after his hasty departure. He had to be in constant contact. His company was in the middle of conducting a major deal that would affect the future of the company. He just would not leave it in the hands of the board or the laissez.

Dmitri eased back in his chair, and put his hands behind his head. He stared at her for a moment, roaming over her, mentally recording what he liked and did not like. She found it infuriating and he knew it.

"How long will you be in Austria, Miss Nicholas," he asked becoming serious.

"It depends on how long it takes to resolve this matter."

"A couple days then?" he assumed.

"Is that how long you think it's going to take?"

"Possibly," he smiled. "Do you have any plans while you're here besides business?"

"Not particularly," she answered, finding these lines of questions odd.

"In that case, are you busy tonight?"

"Uh..no," she replied becoming uncomfortable.

"Perfect," he grinned. "How about dinner?"

"Dinner," she repeated taken back.

"Yes, you do eat, don't you?"

"Uh...yes but.."

"Great! Shall we say seven o'clock?"

"Uh..err..."

"You know, let's make it eight. I have a four thirty meeting with the board and knowing it'll be a long one."

"Mr. Dmitri-"

"Call me Vincent," he reminded her.

"Okay, fine, Vincent," she started only to be silenced by the buzz of the intercom.

"Excuse me." He pressed a button."Yes Miss Hans, what is it?"

"I'm sorry to bother you sir, but I've tracked down Krestyanov for you," she reported.

"He's on the way back to his office."

"Thanks Miss Hans."

He stood and slipped a pile of files into a brown leather brief case. He paused and looked at her.

"I hate to rush off like this, but I've got to see this guy," he rushed on, putting on his jacket. "I'll see you tonight."

He started to leave but then stopped as if he forgot something.

"I don't know where you're staying," he commented realizing that would be a problem. "Just relay the information to my secretary."

"But..."

She fell silent, staring at him perplexed, knowing it was useless to try to continue to talk to him. He just walked out ending their conversation abruptly without giving her a second glance. It irked her he did not let her get a word in edgewise. He just took it for granted she would go to dinner with him. The nerve of him!

She stood up and strolled out, feeling as if she was just walked all over and she did not like it one bit.

CHAPTER 3

Cheyenne paced back and forth across her hotel room, debating if she should appear ready and waiting for Dmitri. He had phoned earlier to verify the time he was picking her up and that evening would be formal. How formal, he did not divulge. If they were just going to dinner she thought a simple dressy black dress would suffice. The problem was she did not pack any formal wear. She had not planned on going out to town let alone on a date, if that's what it was, with an arresting, infuriating businessman.

She stared at her clothes scattered about her bed and groaned. She had nothing appropriate to wear and she could not afford to go to one of the boutiques in the hotel to find a suitable outfit. She knew she would pay an arm and leg for something halfway decent. Moreover, to find a bargain at any other shop she could find on short notice would take hours she did not have.

She sat down on the bed feeling dejected. She should just call the arrogant man and make up some excuse why she had to cancel. She doubted he would buy it. He seemed very perceptive of people and would see right through her lie like an hourglass. She wasn't sure if that was good or bad.

She stood up and began pacing wondering what she should do. She could always buy a dress then return it. However, that would be dishonest and it would distract her to no end. She continued to ponder when it hit her. She could rent a dress.

"Idiot," she muttered.

She picked up the phone and dialed the front desk. The clerk referred her to a shop tucked away in a remote area in Vienna, situated down a narrow but cozy alleyway.

She browsed, flipping through dresses on the racks, not really finding anything that appealed to her. She was about to give up when her eyes rested on a dark purple cocktail dress made out of a light silk material. She took it off the rack and went into the dressing room.

She stood in front of a full-length mirror analytically studying herself. She did not look half-bad she mused. It flowed over her nicely and fanned out slightly on the bottom. It was flirty, classical, not too seductive or flashy. The bodice was V cut and enhanced what little bosom she had. It would have to do. She did not have time to scour the racks for anything better.

She wished she had time to go to a tanning salon. She looked like a white ghost against the purple. She would have to add more color to her makeup regime so she did not look so drawn and pale. She noted something had to be done with her mousy brown hair. She wondered if it was possible to have her locks highlighted and styled. She glanced at her watch to see she didn't have much time to get a trim let alone a dye job before Dmitri made an appearance. If she managed it right, she probably could dye it herself to spruce it up. She just had to find a drug store and then shoes to go with the dress; a nice pair of sleek black stilettos to give her 5'6 frame some height, so she didn't look like dwarf next to his tall, broad stature.

Paying the rental fee, she headed to the closest shoe store.

She returned to the hotel, with dress, shoes and hair color in hand. Once the transformation was complete Cheyenne stared at her reflection, noticing the lighter shade she picked enhanced her deep brown eyes and added a warm hue to her fair skin. She had never gone natural blonde before but it was a good look on her.

After curling it and pinning it up, she began to put on the last details of her make-up when the phone rang. Inwardly she groaned, cursing whoever was calling and stood up to answer it. She prayed it was not Dmitri phoning to cancel. She would be sorely upset if she went to all this trouble for nothing.

"Hello," she said, a little hesitate.

"Hi my lovely," a familiar voice purred.

"Gary," she said not sure, if she was relieved or not.

"Who else would it be love," he said seductively, but in a teasing manner.

"I don't know, maybe Hugh Jackman."

He laughed. "Did you get my texts?"

"I always do Gary. You send them like clockwork."

"And you don't like that."

"It's not that I don't like it," she stressed. "It's nice of you to think of me but we've talked about this. You are my supervisor and it is not appropriate for you to be paying me special attention, especially when we are not dating anymore. *You* should not have been doing it then. If you feel the need to send me text out of politeness or kindness then you should show that same courtesy to the other couriers in your department. Not just me. There are other international carriers besides myself that go out of town like Mike, Jerry and Louise."

"First of all, I am not going to send texts to Mike and Jerry out of courtesy. They might get the wrong idea," he pointed out. "As for Louise, you can forget it. She reads enough into things that if I start sending her texts when she's out of town she'll think I'm coming onto her."

"She does kind of have a thing for you."

"Look if they make you uncomfortable, I'll just send flowers."

"Gary," she drawled.

"What, you don't like flowers?"

"You know that's not it. We aren't together anymore." She reminded him.

"You're decision, not mine?"

"Oh, come on Gary, you would have ended it eventually if I hadn't." she shot back. "You were growing tired of the chase and becoming more and more restless with chasteness of our relationship."

"That's not true. I cared about…. that is, I do care about you. That's the point," he stressed. "I backed off, gave you space and sacrificed my own selfish needs."

"Yes, but it wasn't because you had real, true feelings for me. You were hoping if you gave me things, said the right thing or acted a certain way you would eventually get me into bed but I always knew it was a put on. Your attention were not genuine or honest, and that is why we are not together anymore. Now I have to go."

"Go? Go where?"

"Out. I'm going to check out the city and it's night life."

"When were you ever into the club scene or checking out hot spots?" he questioned. "You preferred quiet, intimate cafes or art exhibits."

"Pardon me for having cultural and artistic tastes," she expressed. "But if you must know, I'm not going clubbing or to a dance club, though they do have museums and art galleries here I can explore but that's beside the point. I'm actually, going on a date."

She was not actually sure if she was really looking forward to it or not. Dmitri intimidated her and she did not like his *'I do not take no for an answer'* attitude. Why he asked her out to begin with puzzled her. It did not make sense unless he considered it a business date in which he was going to manipulate the situation into his favor. It sounded like something the man would do.

"You've been in Austria one day and you have a date," he questioned. "He must be something else for you to agree to go out with him on the first try. You turned me down four times before you agreed to have coffee with me. What is he, a man of the cloth?"

"No," she snapped thinking Dmitri was far from being virtuous and abstinent. "He's the laissez for Krantz and Hurst."

"The laissez? I didn't know they had someone negotiating the merger."

"Apparently they do," she countered. "His name is Vincent Dmitri."

"Dmitri," he repeated rolling it off his tongue. "Did Lindbergh introduce you to him?"

"No…he was just there. He's apparently using one of their offices for the merger."

She explained the circumstances of how they came to meet, and about Lindbergh's unexpected absence.

"I wonder what could have happened that Lindbergh would drop everything and leave?" Gary pondered. "It's awful strange."

"Maybe there was a family emergency," she reflected. "Who knows but his absence has complicated things. I cannot deliver the package now until he has contacted and made aware either that he has to authorize the board or Dmitri to accept it. I tried to get in touch with Rachel to get it rolling but Denise said she'd be out all day."

"She was out with the partners all afternoon." Gary reported. "Then she had business to discuss with Royden."

"That explains why I couldn't get her on her cell."

"I'm sure it will be taken cared of by this time tomorrow," he said, confidently.

"Now what is this Dmitri guy like? Is he a boring, stuffy fellow or he is still wet beyond the ears?"

"I don't know," she said, getting frustrated. "I've just met him."

"But that didn't stop you from agreeing to go out with him."

"It's just dinner, not a life time commitment," she argued. "And secondly what I do on my personal time is none of your business. Not anymore."

"Again, your choice but maybe that's because the reality of it is, is that I really never did it for you. You did not have chemistry with me. That would explain your reluctant to immerse yourself fully into the relationship. You have to have a balance of both for it to work."

She rolled her eyes. "Good night Gary."

Why did men always blame it on the woman or chemistry when the woman refused them physically? Just because she had chosen to stay virtuous throughout their relationship, did not mean she had not been attracted to him. She was just being wise with her choices. It showed how small-minded and clueless he was.

Shaking off her anger, she grabbed her purse and scurried out the door. She heard the elevator chime and called out to the person stepping on to hold the door.

Once in the lobby she scanned the area to see if she could spot Dmitri but he was nowhere to be seen. She checked the bar and the lounge, but he was not there. His meeting probably went over longer than he expected. Here she was worried about keeping him when it turned out she would be the one waiting.

"Miss Nicholas," a voice said from behind her.

Startled, she bolted around to see an older gentleman whom she assessed was a chauffeur. He fit the bill to a tee with the cap and dark attire.

"I'm sorry," he apologized. "I didn't mean to scare you, Ma'am."

"That's quite all right," she expressed a little flustered.

"I'm Mr. Dmitri's driver, Hubert Grace," he explained giving her a gentle smile.

"He's waiting for you in the car."

"Oh." was all she could say.

Why he did not meet her himself, only one could wonder but she had a feeling it had to do with his arrogant nature of *I do not come to you, you come to me* mentality.

"Please don't be offended, Miss Nicholas. The reason he didn't personally meet you, is because of an important call he had to take," Hubert said as if he read her thoughts.

"I see," she said chiding herself for prejudging the man.

"Are you ready?"

"Yes, of course," she answered following his lead.

He opened the door for her and stepped out to see a white stretch limousine parked at the curb. The back door opened and out stepped Dmitri, looking dashing and devastatingly handsome in a pressed European black suit. She never thought anyone could look so enticing in a get up like that. It amazed her how clothes added to a person's appeal. She swallowed hard as he came closer.

"Miss Nicholas I must say you look beautiful, if you don't mind me saying so," he grinned admiring how her dress showed off her figure, his gaze resting on her hair. "The lighter color suits you. I've always heard blondes have more fun." He smiled.

She let out a short laugh and murmured, "Thank you."

She slid into the limo and he soon followed.

"We're dining at *Sirks*. It's in the Bristol Hotel," he told her as he poured her a glass of champagne. "Then we're taking in an Opera at the Vienna State Opera House"

"An Opera," she said in wonderment.

"Yes. The Opera is called Die Fledermaus . It's about…."

"But do you think I'm dressed right for a night at the Opera," she said worry evident.

He smiled. "It's perfect. I like it. Isn't that what's important?"

She let out another short nervous laugh and took a sip of her champagne.

The limo came to a halt shortly after and Herbert opened the door for them.

They entered Bristol Hotel and made their way over to Sirks. They were shown to a private table upstairs overlooking the Vienna State Opera House.

A waiter set down two menus.

"I'm Clovis. I'll be your server tonight. Is there anything I can start you off with? Perhaps drinks?"

"Yes. Can we see your wine list please," Dmitri said.

"Of course," Clovis said. "Would you care to order an appetizer?"

"No thank you." Cheyenne replied without thinking.

She cringed when she realized she made a blunder. She was used to declining that request because on most occasions she dined alone. It just showed how pathetic her social life had become. She gave him an apologetic look, chastising herself for being a dunce. Ever since she laid eyes on Dmitri she's felt inadequate and self-conscious as if her conduct and behavior would have great impact on his opinions of her. It was ridiculous. He meant nothing to her, so why should she care what he thought of her.

She noticed the waiter look inquiringly at Dmitri for a second motion on the subject. He was silent for a moment, contemplating it.

"I believe we'll pass. We want to save room for dessert." He smiled wickedly at her and she glanced away in disgust. She stared out the window feeling a pit form in her stomach. He was another Gary, out for a good time, she thought miserably.

Once the waiter left, she felt obliged to apologize and change the subject.

"Mr. Dmitri..."

"Please call me Vincent," he proposed interrupting as he leaned forward, placing his elbows on the table. "You seem to have difficulty in addressing me by my first name. Why is that, too personal for you?"

"No, not really," she lied.

"Why then be so formal?"

"It's out of habit, I guess. I don't normally socialize with people I.....that is ICS does business with."

"Why not?"

"Because that's how I like it," she said. "I don't mix business with pleasure."

"Too conflicting," he prodded.

"You can say that."

"Do you go out at all?"

She gave him a look and quickly added, "I mean with people you work with, other couriers."

She was about to answer when Clovis returned with the wine list. Vincent, she decided to refer to in her thoughts, scanned the list and picked out his choice. Clovis returned moments later with the selection and poured them each a glass.

"Are you ready to order?" Clovis asked.

"Give us a few more minutes."

"As you wish sir."

"Where were we," he asked more to himself than to her.

"You asked if I socialize with my colleagues."

"Right," he said taking a sip of his wine. "And do you?"

"Sometimes but not often," she answered. "Our schedules often don't coincide."

"Are you married?"

"No," she replied not liking where their conversation was going. It was obvious she was not.

"Boyfriend?"

"Only imaginary ones," she joked wishing he got off her personal life as she roamed over the menu.

He laughed. "What are you going to have?"

"I think the stelze."

He signaled Clovis. "We are ready to order. I'll have the Baurenschmus."

"Very good sir," he said. "And the lady?"

"She'll have the Stelze," he replied before she could.

Clovis nodded, gathered the menus and departed swiftly as he came.

"I'm must say I'm impressed with your German," he complimented changing the subject. "I suspect you are required to speak a variety of languages because of your profession."

"Yes, it does help when I'm jet setting to different parts of the world."

"What other languages do you speak?"

"Russian, French, Spanish and a little of Italian."

"I'm impressed even more," he said saluting his glass to her.

He recited a poem in French that left her memorized. The dialect rolled off his tongue so eloquently it was as if it was his primary language.

"That was beautiful."

She smiled thinking he was not at all what she suspected. He was definitely an enigma. One moment he is egotistical and intimidating then the next, he is charming and easygoing. It baffled her the way he changed moods.

It was apparent when they first met her presence put him on edge or at least that was how she took it. He had purposely set out to put her in her in place. He wanted to ruffle her to see what made her tick. Why she had no idea? Maybe he was this self-absorbed jerk who wanted to show he was in control and could make anybody jump at the snap of his fingers. As for asking her out to dinner, she was still trying to figure that one out.

"What made you want to study different languages?" he asked, breaking into her thoughts.

"Growing up, one of my dreams was to travel the world," she said. "I thought learning other languages would bring me closer to the countries I wanted to visit. In actuality it was a hobby I picked up."

"It seems your *hobby* paid off for you're working for a company who has you traveling all over the place. It's ironic in a way."

"I guess it is, but I didn't apply for this job."

"You didn't."

"No. I applied for an unimportant job in the mail room."

"Really?"

She nodded. "What about you?"

"What about me," he asked.

"Why did you learn French and German?"

"To impress a girl in college," he answered, honestly. "She was an exchange student, Josette Roux."

"Was she impressed?"

"Are you?"

"I'm irrelevant."

"I don't think so. I think you are very relevant." he said, pointedly, his eyes conveying so. "You sell yourself short."

She smiled nervously, not agreeing or disagreeing with his assessment. She took a sip of her wine and sat back.

"You have a unique name," he complimented moments later, changing the subject once again, noticing his attentions were a turn off. "What made your parents pick the name Cheyenne for you?"

"My great grandmother had said our ancestry went back to the Cheyenne Indian Tribe," she said, sitting back. "An ancestor supposedly had married a Cheyenne Indian. She also claimed we were related to Pocahontas, so who knows if any of it is true, but it really doesn't matter." She paused taking another sip of her wine before continuing. "Before I was born, my parents did a lot of hiking and back packing. One year they had taken a camping trip to the Cheyenne Mountains in Colorado. They went off exploring one afternoon, gotten off the beaten track and were caught in a hailstorm. Since it was late in the day, they unrolled their sleeping bags and ended up sleeping out there that night."

He smiled. "And when you were born your mother remembered what your Great-grandmother had said and the Cheyenne mountains, and called you Cheyenne."

She nodded. "Do you have any brothers or sisters?"

"Yes," she replied suddenly becoming despondent. "I had a younger brother. He was killed two years ago in a car accident."

"I'm sorry," he said quietly reaching out for her hand to lend comfort. "I didn't mean...."

"It's okay, you didn't know. Even though he's gone, I carry him with me here," she said pointing to her heart. "and here."

She held up her locket. "My mother gave me this after he died. He had given it to her as a present but she felt I should have it. I place his picture in it in hopes to keep his memory alive. I know that sounds silly but..."

"No, it doesn't," he firmly declared touching her cheek, gently caressing it with his hand. "My daughter keeps a..."

"Your daughter," she said jolting back as if she was burned.

"Yes," he said regrettably. "Her name is Samantha. She's eleven."

"Then you're...."

"Divorced," he finished for her.

"Oh," she responded, feeling the knot in her stomach unwind and subside. She quickly eyed his hands to see if there was any evidence of a missing wedding band and noted in relief there was not any.

"That pleases you, doesn't it?"

"Whether you're married or not isn't any of my concern," she stated. "We're just business associates out to dinner."

"But the fact that I'm not does ease your mind," he argued.

"Listen Mr. Dmitri, I appreciate...."

"It's Vincent," he stated, evenly.

"Vincent," she corrected. "As I was going to say, I appreciate the evening out but I'm here on business pure and simple."

"As am I?"

"If that's the case," she said, calling him on it. "you must have some news to report on how we are to proceed with the situation. Have you contacted Lindbergh?"

"Yes, but he wasn't available."

"Not available," she questioned.

"That's correct."

"When we'll he be available," she asked, irritated at his answer.

She did not know why it matter to her they took their precious time on the resolving the matter. It did not concern her. She was just the messenger. She realized it had to with the man before her.

Having to deal with him was frustrating and nerve racking. His attentions disturbed her and made her uncomfortable. With the exception with Gary, men did not seek her out especially one's she met on her travels.

"Look I'm sorry this has been an inconvenience for you," he said, pointedly. "But we are doing the best we can under the circumstances. It could take a day or a week to resolve it but it will be done. I apologize if that is not to your liking or time frame but if you had handed over the package to me in the first place we wouldn't be here."

"This is not my fault," she stressed. "I was following procedures."

"Yes, I know and I apologize," he said. "Placing blame isn't going to make it go any faster, so we should take advantage of it. Vienna has a lot to offer. Have you done any sightseeing since you arrived?"

"No."

"I can show you around if you like," he said as Clovis appeared with their meals.

"That's very kind of you, but I think I can manage on my own."

"You don't have to be afraid of me," he said, quietly leaning forward. "I'm not going to bite."

She smiled at that. "I appreciate the gesture really, but you don't have to entertain me."

"I don't mind at all. It would be my pleasure. And secondly it's more enjoyable and fun seeing Vienna with someone else."

"True, but don't you have to work. I'm sure you're quite busy with the merger."

"Well, there isn't much I can do at this point until the papers are signed and returned to Hurst," he said, cutting his steak. "Everything is on hold until then."

"You must have other obligations, meetings, phone conferences and such."

"Nope," he said. "My calendar is free-at least for the moment."

"You're not going to take no for an answer are you?"

"I wouldn't be in the business I'm in if I did," he commented. "I'll pick up around eleven thirty tomorrow morning."

It appeared the decision was final for he moved onto another subject.

CHAPTER 4

Sitting back, Cheyenne began to unwind and relax as Dmitri dominated the conversation, his deep, baritone voice sooth the tension from her body. She listened attentively as he spoke tidbits of his life but his travels were what captivated her the most. He told her after collage he took off a year to back pack across Europe using the money he saved to buy a car. He managed to live off it for three months then he had to find work to support himself. He might stay in one place for a few days, others weeks, even months. He seemed to know what parts of his travels would hold her attention and he was very detailed when he described a place; whether it was the lands itself, its people or the day to day experiences like watching Egyptian women wash their laundry in the Nile.

And unlike her, he learned several of languages because of circumstance. It was inevitable he would pick up a little of the local language if he was there for an indefinite amount of time. His knowledge of languages is what had helped him in his field. She found it interesting and a bit…ironic that in some ways their history paralleled with each other on that note.

Looking at him now, she thought, he certainly came across as the ideal package if one was looking for that *one*. Whether it was all for show, or not, he sure did it well. He would be a historical romance novelist's dream. He had all the characteristics and aristocratic good looks of an era that had long time passed. He had that mysterious, dangerous look about him that appealed to so many women. Unfortunately, he seemed to know it too.

It was also obvious he was the type who liked to be in control and in charge, no matter if it was business or socially related. He wanted to be the one holding the cards. Something told her it went beyond being a personal trait that had been formed and harden by some past heartache or painful experience. He did it on purpose. How she knew this, she didn't know? She just sensed it. She had always had the unique ability to see right through people since she was a child. She found it easy to read people. However, if she was honest with herself, Vincent Dmitri, was not exactly an open book. There were certain things about him that could not be perceived or understood, like his unexpected interest in her. Men of his statue normally overlooked her, and did not consider her worth their time.

What was his game, she wondered? Was he some Don Juan who hit on women no matter what position they held or were they for his own amusement or was it out of obligation and guilt? She doubted it but it seemed the most logical reason.

She was aware he had stopped talking and noticed he stared at her intently as if she was a specimen that needed to be analyzed. It annoyed her. What could he possibly find so appealing to look at her in such a manner?

Vincent could tell she did not like how he openly studied her, which surprised him. Most women he came in contact with didn't shy away from his intimate appraisal but lapped it up like one would a pretty trinket they desired. They never were embarrassed by it. She must not be used to having men admire her in such a way. It was as if she knew of worldly things but was not a part of them herself. One did not find that kind of innocence and purity in a woman in today's society often. He found it oddly enticing.

She was going to be a challenge he knew that, but he liked women who were.

It made the pursuit even more gratifying. Secondly, he always got what he wanted, matter it be man, beast or the fairer sex.

His eyes roamed over her, taking in the elegant but unpretentious dress that flowed over her body like a second skin, yet it disguised her form subtly. It was modest in designed-at least to today's standards but it was sexy as hell. It showed enough to tantalize the senses but not to overload them. It left mystery, which was more enticing than the dress itself. The silky material it was made out of called out to him to touch and run his hands over. The purple color was an exotic contrast to her snowy white complexion. Her alluring fragrant hair which she lightened, were curled in corkscrew curls that flowed over her delicate shoulders. She had it pulled back with barrettes adorned with diamonds. He loved how the wispy curls that had escaped, framed her face.

Then there were her beautiful brown eyes that called out to him. They had their own personality and spark even though they were in tuned with her emotions, as if they were a window to her soul. They changed with her moods. When she smiled, they twinkled. When she was angry or annoyed, they deepened in color. When she blushed, they became a glassy color like crystal. He wondered what they would do in the heat of passion. Would they smolder into a shade of amber or would they turn opal like a semi-precious stone?

He saw her cheeks turn scarlet. She knew what he was thinking and he chastised himself for it. He was going to scare her off if he continued lusting after with his eyes. She already detested his behavior toward her and if he were not careful, he would blow it. He could not afford that. He had to play it cool and gain her trust before he made his move.

After dinner, they headed over to the Vienna State Opera House.

As they walked up the grand staircase to their seats, Cheyenne gazed upon the interior in awe. She felt she had been transported back in time. She was flooded with images of what it must have been like in Shakespeare era and Queen Victoria's reign. She could just imagine the drama that took place to where she could feel the excitement and anticipation of the individuals who had experienced them before hand.

They sat up in a balcony away from onlookers. The Opera began and she became lost in it. The music was potent and alive it consumed her. She did not even have to understand the words, even though she did. The expressions on the actor's faces and their movements were so defined that what was being presented came through clearly.

Heading back to her hotel, Vincent offered her a glass of wine and she said, "Are you trying to get me drunk?"

"No of course not," he said, sounding insulted. "Even if I wanted to I wouldn't have to. You are already drunk from the opera."

"You can't get intoxicated by experiencing the beauty of music and movement," she stated.

"Yes you can," he argued. "It is a different type of intoxication. It is not a chemical reaction but an emotional one that touches your soul leaving you this utopia state which sometimes alcohol does. Only difference is it is not as gratifying and you do not have a hang over the next morning."

"Then I'm going to have a double dose of it if I keep consuming this wine," she said. "This will be my third glass."

"We'll just have to suffer together then," he grinned. "I'm just as intoxicated. But not from the wine or the opera but from you which I've been drinking in all night."

She gave a little nervous laugh. "You're good, you know that. You must have learned from the masters. Did they give you some secret manual on how to seduce..."?

She did not get a chance to finish for his mouth came down on hers silencing her.

Her whole body automatically stiffened and coiled. His onslaught had her drowning in potent sensations that frightened and surprised her. She seemed to liquefy in his embrace.

He withdrew, leaving her dazed and confused as the limo came to a halt. What had just happened, her fuzzy mind questioned? It had to be alcohol she concluded. It had to be for her to respond to him so easily. Secondly, she was not in the habit of making out with men who she just met.

Suddenly the confines of the car seemed too much to bear. She fumbled for the door handle. She had to get out of there and gather herself.

"Cheyenne," he breathed, clasping her hand.

"I.... good-night, Vincent."

With that, she shoved opened the door and scrambled out of the car.

Once her feet hit the pavement, she rushed towards the entrance of the hotel. She did not notice Vincent had followed her until she stepped onto the elevator. He placed his hands on the doors preventing them from closing and joined her.

"What are you doing?"

"Don't you know it's proper for a gentleman to escort a lady to her door after taking her out," he said.

"If you think I'm going to invite you in for a night cap you're in for a rude awakening," she stated, moving away from him.

"That was not my intention," he stressed. "What happened in the car was a natural thing to occur. It was instinct, not seduction."

She begged a differ and gave him a look that expressed it.

"I'm not naïve, Mr. Dmitri," she stressed. "Nor am I stupid. I might be a little tipsy but I know what you are after. I know the signs because my ex-boyfriend is just like you."

The elevator chimed and she proceeded off.

She walked ahead hoping he got the message their association ended there but he caught up with her moments later.

She grumbled under her breath searching for her card key wishing he would leave her alone.

Couldn't he take a hint?

She stopped in front of her room when he cupped her elbow and turned her around to face him. Her eyes held contempt as she stared up at him. It appeared he was not going to give up easily.

"Listen I'm sorry," he said honestly. "If I came on too strong, I apologize. You weren't what I expected and I couldn't help myself."

He stepped closer, eating up the space between them. She grew rigid and straightened her back wondering what he meant by that when he said, "You don't have to be afraid of me. I'm not here to hurt you."

He gently caressed her face before claiming her mouth once again to prove his case.

He pressed her up against the door as he kissed her thoroughly. She felt her stomach tighten and her knees go weak. Her nails dug into his shoulders blades as the sweet havoc he created swelled inside her. She cursed him because he was trying to break her defenses with his seductive kisses.

He released her. "Until tomorrow."

She blinked up at him and he smiled. He gave her another searing kiss and took leave.

She stood there transfixed, wondering what the matter with her. Gary never had this effect on her. Not that she was comparing the two, but he never left her breathless or confused, nor did any other man. She felt ashamed she enjoyed being with this man, this virtual stranger.

What was happening to her? This was why she was not with Gary because he based their relationship on physics. The chemistry between two people could only go so far and Vincent was not going to be a permanent fixture in her life. Nor was he going to be some cheap fling she had while out of town. She was not into one-night stands and she had to make that clear to him.

She nudged the door open to her hotel room and stepped over the threshold only to stop short.

"Oh my god," she exclaimed, eyes going wide at the sight of her ransacked room. "What the…"

The words escaped her as she felt her legs buckle. She cried out for Vincent, as she slumped to the floor.

CHAPTER 5

Vincent had just entered onto the elevator when he heard his name echoed down the corridor. He pushed the button to open the doors, but they did not respond. The elevator began descending so he pushed the button for the next floor. When it stopped, he rushed out and headed for the exit.

Shoving the door open, he proceeded up taking two at a time. He reached her room moments later to see it trashed but no signs of her. He stepped further into the room and heard noise coming from the bathroom. He turned to see the door ajar and pushed it opened. Cheyenne was hunched over the toilet, gripping the rim. He gave her a moment and went to back out to see what the damage was to her room. Her friendly intruder did a number on the place. He certainly knew his trade. Nothing was missed. It appeared from the looks of it he was looking for something. Drawers were pulled out and dumped; papers and magazines were scattered about; the pillows and cushions were slashed opened. The bed was turned over and dissected.

The intruder had gone through all her belongings only taking certain valuables. It told Vincent that their intentions were not solely on stealing and selling what they obtained for a few bucks. It was made to look like your typical larceny job. They were looking for something specific and he had a good idea what that was and it angered him.

He dug into his back pocket and retrieved his cell. He flipped it opened and began dialing security when he noticed Cheyenne emerge from the bathroom. She groaned and glanced around taking in the chaotic surroundings. It looked worse than she had recalled. Her gaze met Vincent's and she felt nauseated all over again.

"I'm sorry."

"Sorry, sorry for what? Your room was burglarized," he stated, matter of fact.

"I don't mean that," she said, glancing around the chaotic surroundings. "I meant the scene in the bathroom. I am sorry you had to witness that. I guess the wine and the rich food didn't agree with me."

"It's no big deal Cheyenne," he commented. "It happens to the best of us."

She sighed heavily. "I can't believe this. This is a nightmare."

She slumped into the only chair that had not been sliced and ripped apart.

"It's going to be okay," he reassured her, flipping open his cell once again and dialing security.

After being questioned, Cheyenne sorted through the mess to see what was salvageable while Vincent dealt with any other details that needed to be tended to. Tallying the items and articles that was damaged and stolen for the insurance company, was a tedious job. She could not think straight for one and could not remember clearly, what she had brought with her to calculate the loss. If Vincent had not been there to take control nothing would have been done or ran smoothly as it did. He just took command and took over. She did not know how he did it. He had to be exhausted after working all day and entertaining her for the evening, but there he was dealing with her problems.

It was close to two in the morning by the time things were settled. She was half-asleep. She wanted to fall into bed and know no more until morning.

The hotel set her up in another room, a suite that was a size of an apartment. She was too tired to admire it. She sluggishly walked into the master bedroom and sat on the plush, rich, brass bed.

She slipped off her heels and relaxed back, wishing to God she could go through another day without something horrible happening. She never had this much bad luck and misfortune in her life.

Had her roommate been right? Was there some force at work here making her stay in Austria miserable? No, that was ludicrous. The only way black magic or witchcraft could exist is if you believed it and she did not. There might not be a logical answer for it but whatever was behind it, she thanked God she had Vincent. He had been the only good thing that came out of it. She was still leery of him but nonetheless it was hard not to like him.

She sat up and started to undress. She began to unzip it, when she heard the outer door in the living area open and close.

Vincent strolled in moments later just as she zipped it back up. He carried the unattractive, worn, cloth suitcases she obtained after her incident at the airport.

Did she forget to lock the door? She did not recall the manager giving him a key, she thought as he set them down.

"How did you...."

"Get in," he finished for her taking a seat next to her.

"Yes."

"You didn't shut the door all the way," he answered.

Her eyebrows went up at that. "If I had left it open, it was an oversight. No offense."

"None taken," he said.

"It's just I didn't expect you to follow. I thought you had left."

"I couldn't leave without bringing your clothes to you," he commented. "Hotel security has taped your room off and I don't think you want to go back there in the morning in a towel. Nor go sightseeing in that snazzy frock your wearing."

She smiled. "No, I wouldn't."

"Would you like me to put these on the dresser," he asked standing up.

"How about the closet," she said. "I wouldn't want to insult the dresser."

"Not too fond of your traveling gear, eh?"

"I know it's ridiculous and snobbish, but I'm embarrassed to be seen with them."

He smiled at her. "You like the finer things, do you?"

"When it comes to my luggage, yes," she said. "I don't want you thinking I'm some material girl."

"So, if a man showered you with diamonds and expensive trinkets, you would refuse them?"

"It would have to depend on the occasion and the meaning behind it," she said. "Flowers can be as valuable as jewels because of the intent behind it."

He did not comment but stared at her in wonderment.

"What," she asked.

"Nothing," he said. "Is there anything else I can do for you?"

"You've already done a great deal as it is. I would not dream of asking anything else of you," she said. "You've been gracious enough tonight."

Unconsciously, she placed her hand over his in a thankful gesture. She started to withdrawal when he captured her hand in his. He turned it over, placing his mouth on the softness of her palm, kissing it.

Her stomached tighten as the sensations of the physical contact, rioted through her. He reached for her and sought out her lips with his own. He pulled her close, his hands caressing her as he urged her to return his desires with his sensual kisses.

She was suddenly lost in his arms, drowning in the sensual sensations he erected that coursed through her body. Any sense of morality or caution was obligate.

Intertwined on the bed Vincent caressed her passionately, planting feverous kisses on her throat slowly moving downward. He pushed aside the material of her dress so he would have more access to her lovely form only reveal another barrier. He sought out the delicate straps of her bra and slid them off her shoulders.

Breathing heavily, Cheyenne came aware of his movements and was jolted back to reality.

"Vincent, please," she murmured, distractedly.

Her plea did not hinder him but told him something else. He slid one of his hands up her thigh pushing up the hemline when her hand snaked out to stop him.

"No, please don't."

Her outcry stilled him. He gazed down at her transfixed and saw the panic in her eyes. He rolled off her and swore. What was the matter with him? He knew he was going to have to take it slow with her and what did he do? He makes a play for her after knowing her for what, a couple hours? If she's been more experienced as he expected her to be, seducing her would have been easy, but she was not, so he had to do things differently. He knew she was not afraid of him or sex. She was just hesitating because of what he aroused in her. At least that is what his male ego told him. He would be lying if he said her rejection did not bother him. He was not used to being refused or denied in that area. Not that he ever pressed a woman into doing something they did not want to do. He just never really had to. They were always willing.

He had to figure out a way to apologize without embarrassing her and scaring her off. He turned her and was about to speak when the phone rang. He swore again. "Ignore it."

"It could be something important," she said sitting up, trying to gather herself.

"We need to talk about what just happened," he stressed. "Whoever it is can call back."

"I know but it could be the office," she said.

"This early in the morning?"

"There is a seven-hour time difference," she argued as she picked up the receiver.

"Hello."

"Cheyenne?"

"Gary," she questioned, wishing she had ignored it. What in the world was he calling her for now and how did he get through when she changed rooms? The front desk must have patched him through or gave him the new room number, she thought. She hoped his call was business related or she hang up on him.

"Do you always have to sound surprised when I call," he asked.

"No, but it's almost three in the morning in Austria," she explained wrapping the phone cord around her finger. "I didn't expect to hear from you so soon after out last conversation."

She turned around to see Vincent had left. The outer door slammed. She was not sure if she was relieved or annoyed. The insane attraction they had for each other confused and disturbed her. It did not make sense to her. She was not desirable. She did not possess the outer beauty that drove men into wanting. Men usually didn't give her a second glance so why was Vincent?

"Cheyenne." Gary's voice vibrated over the line in an irritated tone. "Is this a one way conversation?"

"Huh, oh no, of course not," she replied shaking the cobwebs out of her head. "What did you say?"

"I asked you why you changed rooms."

"Because the other one was broken into," she said matter of fact, sounding more annoyed than upset about it.

"Why didn't you call me and let me know," he demanded.

"Because I didn't think about it," she snapped becoming impatient with him. "I don't have to report my every move to you. I'm not a possession of yours!"

"Aren't we in a grouchy mood," he muttered. "Did your date with the laissez turn sour?"

"What do you want?"

"A nice hello for starters."

"I'm sorry Gary if I'm being snippy and rude, but I'm extremely tired, so will you get on with it."

"Yes love," he said, holding his temper. "I have good news for you."

"And what is that?"

"Lindbergh has contacted Rachel," he answered. "You're delivery problems have been solved. You are now authorized to hand over the package to the Laissez- what's his name?"

"Vincent Dmitri."

"Right Dmitri," he said. "Anyhow Lindbergh faxed over a written authorization to her office, so you're set to go."

"That's a relief," she sighed. She would not have to deal with Vincent anymore. The news could not have come at a better time. "Thanks for letting me know."

"At least I'm good for something," he commented.

"Good-night Gary."

"Night."

Vincent unlocked the door to his suite and strolled in, in deep thought. He threw his jacket on the couch and grabbed a water out of the mini frig. He slumped down into a chair and stared at the monitor. He debated if he should turn it on when the phone rang. He swore.

"What," he said into the mouthpiece of the receiver.

"Where have you been West?" A dry voice said on the other end.

"Doing my job Stewart," he said taking a gulp of his water.

"You missed your check in and you didn't call in the recent events."

"I just returned to the room. I haven't had a chance to do a report let alone watch the surveillance footage." he said, slumping into the desk chair.

"That's not what I meant and you know it." Stewart conveyed.

"I'm sorry. I didn't have a moment to notify you. Things were a little chaotic".

"Any leads?"

"Not as of yet, but from just studying the scene it was evident it was staged to look like a typical break in. Even though some valuables and cash were taken; they were definitely looking for something pacific."

"Micro-film."

"Possibly."

"Possibly," Stewart snorted. "What else could they have been after if it wasn't the micro-film?"

"I don't know." he argued. "If she doesn't have knowledge of it, the transaction would have been completed and we would have both in our possessions but we don't."

"Exactly. It's why you're here." Stewart reminded him. "We now know she has to be working with Lopez since she doubled crossed the buyers at the airport. Tretan was evidently unhappy when it was discovered he only got half for what he or his associates paid for. The product is useless if it doesn't have the codes."

"But she doesn't fit the profile Stewart. She has no criminal record. Her finances are clean. You would think if she had a history of criminal activity there be evidence of it."

"Our INTEL is rarely wrong." Stewart reminded him. "We have her in connection with the original seller Hayden Davis. She is involved with Lopez both on a personal and business level. We have photos and documented evidence of her involvement. Then there's the exchange at the airport where she screwed over Roderick."

"But we don't know that for sure." he stated, standing up. "It's possible Lopez was aware we were onto him and used her as a diversion and there were two curriers in play, instead of one; her to lead us astray and the other to deliver the product to the buyers."

"But why would Lopez give her the essential product if he knew it would fall back into our hands."

"There's a lot that can't be explained, but just like the buyers, the program is useless to us." He pointed out. "Having it really isn't a threat unless you have the codes, especially since you can remotely upload it from any device, be a flash drive or a laptop. And since the only person who knows the key codes is dead, the micro- film is the only evidence we have that proves it exists in the real world, not someone's brain."

"I'm certain you'll be able to seduce that knowledge out of Ms. Nicholas." Stewart pointed out. "If anyone knows about it, it would be her since our recent INTEL reported that she met with the man who reportedly fused the codes onto the micro-film."

"But video surveillance can be tampered or doctored with." he argued, "Secondly she's not physically seen with him. She's only seen walking into the building and leaving."

"Yes, with Lopez not too far behind." Stewart interjected. "Not to mention the man identified her being with Lopez."

"Yes, there is that but…my gut tells me this more to this than were seeing." he stressed, running his hands through his hair. "If she had part in this, she would have taken the first flight out of here and disappeared."

"Not necessarily. Whoever she was supposed to meet at St. Stephens this afternoon could have been another buyer."

"But again, we aren't certain of that either," he said. "It's possible it was delivered to the wrong room and it was meant for someone else, possibly the other courier since there was no name on the envelope."

"Then why did she decipher the note?"

"I don't know. Maybe she was curious about it and is the type who likes riddles."

"Look Vincent our objective is to retrieve the activation codes." Stewart pointed out. "That's your focus and mission, not her guilt or innocence."

"I know that but the seduction angle isn't going to work on this one."

"Then figure out another way to close to her. You have a lot of other talents."

He did not comment and Stewart said, "Get back with me when you've viewed surveillance tapes."

"Will do."

Vincent hung up and leaned back. He turned on the monitor and replayed the night's occurrences. He noted there was only one perpetrator but he could not be identified because his face was covered with a fitted mask. He was dressed in black attire like a professional. Whomever Cheyenne was mixed up with were serious players and they would not back off until they got what they paid for. Time was running out. If he did not succeed in discovering and retrieving the codes, they would.

He wished he could survey what she was doing at the particular moment. She was probably laying there unable to sleep wishing she never met him. He knew he had blown it. There was no way he was going to be able to get close to her, at least not romantically at this point. He had to go about it another way. He had to make her come to him. She had a taste of what it would be like between them and he could use that to his advantage. He just had to play his cards right.

CHAPTER 6

Cheyenne awoke the next morning to the sound of knocking. Her eyes fluttered opened and she raised her tousled head to see it was after eight. She groaned and rolled onto her back. The knocking continued and she slowly sat up.

"Room service," a foreign muffled voice echoed.

"Room service," she questioned as she threw the covers off and slipped out of bed. "I didn't order anything."

She slipped on her robe and went out into the living area. She unlatched the lock and opened the door. A bellhop stood in attendance next to a silver cart, holding a bouquet of flowers.

"I think there has been some mistake," she said. "I didn't order room service."

"Its compliments of Mr. Dmitri Miss Nicholas," he reported.

"He's here," she exclaimed, pulling her robe tighter as she glanced out into the hall.

"No Ma'am," he responded trying to hide a smile. "Where would you like me to put this?"

"Uh...well...I guess there," she replied pointing to the table situated by the window.

He handed her the flowers and pushed the cart in. He lifted the tray covers to reveal array of food. There were pancakes, eggs, sausage, bacon, hash browns, and fruit. There was a serving of coffee and juice that he placed on the table.

"Is this to your satisfactory," he asked.

"Yes, everything looks delicious," she responded wondering how Vincent could think she could eat it all. Had she come off the night before having a big appetite?

"Would you like me to put those in water," he asked.

"No that's all right," she responded. "I can do it myself. Thank you."

"You're welcome."

He was about to take leave when she said, "Wait."

She ran into the bedroom and returned moments later with her purse. She handed him a ten and thanked him again.

She strolled back over to the table breathing in the flagrance of the flowers, as she did so. She sat down and lifted out the small card out of the plastic prongs that held it.

"Cheyenne I'm sorry, I don't know what came over me last night. Please forgive me. I know these flowers do not make up for my behavior but I hope they will give me a second chance. I still would like to show you around Vienna, if you let me. I will be down in the lobby at ten. Hope to see you. Vincent"

She walked over to the breakfast bar and grabbed the silver ice bucket filling it with water. She arranged the flowers and brought it to the table setting in it in the middle. She slid down into the chair, made herself a plate of food wondering if this gesture of an apology was sincere or just customary ritual men did to get back into your graces.

Vincent was certainly a charmer and the type who played the field. She did not trust him or his motives. She did not trust herself when she was with him for that matter. She would have to politely thank him and decline his offer but she could not do it on the phone. It would make her look like she was a coward and could not face him. It would only stroke his ego and she was not going to give him the pleasure. She had to do it in person.

She had to see him to hand over the documents for Lindbergh anyhow giving her the opportunity to set him straight.

Once she showered, she slipped on simple white blouse and tan slacks, going for the causal, business look. She pulled her hair back, into a pony tail. Simple, nor frills do. She dabbed on a little make-up and breezed out the door.

She strolled off the elevator scanning the lobby area for Vincent as she headed toward the front desk. He was nowhere to be seen. She asked the clerk if there were any messages for her and was told no. Noticing it was thirteen past the hour, she sat down in one of the sitting areas by the water fountain that was provided, wondering if Vincent was going to show.

Her fingers began drumming on the side rests of the chair. Her eyes rested on the magazines on the side tables. She picked one up and began breezing through it.

"Miss Nicholas."

She looked up to see a tall, well-built man dressed casually with a sports coat draped over his shoulder. He had a chiseled, angled face that was stern, and blank of emotion. It was apparent time had not been kind for his complexion was ruddy and splotchy like a dirt road with potholes that fell to neglect. His straw like, blonde hair was all unruly, a style popular with the twenty-to-thirtyish young men sported these days.

He did not look like he worked for the hotel. He had to be one of Vincent's messengers. It annoyed her the man couldn't pick up a phone and have the decency to speak to her directly.

She shook her head. "Yes, I'm Miss Nicholas."

"We have some business to discuss." he replied taking a step closer.

"Business," she questioned, confused. "I'm not quite sure what you mean? Are you from Krantz?"

"Don't play coy Miss Nicholas, it's very unbecoming," the man bit out which had her sinking further back into the chair. "You know why I'm here."

"I'm sorry but I don't know what you're....."

She did not get a chance to finish, for the words died on her lips. Nestled comfortable in the stranger's hand was a gun. It was obscure from on lookers by his sports coat, its deadly barrel trained on her.

She swallowed hard. "What do you want?"

"You know what I want," he snarled. "so don't play games with me, Miss Nicholas."

"I'm not," she stressed. "If I knew what you meant, I would tell you."

His features turned dark and hard. "Stand up."

"What," she said her eyes going wide.

"I said stand up," he gritted out.

Trembling, she did as he asked. He slipped his arm around her waist and motioned her forward.

"Where are we going," she asked, panic evident in her voice.

"For a walk to jog your memory."

"But I don't know anything."

"I beg a differ," he smirked pressing the gun into her ribs.

This could not be happening; it just could not be. She scanned for Vincent or anyone else who might be able to help her but she could not make any eye contact with any of guests roaming around. They were getting closer to entrance and if she did not do anything, she might never return. Think, Cheyenne think!

"I see the wheels turning in your head," he said tightening his hold on her. "If you want to live, I suggest you don't try anything stupid."

He jerked her forward through the revolving doors making her stumble. Once outside she half expected to be shoved into van and whisked away, but her captor veered her down the road towards the poorer section of town.

Panic began to escalate in her. She thought her heart would pound out of her chest at the rate it was going. Her palms began sweat. The farther they walked, the more frantic she got. She felt like she was being sucked down a black hole, getting lost in its darkness. Idiot, she thought. She should have retaliated when she had the chance but she had been too num and scared. Now it was too late.

They walked down two more blocks, when she was dragged around a corner.

When they were some ways away from the main road, she was shoved up against the wall and pinned.

"Where is it bitch," the man growled.

"Where's...what," she whimpered.

"Package," he growled. "We know you still have it."

"Package," she questioned not understanding until it hit her. Her eyes lit up. "You mean the ...package I delivered to Krantz Steel Corporation."

"No, you stupid broad," he said, looking like he wanted to strike her. "You were to supposed to give us the other half of the package St. Stephen's yesterday afternoon but failed to do so."

"St. Stephens," she said, remembering the note that had been slipped under her door.

"Yes, and from the look on your face you know what I'm talking about. "

"Only by mistake," she insisted. "I didn't decipher it because I knew about it. It was....out of curiosity that I did."

"You expect me to believe that," he sneered. "What do you play me for a fool?"

He cocked his gun and pointed it to her head.

"No of course not," her voice trembled to a high pitch. "It's just this is all a mistake. I'm not the person you think I am."

"You got that right," he bit out. "You're a two-timing thieving bitch, who's going to end up in pool of her own blood if she does not snap out of the dumb blonde act and tell me where it is."

Trying to hold down the nausea, she uttered bravely, "I'm not stupid. Even if I knew what you were talking about you would not kill me until you got what you wanted. You can threaten me all you want, but I can't tell you what I don't know."

"*Liar*," he bellowed, striking her across the face with the gun. A starburst of pain exploded followed by the warm sensation of blood.

"Your visitors last night wouldn't have come up empty handed if that were true."

She trembled "You're the one who ransacked my room?"

"No sweetheart, that was my associates work," he said. "I don't do the cloak and dagger crap. I'm just the enforcer. Now where is the micro-film?"

"Micro-film." She uttered, becoming more confused by the minute. "I don't know what you mean?"

"Listen bitch, I don't have time for your games." he said, jerking her forward and then shoving her back. "You sent us a message with the file that you had the codes and to set up a meet. You didn't show so I ask again, where is the god damn micro-film?"

"For the millionth time I don't know anything," she cried out, before breaking down.

"You are really trying my patience," he said, his hand intertwining roughly in her hair, jerking her head back. "No more stalling. *Tell me where it is!*"

"YOU!" A voice echoed from the mouth of the ally. "Step away from her!"

Cheyenne turned her head to see a policeman slowly closing in on their position. There was someone else with him hanging back but she could not make him out.

Her assailant let out a yell and shoved her down with force before breaking into a run. The police officer shouted out for the man to stop or he would shoot but that did not faze her attacker. Shots were fired and the sound of feet hitting payment echoed in her ears. She heard a ruff, out of breath voice say, "I'll take care of her. You go after him".

The next thing she knew she was being helped up and encased in strong arms. She looked up and focused in on the face that had enveloped hers. It was Vincent. He cupped her face and swore. He withdrew a handkerchief and pressed it against the gash across her cheekbone.

"Did he do that," he said, in a cold steely voice.

She nodded. "Did he hurt you anywhere else?"

He patted her down before she could reply; sighing in relief he did not find any other injuries.

Her body shook from the emotional distress and she broke down. His arms went around her and he held her until she was spent out.

"How did you know I was here," she asked, after she collected herself.

"I followed you,"

"Followed me," she said in surprise.

"Yes. I saw you leave with that guy and thought I had been put out to pasture. I was angry you did not tell me face to face you were brushing me off, so I followed you to confront you."

"I wasn't brushing you off," she lied, feeling like a heel because that was exactly what she had planned to do it but not that subtly.

"Apparently not since you didn't leave with him willing," he said removing his handkerchief to examine the wound. "It doesn't look like you'll need stitches."

"Really," she said in false disappointment. "I was looking forward to having a scar as a memento."

"You're lucky you're only going away with a scratch. He could have done a lot more damage," he said. "What did he want from you anyway, money?"

She did not know how to answer that. She had wished that had been the case but he wanted some package/micro-film/codes. She felt like she stepped into some old black and white spy movie. Who used micro-film in this day and age? And what codes was he referring to? What were they and what did it all have to do with her?

She did not know what to make of it all. She had heard of similar incidents happening to travelers who have gone abroad and have been accused of carrying stolen items; drugs and other illegal substances, without their knowledge and in the business, she was in, anything was possible. Someone could have slipped her this micro-film before she left home. They could have been scouting the international flights and thought she would be a perfect host. Though her assailant had known her name, which he could have easily gotten off the passenger manifest but he said she contacted them for a meet after she arrived which meant someone had to be impersonating her. That's why that note was slipped under door. It was their response to the meet. Not knowing what all this meant, she decided to hold back this knowledge until she could make sense of it all.

"Cheyenne," Vincent said, lifting her chin when she did not answer.

She blinked. "I'm sorry, I'm a little bit out of it."

"That's understandable," he said. "Did he take anything important like your identification, your credit cards?"

"Uh....." She drew a blank for moment and looked discreetly around to see if she had dropped her purse but she did not see it anywhere. She did not remember having it when her assailant forced her out of the hotel. She must have left in hotel lobby on either the table or the chair. She decided to use that to her advantage.

"No. I remember now that he got angry with me when I could not account for my purse. I must have dropped it or left it when he took me out of the hotel at gun point," she explained.

"Is that why he got rough with you?"

"I suppose so. I could not understand him very well. His German was choppy and laced with another dialect I didn't recognize," she lied. "I did make out a few words and I believe one of them was money but I can't be sure. He was yelling and screaming at me that it was hard to make out what he wanted. I remember him patting me down as if he was looking to see if I had my purse and when he came up empty handed, he struck me. I was so scared he might kill me that, that's all I thought about."

He took her in his arms and felt the anger rise up in him. Even though she appeared distressed and frightened over the ordeal, he knew she was not telling him the whole truth. There was more to it than she was telling, which only confirmed that she was deceptive and a liar.

The policeman who had chased her assailant appeared at the mouth of it and jogged towards them. He was beat and out of breath. He informed them he lost her attacker in a crowded square a couple blocks up the road. Regret was evident in his rugged face and he suggested they come to the police station and make a report.

While she gave a description of her attacker, Vincent got a hold of a first aid kit and mended the gash on her cheek. She grimaced when he dabbed peroxide on it. He apologized, smiled and continued to look after her. His closeness distracted her to no end making it hard to concentrate on what she was doing.

When he finally sat back, she almost let out a sigh of relief. Her heart went back down to a normal rhythm and the tension in her body subsided. It infuriated her that her body betrayed her every time he was near. Why was that? Why did he have this effect on her after only knowing him for 48 hour? She dated Gary for four months and she never once was attracted to him the way she was attracted to Vincent. It did not make sense to her. Gary was just as attractive, and charming as he was so why didn't Gary have the same effect? Why did she have to struggle with the attraction she had for him? It was physics after all. It should have the same results but apparently, she was wrong for Vincent had some hold over her. Thank God, she was leaving in two days. It would be severed and she would not have to deal with it anymore.

As for the mystery surrounding her involvement in something criminal, she had no clue on how that was going to be resolved. She doubted it would stay put in Vienna. She would have to contact a lawyer to see how she would handle it. He probably would tell her to bring it to the police attentions but she had mixed feelings on it. If she revealed the man's real purpose for grabbing her and related what he had told her now, they will think she was hiding something because she lied. She might incriminate herself. However, is she didn't say something now, it will make her look bad down the road. It was damn, if you do and damn if you don't.

She was certain someone had stolen her identity. It was not that uncommon these days. Identity theft was real concern when crafty, clever people could tap into the information highway.

They say knowledge is power. It was very possible someone with criminal intentions could have stolen her name and had been using it in an illegal manner. If the law got whiff of this person's activities, there would be a less of a chance of being exposed for, they would be chasing a name not the person-per-say. By the time, they figure out the deception, they are long gone with a new name and she would be in prison. There was no guarantee it could be proven that she was a victim of identity theft. That terrified her. The idea of that happening made her ill.

Trying to fight off a headache, she massaged her temples as they walked out of the police station.

"Would you like to go get a drink?" Vincent suggested descending the stairs to the street. "I know I could use one and I'm sure you could too."

"You're very welcome to indulge yourself but I think I'll pass," she said her smile apologetic knowing very well a glass of wine or two wouldn't mix well with her vulnerable state, especially where he was concerned. "Secondly I have the matter of locating my purse."

"You have to go back to your hotel sometime today anyway," he said. "We'll just take care what needs to be done, and then take some time out for ourselves. If going for a drink doesn't tempt you we could go for a drive and take in a little bit of the city."

From his tone, she knew he was determined to stay in her company, and opted to take him up on it.

Upon entering the hotel, Cheyenne automatically scanned the lobby, a shiver going though her, as she noted everyone roaming around. She knew she was being ridiculous but it had only been two hours earlier when she had been taken out of the hotel at gunpoint. Granted it would probably not happen again but she did not feel safe anymore. He had shattered any sense of it. Vincent must have sensed her uneasiness for he stopped in mid-stride and turned to her.

He rested his hands on the base of her neck. "It's going to be okay. I'm here and I won't let anything happen to you."

He kissed her deeply, and tenderly, not carrying one way or the other he was doing it front of strangers.

Cheyenne did not have time to reflect or recover from the kiss for he took her hand and led over to the area where she had been sitting earlier.

Shaking herself out of the daze he had put her in, she began to look over the areas she might have laid or dropped her purse, only to come up empty handed.

They walked over to the front desk and asked if her purse had been turned in and sure enough, it had. Cheyenne was kind of hoping it would have stayed lost. It would have given her a distraction and some distance from Vincent, even if it were for only a couple hours. Why couldn't she be firm with him and tell him to leave her alone?

'Because deep down you don't want him to' her voiced echoed in her head.

"That's not true," she said in an exasperated tone.

Vincent and the desk clerk looked at her. She inwardly groaned and smiled nonchalantly not granting them an explanation to her outburst and thanked the clerk excusing herself.

"Cheyenne." Vincent called after her.

"Sorry," she said. "If you don't mind, I'm just going upstairs to my room to freshen up. I'll be right back."

As gracefully as possible, she rushed to the elevator hoping Vincent did not follow.

CHAPTER 7

Stepping off the elevator, Cheyenne reached her room in record time. She hesitated. What if her room was ransacked again? No, they would not try so soon. Secondly, if they did not find what they were looking for the first time it would be pointless to try again.

Taking a deep breath, she went in. Everything was in right order. Nothing was out of place.

She sighed and went into the bedroom. She shed her clothes and slipped on a basic blue top and a long, flowing, flowery skirt. It was simple and to the point, nothing remotely sexy or provocative about it. If Vincent saw anything attractive about her attire, there was something seriously wrong with him.

She went into the bathroom to see the damage to her hair and face. She had not had a chance to glance in a mirror. It was not as bad as she feared. Her hair was in disarray and her make-up had melted away with her tears. Her eyes were all red and puffy. The band-aid covering the gash stood out like a sore thumb. She removed it and noticed the swelling and irritation had gone down. A dab of foundation would cover it enough not to be noticeable, she thought.

As she reapplied her make-up, she tried not to think about how it got there.

Satisfied with the results she made her way back down to the lobby.

Vincent was leaning against the front desk on the phone when she appeared.

He hung up ."I was just ringing your room. Is everything okay?"

"Yes, I'm fine," she reported.

"I wasn't sure if you were going to come back down," he said as they walked through the lobby.

"Really" was all she said.

Once outside, he led her over to a black Mercedes parked at the curb on a side street. He pushed a button on his key chain and his front lights flashed on and off.

Holding the passenger's side door open, she slipped in and settled back in the soft, rich brown leather seat. She took a deep breath letting the aroma of the leather fill her nostrils. She loved the smell of it. If it were possible, she would have everything around her made of it.

The interior of the car was plush and lustrous. It had state of the art stereo equipment mounted into the dashboard; a car phone, GPS device and ports to plug in any other portable device such as a MP3 player.

"You like?" Vincent asked, giving her debonair smile.

She laughed. "It's very.....luxurious."

"I suspect that's why women love it," he said putting it in gear.

She laughed again. "I think it's the man behind the wheel that does it for them."

He looked at her. "I think I'm corrupting you. You just made a flirtatious remark. "

"It wasn't meant to be."

"Too bad, I like women who flirt," he teased.

She did not answer or comment. She knew it was a perfect time for her to speak to him but she did not want to have a debate. She just wanted some peace.

"I have a surprise for you." he commented moments later.

She looked over at him. "A surprise!"

"Yes. I made arrangements for us to see the Lipizzan's."

"As in the famous Lipizzan Stallions?"

He laughed. "Yes, very ones. You cannot come to Vienna and not see them. It would be sacrilegious and an insult to the institution if you pass up the opportunity to see the greatest beloved horses in the world."

She gave a little laugh. "Well I wouldn't want to do that."

"Precisely," he said. "I've saved you from it."

"My hero,"

"Seriously though, are you up for taking in a show?"

"Of course," she said. "Seeing them perform would be delightful. The diversion would do me good and it would be a pleasant memory to overpower all the other unpleasant ones. It is the best gift I could receive. Thank you."

"I've been bred to please," he said giving her a brief smile.

"Yes, that's very apparent for it has been substantiated on many occasions," she said matter of fact.

"Really," he said in surprise. "I thought I had fallen short in that department with you. I'm glad to see I was mistaken."

She gave a little nervous laugh but did not comment.

As he drove west to Hofburg, she took in the life of Vienna. People mostly swarmed the streets and sidewalks content in window shopping or just browsing to see what the city offered. Some sat outside of cafes and restaurant relaxing and chatting amongst themselves. Musicians could be found on corners or squares entertaining whoever would listen to their montage of music.

Local painters and artists could be seen sitting on a sidewalk or standing behind an easel capturing scenes that inspired them.

The architecture of the city is what really captivated her eye. Each building had a historical value and character of the old world. A few were distinctively Gothic, while others were Baroque in style. Many were a combination of both arrayed with many flavors of designs and styles.

She saw a pattern of certain figures that were present; eagles, lovers, children, kings, and ancient rulers that had once ruled Austria.

In a neighboring suburb, there was an edifice-an apartment complex of sorts-that took up a block that definitely had modern flare to it, but in an artistic way. It was not your ordinary, straight lined, geometrical structure. The outer shell had an adobe feel with its soft curved edges, but the core of it was uneven, and sported unusual geometric shapes for the windows and doors. They were arrayed in many colors from a sunny yellow to a gloomy grey. Then there were sections-splotches of areas- that looked like the outer surface was chiseled away to reveal a brick or tiled pattern within the wall.

Vincent had commented as they drove pass that a famous artist, whose name eluded him, had designed it. It certainly explained the idea behind it. Only an artist could create a building that looked like it belonged in a museum of Modern Art.

On the way back through town, Vincent drove by the Winter Riding School, also known as the Spanish Riding School, where the Lipizzan Stallions preformed. She had seen them once perform when they toured America and had found the performance fascinating. She had taken her mother to the show as a birthday present for the Lippizans were favorite horses. To get see them in the country they came from was one of those once in a lifetime occasion. She wished she had her camera.

Vincent found a spot a few blocks down from the school and parked.

While he picked up the tickets from the ticket office, she strolled around the school, taking in its Corinthian style, finding its simplicity surprising and peaceful. Generally, though arena's, theaters and other theatrical places were rarely overly elaborate with decoration. It took the focus away from the performance.

Inching by spectators, they made their way to their seats. Cheyenne took a seat and took in the ring below, her gaze lifting up towards the high ceilings, making more of a study of the building.

Chatter echoed in her ears, picking up a remark made by the couple sitting next to them. They were snickering how they lucked out on getting tickets for the full performance and their friends not, because they had to be bought way in advance. She wondered how Vincent managed to obtain their tickets on such short notice. It was a packed house. Did he have connections or did he just flash a couple hundred acquiring them? He appeared to have money but that did not guarantee he could get into any place no questions ask.

"What are you thinking about?" he asked.

"Huh?"

"You have this thoughtful look on your face."

"Oh," she smiled. "I was just wondering about something."

"And what was that?"

"Well it's just amazing how you managed to get tickets for this show when most of the spectators had to get them way in advance."

"You're worried I had bought them for someone else?"

That had not entered her mind, nor was that what she had been thinking, but now that he mentioned it; it could have very well been the case. He probably had set on taking some woman he would romance during his stay in Vienna prior to her arrival and she or he backed out. It was probably that hot looking secretary in the lobby or the one up in Lindbergh's office.

"Cheyenne."

"Hmmm," she said, distractedly.

"You've been doing that a lot lately."

"What?"

"Starting something then phasing out on me going somewhere else."

"I'm sorry," she said. "I don't mean to. Maybe's it is some heredity dysfunction I inherited from my family"

He laughed. "I doubt that."

She smiled. "Did you purchase the tickets for someone else in mind?"

"No." he said. "Actually, they were given to me by Lindbergh as a gift of appreciation."

"Oh."

"You sound disappointed."

"No, not at all," she said. "I'm honored you picked me to accompany you when you could have taken plenty of other women you've met while you've been in Vienna."

"I don't know if I should take that as a compliment or an insult," he said. "For with that remark it could be perceived that you're stating I'm a player who entertains a lot of women, and I picked you as my next diversion."

"I didn't mean it like that," she said not sure, if that was the truth. If he wasn't out for a good time then what was he really doing out with her? If causal dating did not come into play then why was he pursing her when he knew it was just going to be a brief fling, he had on a business trip. She did not understand him or get him sometimes. She felt she was dealing with two different people half the time.

"I'm sure you didn't." He smiled, and then went on. "If you're up to, there are many other historical and inspiring things I could show you. It would be a shame if you go home and not take in as much as you can while you're here."

"I had thought the same. I had been hoping to cram in much as possible since my time here has been cut short. Though I leave the day after tomorrow so I don't know how much we could really fit in."

"Yes, that's....." He stopped speaking and stared at her. "What did you just say?"

"I said I had thought the..."

"No not that part," he interjected. "the last part."

"About me leaving?"

"Yes."

She put her hand up to her face. "That's right we haven't set up a time for me to hand over the documents. With everything that happened today, I spaced it."

"Wait, back up a moment, am I missing something here because as I recall you were very adamant about following ICS's protocols and refused to give me the documents until Lindbergh gave the OK."

"Yes, that's true, and as far as I know Lindbergh did give the OK, last night in fact," she explained. "Didn't you get the message?"

"What message?"

"The one that authorizes me to give you the documents," she said puzzled he had no knowledge of this. "Lindbergh contacted my boss yesterday and over-nighted a notarized release form. You should have gotten a copy."

"I probably did," he said off handily. "I just wasn't notified of it."

"Didn't you go into work today?"

"No. I took off the day for our sightseeing tour."

"Perhaps they left you a message on your cell," she said wondering how in the world they got anything done with this 'laid back' mentality they seemed to be sporting. Did these people not communicate with each other?

He pulled out his cell and flipped it opened. There were no missed calls. What the hell was going on, he thought, angrily.

"Well," she questioned.

"Um...yeah it looks like I missed a few calls," he said. "Would you excuse me?"

He stood up and made his way to the entrance thinking there had to be a mistake. There was no way Lindbergh could have contacted Rachel Sullivan or Alan J. Royden for that matter. The man was dead. His death of course was not publically known or officially declared yet. Only he and the CIA knew of it. Vincent felt partly responsible-at least indirectly, because Lindbergh was cooperating with them, so he could set up his cover as a liaison. Lindbergh's unexpected departure was part of the agreement so Cheyenne had to deal with Vincent directly if the arrangements at the airport fell through, which they had.

When it was discovered, the flash drive was just what Vincent had thought it was, a sophisticated version of Spyware, the CIA had no choice but to go to plan B. There had been speculation she might be an accomplice rather than a victim so Vincent fell into role. Unfortunately, his involvement cost Lindbergh his life.

It had been some sort of twisted fate that Lindbergh's private plane was caught in a violent storm in mid flight to London and crashed into the sea. As far as Vincent knew, the dead could not make phone calls from the grave. The possibility of Lindbergh surviving the crash was slim at best and even by some miracle he did, he had no knowledge of the situation. The only conclusion there was, was that someone was impersonating him, but who?

No one other than he and CIA knew about his demise. The only logical explanation was someone, possibly Cheyenne, wanted their business dealings to come to an end and made it so by improvising and speeding up the process by pretending to be Lindbergh.

If Cheyenne had any part in this whole conspiracy, which he was becoming to believe she was, she would want to make her departure look as normal as possible.

With the implications she doubled crossed the buyers, possibly her accomplice, Gary Lopez, the urgency to leave Austria would be impertinent to her. However, she had failed to meet with the buyers at St. Stephen's which meant she still had the micro-film and was either holding out for more money before she gave them the codes or she had another buyer lined up who had a higher bid. The question was had she gone rogue or was she a pawn in all this? And if it was the latter, she must have arranged another meeting for a trade off if she was leaving in two days. She would not have gone through all the deception and planning just to abandon it. However, it was very possible the incident in the ally had been a drop off staged to look like something else not to arouse suspicion. He could not be sure, but he had to find out.

After phoning Stewart, he returned to her side. The show had already started and her attentions were focused on the performance when he sat down.

She smiled and leaned towards him. "Is everything okay?"

"Yes," he replied. "I'm sorry I was so long."

"It's all right," she expressed. "You're here now."

He did not comment but sat back. He crossed his arms and watched her out of the corner of his eye. She baffled and confused him. She played the innocent, down to earth, hometown girl like a pro. She was so good in fact, that it drew him in like a fly being seduced by a flicker of light, turning the tables on him. He was supposed to be the seducer not the Sadducee. She was not supposed to be the one who threw him off balance and put him in a tailspin.

Even though it appeared her defenses were wading, she was still guarded where it was becoming harder and harder for him not to let his down. Whenever he was with her, he was in danger of showing her who Troy Vincent West was, not his persona Vincent Dmitri. He had already revealed too much of himself as it was. If he was not careful, he was going to blow it. He had to keep the ball in his court. He had to stay focus and keep to the objective, which was easier said than done. Seducing her for the information was becoming more than just a role for him and with the recent events; it was not an option anymore.

They returned to her hotel after catching a bite to eat at Braunerof Café. Vincent made no attempt to escort her to her room or take her in his embrace for a passionate goodnight kiss. In a way, she was disappointed. She was becoming accustomed to it as if one would become accustom to a wealthier state of living, where she had gone without.

He did express he wanted to see her before she left and persuaded her to join him for a day in the country, promising she would be back in plenty of time to prepare for her flight home.

At first, she had regretted agreeing to go, but when they drove out of the city into the countryside the following morning her regret vanished. She could not imagine a better way of ending her trip than being flooded with beautiful scenery of Austria. She was in awe at the landscape. Everything spoke to her, the deep blue sky, the grassy knolls and valleys, the majestic snow capped mountains.

About mid-morning, she found herself staring up at a modern-day medieval Castle built by Emperor Franz II. Vincent took her hand, and they meander alongside the moat with its islands and bridges before taking the tour. Afterwards, they sat under a big maple tree and lazily ate the picnic lunch Vincent had brought.

For the first time, since she arrived in Austria, she found she could relax and enjoy herself. There were no interruptions, no inconveniences, or mishaps. Vincent was companionable and less intimidating. He was desirable and charming as ever. He was not as intense or obviously seductive as he had been before, but more at ease, which made him more approachable. However, who was she fooling? Just because she was becoming to like him, did not mean it would bloom into something else. She knew what that something else would be, and it would be fleeting. She did not want that. As much as she wanted to entertain that there was something there, she could not. She would be gone the next day and would never see him again. There was no reason to give her heart that much hope only to be disappointed.

As the sun began to sink in the horizon, they leisurely headed back towards Vienna, driving through quaint villages and towns in between. She rested back, gazing out, getting lost in shadows of light that played across landscape when Vincent's car began acting up. It started out shuddering then there was a grinning noise followed by a series of other unfamiliar noises. Before she knew it, Vincent was rolling to a stop on the side of the road. He swore, and popped the hood. He got out and began tinkering under it. He swore again, and came around the passenger side, asking her for his cell phone. Once in hand, he flipped it opened and dialed a number.

An hour later, a tow truck arrived hitching Vincent's rented Mercedes to the trailer. They were brought to a local repair shop where Vincent went off with the tow truck driver, Heinrich, to fill out paper work. They seemed to be having an amusing conversation for Heinrich was smiling as if they shared some private joke. When he spotted her observing, he coughed and became serious. She found it odd. Vincent waved off to him and joined her moments later informing her that Heinrich had to check the car out and would let them know the problem.

Spotting an Inn, a little way up the road, Vincent suggested they go wait out there. Heinrich had mentioned they had a restaurant and they should try it.

Stepping under the threshold of the Marienhof, Cheyenne took in the quaintness and warmth of the place. A waitress showed them to a table, near the back where the lighting was low and private. She rolled out a list of specials in a droll voice and asked them what they liked to drink.

Once she departed Vincent said, "I'm sorry. I know this isn't something you need right now since this is your last day here and you have to catch a flight in the morning."

"Do you think it's serious?"

"It could be," he said. "It's possible it's the timing belt or the battery. If that is the case were okay. But if it's the alternator or carburetor were screwed."

"Lovely," she smirked.

"Look I know your trip hasn't been what you expected it to be and all you want to to do is put it all behind you, but would it be that bad if you stayed a few days longer. I mean you have been enjoying yourself, haven't you?"

"Yes, but you seemed to forget I'm in Vienna on business, not pleasure," she reminded him. "Granted if it can't be avoided, I'll have to cancel my flight but my boss isn't going to be happy about it. If she finds out I had to delay my flight to Houston because I was fraternizing with Krantz's liaison, she'll fire me."

"I think we've been more than fraternizing but......."

"I'm serious Vincent," she flared, cutting him off. "This is my job we're...."

"I know darling," he said taking her hand into his, kissing it affectionately. "I would in no way let our personal relations get you in trouble with your place of employment. If it becomes an issue, I will handle it. You need not to worry. But if that doesn't bring you comfort; I can always call you a cab."

"Can you actually get one way out here?"

"I'd probably would have to call a company in Vienna and have them come pick us up."

"Wouldn't that be pretty expensive?"

"You needn't concern yourself with that," he said.

"Maybe we should just wait until we find out how bad your car is off before we make that decision," she said taking another sip of water. "Like you said it could be something simple that can be fixed right off."

Dropping the subject, Cheyenne studied the menu. The waitress returned with their drinks and promptly took their orders.

Knowing Cheyenne was feeling restless and awkward, Vincent drew her into a casual conversation about subjects not relative to her stay in Vienna. It kept her distracted until their meals came.

They continued to converse as they ate but halfway through the meal Cheyenne began not to feel well. Heaviness fell over her and she found it hard to concentrate on what she was doing.

Everything around her began to become blurry and hazy. Vincent's words slurred as if he was in slow motion. Her heart started to beat rapidly and she felt like she was going to pass out.

What was happening to her? She did not consume that much wine to become drunk. What was going on? Did she have food poisoning?

"Are you okay?" She heard Vincent's worried voice echo.

"I don't think so," she murmured, trying to stand up. "I think I need some fresh air or......"

Collapsing, Vincent caught her before she hit the floor. He announced to the concerned patrons she was all right explaining she only fainted and carried her out.

A dark green Volvo pulled up shortly after and Vincent opened the back door. He gently laid her down and situated her comfortable on the back seat. He stared down at her for moment, caressed her cheek.

"I'm sorry." Then against his better judgment, he kissed her. He knew she would not respond it or remember it for that matter but he would.

"Should I leave you two alone?"

"Shut up and drive," he barked slipping into the passenger's side.

"And hi to you too mate," his companion said pulling out onto the road.

"I don't have time for pleasantries, Merrick."

"But you have time to lay one on the lassie back there who I might add is pretty much dead to the world right now." Merrick Donovan pointed out.

"I know what you're thinking so drop it," he said. "I don't have to explain myself."

"Apparently not," Merrick said turning off onto a country road.

He looked into his rear-view mirror, and back at Vincent. "Are you going to tell me why you're working for the CIA again? I thought you retired."

"I did," he answered. "I only came back for this one job."

"Are you sure about that," Merrick said. "Because you know they'll try to figure out a way to draw you back in."

"There's nothing they can dangle in front of me that would make me go back into their world on permanent basis," he said matter of fact. "Besides I have a daughter raise. I can't live that life anymore, especially not after what happened to her mother."

"Vincent..."

"I don't want to talk about it," he warned.

Merrick backed off and concentrated on the road.

Vincent was grateful. He did not want to go down memory lane and think about his ex-wife, Victoria. He wanted to keep the happier times they spent and shared together to be what stayed present in his mind. He did not want to dwell on the fact he failed her as a husband and as a man.

If he had been more attentive, supportive, and communicated more she would not have sought out comfort and love from someone else-that some else being his handler, Kevin Rogan.

When he found out it about killed him. The idea his wife sleeping with him left him cold. It was when he confronted him that his whole world fell apart. The next thing he knows the cops show up at his doorstep and arrested him for Kevin's murder. Kevin had been found dead in his apartment shortly after Vincent had gone over there to talk to him. He was shot at close range in the chest, which was later determined the deadly bullet that ended his life came from Vincent's gun. Victoria was devastated.

During the investigation, his present handler, Stewart Mathews, had worked with the local authorities to prove his innocence. In doing so, finding the real killer shattered his life forever for the extensive investigation led to his wife.

With her relationship being substantiated by witnesses who knew her and lived in Kevin's apartment complex, they looked into the jilted lover's angle. Victoria claimed that it was she and Vincent that were having problems, not her and Kevin and would never fathom killing him over their relationship.

Then Vincent's weapon was found a few blocks from Kevin's apartment complex in some shrubby as if it had been carelessly thrown there, suggesting the killer had been in shock when they disposed of it. Her fingerprints were found all over it. She was arrested, found guilty of manslaughter, and sentenced to fifteen years in prison. She holds to this day, that she is innocent, which Vincent believes.

The therapists and doctors he had talked to said she was suppressing it, that the shock had forced the truth to the dark corners of her mind. He did not believe that. Her defense was she did not do it, not that she could not remember killing him. There was more to it and he made a promise to himself that he would find out the truth.

He been working with her lawyer for the past seven years trying to find new evidence to prove she had no part in Kevin's death, only to find dead ends and false hopes.

The longer Victoria stayed in prison, the worse it got for her. Hopefully, if things went as planned those four grey walls that confined her would only be a distant memory not her reality.

"Are you going to stay in stony silence for the whole drive," Merrick asked, unable to take the quietness anymore. "I mean hell mate it's been ten years since we last saw each other. Can't you think of anything to yak about?"

Vincent let out a sigh. "I'm sorry. I have a lot on my mind."

"I've noticed."

"Is Stewart at the chalet?"

"Yes, and he has everything in place."

"Good. We really appreciate your help in this."

"No problem. It's just like, the old days when our agencies would collaborate and swap info." Merrick commented. "Juliet and I occasionally do a job or two for INTERPOL when they need us to, but once the wee one is born, we'll cut back on the work load."

"Wee one?" Vincent questioned looking at him in astonishment.

"Yes, wee one, baby, you know. Juliet's due next month."

"Who's the father?"

"Me, you arse." Merrick said throwing him a dirty look.

"You?"

"Yes me." Merrick countered. "Why does that surprise you? You must have known we had a thing for each other."

"You drove each other crazy."

"Yeah well, now we drive each other crazy in bed as husband and wife."

"Congratulations!" he said. "I hadn't known you had gotten together let alone married."

"Maybe if you had kept in touch you would have."

"I had to sever all ties when I left the CIA," he said. "You know that."

"I don't think there's a security risk in you sending a Christmas card."

"Merrick it is a two-way road," he pointed out. "You could have easily sent me one or an invitation to the wedding."

"Point taken," Merrick glanced in the back and said, "Who is she?"

"Her name is Cheyenne Nicholas. She's a personal courier for a company called ICS, back in the states, Boston area," Vincent said, turning his gaze toward her. "We have reason to believe she's part of a smuggling ring that's either based through company she works for, or is just channeled through it. The FBI has been looking into company for some years now trying to trace the smuggling ring to its source but they have not been able to pin point a pattern. Then about a few months ago they got whiff one of their C.E.O.'s, a fellow named Gary Lopez, came into possession of a computer program that had been developed for government agencies including the military, by a security firm, that provided them a back door into their computer systems that would disable their security protocols so if they are ever compromised, they can retrieve what hasn't been corrupted or lost." He paused for a moment, then continued. "Now because of this, they dug into Lopez's activities and found out he had a connection with the smuggling ring, so they put him under surveillance. To make a long story short, his client, an ex-military officer Haden Davis, who has a degree in software programing and coding, discovered it when he worked at one of their storage facilities. He got caught selling the military equipment that had been retired and stored there on the black market and was discharged. Knowing Cyber terrorism was becoming more prevalent these days, anyone who is tech savvy and knows his/her, way around a computer could use this program to infiltrate their systems undetected and make a large profit on the dark web. To his way of thinking discovering this would make a good pay day and get his revenge on the military at the same time. Since the original program was deactivated when it was compromised, Davis had to rewrite it and adapt it to integrate to the current security programs where you can upload through any computer or laptop via Wi-Fi. Catch is you need a key code to get access to activate and a key code to deactivate it because it has a safeguard in place if it's detected. Not only will the program in sense self-destruct, it will wipe out your whole system." He went on to explain Cheyenne's involvement and how the CIA got involved.

Merrick was quiet moment, going over the details in his head.

"So, there's this glorified, high tech, Spyware-like program out there that's only a threat if you have the codes." Merrick stated. "And this lass," he turned his head toward her. "is the only one that you know of offhand that has physically evidence of them and they're fused onto micro-film?"

"Yes. Lopez made sure the man he hired to do it, was the only one who saw them. He had the guy burn the paper it was written on."

"Well, doesn't that Davis bloke have them?"

"Yes, but he's dead."

"That's convenient. Was it a freak accident or was he murdered?"

"It was determined an accident. It was a house fire, which basically destroyed any evidence that the program and codes ever existed." Vincent explained. "We could not find any off site places he would have kept back up."

"Well that's not ominous or suspicious." Merrick scoffed. "What about the other bloke Lopez. There's no way he wouldn't have the codes written or saved on some device. He could sell the Spyware- like program multiple times. He would have to include the codes or there be no point in selling it."

"He's got a photographic memory." Vincent stated.

"How do you know that?"

"The FBI has profiled him." he responded. "They know every little detail of him."

"Then why isn't he in their custody or yours being interrogated?"

"The FBI has a bigger fish to fry. They want to keep him in play in hopes he leads them to more Intel on the inner workings of the smuggling ring so they can take it down or at least do some damage."

"I see now why you went this avenue instead of the other." Merrick said. "Time is of the essence. If she is as smart and clever as you say she is, it is possible she is ahead of the game and knows you are on to her? She might have already completed the transaction and is just messing with you."

"You think she's duped us."

"I think it's more that she's duped you, but yes it could be a possible she's duped the agency as well." Merrick said, slowing down and pulling up to a gated drive. He punched in a code on a key pad mounted off to the side and the gates parted. "I hope for your sake I'm wrong."

Merrick drove on through and brought the car around to the front of an impressive, very large Chalet. Juliet, Merrick's wife and fellow comrade stood on the stairs waiting for them.

Merrick cut the engine and shook his head.

"What?" Vincent asked, turning to him.

"This might be a stupid question but if the codes can be easily stored on a flash drive, why would this Lopez bloke use micro-film?"

"Because it's more elusive and not obvious. He knew the first thing the authorities would look for would be a flash drive or a USB." He related. "Plus, the codes are just a sequence of letters and numbers. It doesn't need anything fancy to be stored on. A piece of paper would suffice, but that's not very secure. He wanted to keep the two apart, and not on the same device or on two similar devices."

"Understandable I suspect. I can see why you're going with the direct approach." Merrick said, stepping out of the car. "Though I don't envy you."

"Why is that?"

"Because when that lassie discovers you've been lying to her, and pretending to be interested, look out. You'll be saying goodbye to the family jewels mate before you know what hits ya." He grinned. "And from what I observed, she's got you hooked. I wouldn't be surprised if your heart doesn't pop out of your chest and she's eats it for breakfast."

"Okay, Doctor Merrick, you need to stick to your day job and keep your romance advice for the bedroom." Vincent scoffed, heading over to Juliet.

"Hello stranger." she said embracing him. "It's been a long time."

"Yes, it has. I wish it could have been on better circumstances."

"As do I," she replied. "Is that her?"

Vincent looked in the direction of the car to see Merrick lift Cheyenne out.

"Where to love?"

"The second room on the left." she replied taking in Cheyenne's limp body. "She'll have nice view of the grounds from there." She turned to Vincent. "She's very pretty. What's her crime?"

"I'll fill you in later," he said. "Right now, I have pressing matters to attend to."

"I understand." she said following her husband lead. "Just keep it down. I need my rest."

He gave her look and she just smiled.

CHAPTER 8

Slipping off his coat, and tossing it carelessly onto a chair, Vincent paced back and forth, periodically shifting his gaze towards the bed where Cheyenne laid. He noticed her head move, her lips twitch, and her hands flex. She was coming to. It was time to get to work.

He pulled over a chair and sat down. He picked up a small vile of liquid that sat on the side table and grabbed the hypodermic needle that lay next to it. Removing the protective cover, he placed the tip of the needle into the top of the vile and drew in the liquid. Laying it aside, he stretched out Cheyenne's arm towards him, tying off her circulation with one of Juliet's scarf. Patting the area above the crease in her arm, he found a vein that would work. He tapped the hypodermic needle encasement and inserted the drug into Cheyenne's arm, keeping her sedated but conscious enough to answer his questions. Relieving her of the scarf, he sat back and waited a few minutes for the drug to take, effect.

"Cheyenne can you hear me," he said scribbling on a note pad book.

"Yes," she responded, her voice weak and raspy.

"Good. I need your help."

"Help," she repeated.

"Yes. I'm going to ask you a few questions."

"About what?" she breathed.

"About your boyfriend, Gary Lopez."

"He's not my…boyfriend…not anymore." She slurred.

"Ok then your ex-lover."

She let out a short laugh. "He's not… that… either. You've gotten… more action…than he…ever…did and… we dated… four months." She snorted. "Not that he hadn't tried. The only difference…is you…succeeded."

He coughed uncomfortably and cleared his throat.

"Cheyenne…"

"Why is that? Why is it after…knowing you…for what…a hot minute, that any…sense of …morality…just flew…out the door?"

"Cheyenne…"

"Believe me I've seen lot… of attractive men… in my life time…and none…of them…has had…this effect on me…at least not physically. Maybe your endorphins are really potent and…"

His mouth smothered hers silencing her. She went limp and melted into the kiss, the whirl wind of thoughts fading away as pleasure of his kiss washed over her.

He withdrew and settled back, noticing she was complacent and happily distracted. He settled back to see the light flashing on the wall. He picked up the phone next to him. "What?"

"Can we move on and get on with the real reason we brought her here."

"That's what I'm trying to do Stewart."

"Are you sure about that, because from where I'm standing it looks like your trying to satisfy her desires and yours instead of doing your job."

"If I remember correctly *seducing* her was my *job*." he snapped. "I had to shut her up and silence her ramblings so I could get back on track with the questioning. Now let me do that."

He slammed the phone and swore.

"You really should stop swearing. It's not attractive." She murmured.

He broke into smile despite his mood and shook his head.

"Getting back to Gary," he started, hoping it wasn't going to set off another rambling session he had to divert by kissing her, though he be lying if he didn't enjoy it. "He's your supervisor."

"Yes."

"He sent you to Austria?"

"No, Rachel… Sullivan… did. He manages the … department…and usually assigns…currier jobs how he sees fit, but it still…has to be… cleared with Rachel."

"Do you transport any other items or packages not associated with ICS?"

"No…though that man wanted a package?"

"What man?"

"The one who… held me at… gunpoint. He called me a bitch and said I double crossed …them?"

"And who are them?"

"I don't know." she expressed, becoming agitated. "I think someone stole…my identity, someone bad and …"

"And what?" he pressed.

"I don't… know." she stressed. "None of it…makes sense."

"This package he spoke of, was it the package you were to deliver to St. Stephen's Cathedral?"

"No, the only package I had to deliver was Krantz Steel corporation…where I met you." she stated, shifting uncomfortably.

He started to respond when she abruptly blurted, "Why did you ask me out to dinner? I know you didn't think of me… when I first arrived. You took… an instant dislike… to me so… I don't understand…. why you did a 360 and invite me… to dinner. I mean… I could understand if…I looked like Lindbergh secretary…hourglass body…perky chest…flawless skin…beautiful everything but I'm none of those. I'm average, nothing special, a plain Jane."

"You are no plain Jane." he muttered. "You are much more than what you see."

The light flashed again but he ignored it. "Cheyenne you were sent a note the following day after you arrived, an encrypted one," he said. "Do you remember?"

"Yes…I found it…strange."

"Yes, I know, but you figured out how to decipher it. It told you about a meeting at St. Stephen's Cathedral at three o'clock that afternoon," he reminded her. "Why did you not keep the appointment?"

"I'd thought it was…given…to me by mistake," she said distress evident in her voice. "It sounded like…a lovers…rendezvous. I tried to tell that…man…who attacked me…the same…thing, but he did not believe me. That's why he struck me…calling me a thieving bitch…accusing me of all these things, saying I had some package but…I didn't know what he was talking about…I was scared……"

"Okay Cheyenne," he said, resting his hand on hers. "It's all right, I'm here. You have nothing to be frightened about."

Her body relaxed and the stress expressed in her features melted away with his soothing words. He diverted his questions to later that day when they went to see the Lippizans drawing out the pleasantness of it. He then veered it slowly back to the issue of the flash drive.

"Cheyenne why did you give Treten Rodick the flash drive but not the micro-film?"

"Micro-film?" she questioned. "The…man…who attacked me… mentioned something…about micro-film."

"Yes, that's right Cheyenne. Did you pass it over to him?"

"No," she said becoming agitated again.

"Do you still have it?"

"Have what?"

"The micro-film?"

"Why would I…have micro-film." She slurred. "Who uses…that…everything is digital now."

He let out a frustrated sigh and hung his head. He was getting nowhere. She either rambled on about personal feelings or answered a question with a question, denying everything pertinent.

It was possible she was prepped by hypnosis or some sort of mental suppression if she was ever interrogated. That would explain a lot if that was the case. And if not and she really didn't know anything, then God help them. He pressed on.

"Forget about the micro-film." he insisted. "What about the codes Cheyenne. Did you give them to the man in the ally?"

"No," she denied, her head shifting side to side in frustration. "He…hurt…me.."

"He was your contact wasn't he," he pressed on. "And you were going to give him the codes, but you panicked because you knew the authorities were on to you. You knew I was onto you?"

"NO," she bellowed thrashing about. "I don't know what you're…. talking about. I am innocent. I did…nothing wrong…I don't know…anything about a flash drive or codes…the man at the airport or in the ally…this is all a mistake…."

Going to her, he gently pinned her flailing arms and took possession of her mouth once again to calm her. Her body gradually went compliant as before.

Easing off her, Vincent slumped into the chair feeling dejected and at a loss.

Cheyenne slowly opened her eyes with a throbbing headache. Her eyes focused on a brightly lit room that was unfamiliar. She inched up shaking the cobwebs out when she became fully aware, she was naked in a strange bed. She tugged the sheet closer to her as she took in her surroundings. It was evident she was in a bedroom-a turn of the century bedroom that had Jane Austen written all over it. Off to her right was a glorious picture window overlooking the countryside. The lower panes on the bottom were opened to let the breeze in. She spotted her clothes draped over a vanity chair along with a man's shirt and jacket. Panic suddenly surge through her. What was going on? Why was she there naked and more importantly where was Vincent?

The outer door swung open and in came a very striking, very pregnant, Scandinavian woman. She was beautiful Cheyenne noted. She looked like a beam of sunshine that fell from heaven. Cheyenne had never seen a lovelier, natural beauty in her life.

"Good morning Cheyenne." the angelic woman said.

"Morning," Cheyenne replied back, staring at her, thinking she must be dreaming or she was dead.

"Don't be alarmed." The woman smiled. "I'm Juliet Donovan, a friend of Vincent's. We weren't properly introduced last night."

Cheyenne stared at her. She did not remember even being introduced.

"You'll have to forgive me, but I don't recall much of last night. The details are a little fuzzy," she said. "Could you refresh my memory on how I... we ended up here?"

"Vincent called my husband Merrick to pick you at the Marienof." Juliet responded picking up a tie off the floor.

"Why did he do that," she asked not liking the fact she did not remember leaving the Inn or the implication they had been intimate in the very bed she found herself in. What was going on? The last thing she recalled was wanting to get some fresh air because she hadn't felt well. What happened from that time to the present? Did she pass out, what?

"You'll have to ask him about that." Juliet responded evasively.

"Is that so," she stated becoming angry. "Is he here?"

"Yes, he's in the house. He's downstairs with my husband," Juliet said. "Why don't you get dressed and we'll join them."

She handed her, her clothes and retreated.

Cheyenne slipped out bed not liking the feeling she was getting. Why couldn't she remember the night's event's prior to dinner? If she had been ill, why hadn't Vincent brought her to a hospital? Why had he brought her there? She knew it was not because he wanted his way with her for, she would know if she had been violated and she had not. She could not see him do something so heinous. It was not in his nature. Secondly, if that was all he was after, she was sure he could find another willing woman to satisfy him in that area. It was possible he wanted to delay her departure so he could keep her with him a little longer, but if she had become ill, he wouldn't have known she would, unless he just used the situation to benefit him. She did not know what to think.

She dressed and ventured out, making a few wrong turns before finding the stairs that led to the main floor.

As she reached the bottom, she was aware of lot of commotion and men dressed in suits. Two stood by the front door, their demeanor droll and blank. Another one with earpiece walked past her as she stepped off the last stair. He nodded and addressed her.

"Miss. Nicholas."

She swallowed hard, panic surging up in her. How did he know her name?

"This way please," he instructed.

She followed him into what looked like a sitting area. As she entered, the room went silent and six pair of eyes rested on her.

One of those pairs was Vincent's. He was off to her left, standing in a corner.

"Miss. Nicholas."

She turned towards the person whom spoke to see tall, older gentlemen with a receding hairline.

Again, she swallowed. "Yes."

"I'm Stewart Mathews," he informed her. "I work for the Central Intelligence Agency."

It took a moment for that to register.

"The CIA," she questioned evidently confused by the revelation.

"Yes, would you please be seated?"

She did so and asked, "What is this all about?"

"We-that is Vincent brought you here for questioning."

She looked over at him. "You're a CIA agent?"

"Officer, CIA officer," he corrected.

"Pardon me. I didn't know there was a difference," she apologized. "I guess your people don't want to get confused with the FBI."

He did not comment but stood there in stony silence.

"Miss. Nicholas I'm going to cut right to the chase," Officer Stewart Mathews said directing her attentions back to the matter at hand. "We're after an important item, microfilm, that Gary Lopez gave you to be given to a client/buyer along with a flash drive here in Austria. The buyer got the flash drive but no microfilm, which means you still have it, so where is it Miss. Nicholas."

Stunned, she didn't know how to respond. This had been the second time she had been accused of having this micro-film. She had no idea what they were talking about. And then to hear Gary had supposedly given it to her and some flash drive, totally took her by surprise. She had an in clinging when she stepped into the room their presence had to do with the mysteries involving her.

She just did not know she had been so deep in it, that it concerned national security. She knew it would not just go away but she never imagined she be caught up in something so big and frightening, not to mention Gary having some part in it. However, what hurt the most was that she was being deceived not just by him, but by Vincent as well. He had used her, violated her trust in pursuit of gaining information from her. She felt like such a fool.

"Miss. Nicholas where is it?" Stewart Mathews repeated, in a harsh tone.

"I don't know." She shot back. "Maybe it's in the prop room of the 1920's spy movie you're all stuck in."

"Miss. Nicolas…"

"If Gary gave me some micro-film, I'm unaware of it." she argued.

"Look, Miss. Nicholas you have serious allegations against you that can-will-put you in prison for the rest of your life. You do not have many options here. It's best you corporate and give us what we want."

"I can't tell you what I don't know," she balked, her chest tightening, the stress threatening to overcome her.

"Cheyenne don't make this any harder than it is," Vincent put in, going to her. "We know you have it and are working with Gary. Why protect him? Give up its location, and do the right thing." He went to rest his hand on hers when she shoved it away.

"Don't touch me," she snapped forcibly at him. "Don't you ever!"

He retreated. "The only thing I know is, I'm involved in something I don't have control over. I have never in the past or present aided Gary in any of the things you accusing me of. As for the micro-film you're looking for, I know nothing about it or its contents other than what has been told to me by you and the man who attacked me. I don't know where it is."

Officer Stewart Mathews opened a briefcase on the coffee table and took out a folder. He pulled out a black and white photo and placed it in front of her.

"Is this your place of residence?"

"Yes."

"Is that you in the picture?"

"Yes," she answered.

"Who is this man next to you?"

"One of the tenants in my building," she said wondering where they were going with this.

"What's his name?"

"I don't remember." she responded. "I think it was Hayden something."

"Hayden something," Stewart repeated not pleased with her answer.

"I don't know his full name," she expressed. "I only met him once that day. He had just moved in a couple weeks before."

"He gave you something that night outside your apartment," Stewart said moving on. "What was it?"

"My mail. Is there a law against that?"

"Why was he giving you your mail?"

"Because the mailman got my mail mixed up with his," she answered honestly. "He's in apartment nineteen and I'm in sixteen."

"Was it a bill?"

"No. It was a free sample of lipstick."

"This one," he asked withdrawing a silver lipstick container from an evidence bag. "It's called Passion Red? Sound familiar?"

It did but she was not about to admit it. It was useless to.

"If you notice it has a secret compartment." Stewart said showing her, noticing her facial expressions turn from confusion to horror. "See it's a perfect place to hide something small like a flash drive."

He waited for a response but she was loss for words.

"This is your lipstick," Stewart said. "We lifted your prints off of it and encased it was a flash drive that was intended to the buyers that Gary and you sold to but as I mentioned before no micro-film?"

"You went through my things," she exclaimed snapping out of her num state, directing the question at Vincent. "Did you ransack my room too?"

"No, the people you screwed over did the honors."

"I did not cheat anyone out of anything," she insisted. "If I did, I was unaware of it."

Vincent snatched the pictures out of Stewart's hands and slammed each one on the coffee table.

"If you are so damn innocent then explain these pictures of you passing off the lipstick to this man." Vincent growled, pointing to the person he spoke of. She glanced at it to see the man was the one who helped her after she had been rudely rammed into. In one of the photo's he was collecting the items scattered about the floor that had been in her purse, and cleverly pocketed the lipstick. She could not believe it. This was not happening.

"You've become very quiet," Vincent observed. "a sign of guilt perhaps?"

"Those pictures only prove I carried it, not that I had knowledge of it or had a hand in it," she said evenly knowing he was trying to rile her with that comment.

He went over to the desk and brought over another folder of pictures. He placed one out in front of her and said," Is that you?"

She examined it and it was a picture of her walking towards an office building. Here we go again, she thought. Reluctantly she nodded. He placed down another. "And is this you leaving?"

"Yes, is there a point to this?" she snapped. "So, I'm walking in and out of a building. How is that incriminating?"

"Because that's the building, where you and Lopez met Ian Mekinkov, ex-KGB, who fused the information onto micro-film." He laid down two other photos, showing Gary entering and leaving the same building. "The time stamped says he entered five minutes after you and left about ten minutes after. So why you both there not wanting to be seen together or arriving together?"

Cheyenne looked at the photos again trying to remember why she had been there. Her attire told her she had to be working. She had large manilla envelope in her hand, so she had to be delivering to a client. Suddenly she remembered. She was supposed to deliver paperwork to a lawyer's office in that building and come to think of it, it hadn't originally been on her days schedule. Gary had added last minute. That son of--

"Cheyenne."

"I didn't meet up with him there." she stated. "I was delivering a package to a lawyer's office that day. If you look at the logs, you'll see I was there on a job."

"We did verify your whereabouts and there were no entries of you delivering anything to that location so there was no reason you should have been there."

"Well that's convenient." she spat, wanting to scream. "This whole thing has been orchestrated by Gary. He set me up, can't you see that!"

"Why, because he felt rejected and pissed that you wouldn't sleep with him?" Vincent shot back.

She lurched at him in anger, swearing at him, but agents intervened stopping her. She struggled against their hold. "Let go me."

"Miss. Nicholas calm yourself." Stewart ordered. "Or I'll have to consider you as a threat and restrain you. Is that what you want?"

She went still and shook her head.

"All right then. I think we should take a break." he suggested. "Maybe you'll come to see reason when you have some time to think about the consequences of that will happen if you're determined to stay silent." He turned to the agent near him. "Take her upstairs."

Cheyenne paced back and forth her room, her eyes puffy and red from crying. She had to find a way of convince the CIA she was innocent, that her part in it was circumstantial by association. The only thing she was guilty of was knowing Gary Lopez. How could he do this to her? Why was he doing this to her? Why wasn't he in custody being interrogate? Apparently, his involvement did not take precedence over hers. If he was the mastermind behind it all, why weren't they interrogating him? She was sure if they drugged him, he would tell them what they needed to know. It had finally dawned on her why she could not remember the last 12 hours. Vincent had drugged her. He must have failed in his mission, and his superiors decided to go with the direct approach. It did not make much sense to her. If they could not get anything out of her when she was under how were they going to when she was conscious?

She heard the click of the lock and in strolled Juliet carrying in a tray.

"I thought you be hungry."

"Thank you, but I've lost my appetite."

"You have to eat something," Juliet said as if she had authority on the subject. "You want to keep up your strength."

"For what, the trip to prison," she said, sarcastically.

"That can be avoided if you just tell them what they want to know," Juliet said.

"You must have selective hearing as they do because I've already stated I can't tell them what I don't know," she said heatedly.

"Are you protecting someone?"

"Who would I be protecting? If what the CIA is saying is true about me, I wouldn't have any associates to protect."

"What other reason do you have for keeping quiet," Juliet said "It can't be the money because you'll never get a chance to enjoy it spoils when you're spending the rest of your life in prison. Even if you are paroled after twenty years, the money is not going to do you any good. It will probably be worth half of what it is today."

"Well since I don't know what it's worth is, it doesn't really matter, now does it," she said.

"Suit yourself but I advise you to seriously look at your options."

"Look, I'm not holding out because I'm protecting someone or because of the money," she stressed. "You know what, forget it. It is useless talking to you people. You've already have set in your minds I'm guilty anyway."

She walked over to the window hoping Juliet would leave. She could not deal with any more accusations. All she wanted to do was curl up in bed and wake up from this horrible nightmare.

She gazed out, taking in the serene landscape when her view was instantaneously shattered into little pieces. She felt a burning, stinging sensation in her side as she went down. She landed on the floor hard with glass showering down on her. Her hands instinctively sheltered her face from the onslaught. She heard Juliet yell out for her husband and Vincent.

When everything fell into a dead silence, Cheyenne lowered her hands and cradle the pain in her abdomen. She found the area to be warm and sticky. She glanced down to see she was bleeding. She let out stifled cry and tried to stay calm. Tears trickled down her pale, ashen face. She squeezed her eyes shut and tried to sit up when she heard commotion.

Vincent charged into the room and was at her side, taking her into his arms. He cradled her head and covered her hand with his adding pressure to the wound.

"Juliet, get me something to staunch this-a towel, something," he barked out.

She did as he said, and returned shortly after.
"Vincent men are converging on the house."
"How many?"
"Six," she responded handing the towel.
"Go help Merrick and the others."
Cheyenne let out a groan and winced in pain.
"Hold on Cheyenne." He lifted up the soiled towel to see she was still profusely bleeding.
"Vincent," she murmured focusing in on him.
"Yes, I'm here."
"I've been...shot," she rasped.
"I know." He caressed her face, pushing away strands of her hair.
"Am I going to die," she said, fear taking hold of her.
"No, it's flesh wound. You'll be all right."
"Then why...do...you...sound...worried," she said wincing again. "You afraid you'll...lose your only lead?"

"God how you can you think that," he said angrily. "I'm not that heartless Cheyenne. I value life, especially yours and that has precedence over anything else."

She wanted so much to believe him but she did not know if she could trust him or his words. He had lied to her from day one. How could she be sure he was not telling her what she wanted to hear? She was laying there with a bullet in her.

She closed her eyes, trying to shut out the agony and pain rioting through her body. When she reopened them, she caught a glimpse of the windowsill. A pair of gloved hands clutched its rim.

She blinked believing she had to be hallucinating, but when the figure rose, she knew she was not.

"Vincent," she breathed. "There's...."

Before Vincent could fully comprehend her warning, the perpetrator butted him hard with the butt of his gun, knocking him out.

The man, whose identity was hidden by a black mask reached for her. She cried out as he hoisted her up, and braced her over his shoulder. She called out to Vincent in desperation but it fell on death ears. He was out cold, blood trickling down his temple from the blow. She beat her fists on the man's back, but it did not faze him.

He stepped out in the hall, on guard and proceeded down to the first floor using the servant stairs down to the kitchen. The sound of shouts and gunfire echoed off the stonewall as they descended. Her captor was prepared for confrontation for as they reached the bottom, he took out the two men scouting the room. He stepped over them and proceeded out.

"*Going somewhere?*"

Her captor bolted around, gun drawn, only to meet a deadly stare and a bullet to his head.

CHAPTER 9

"What's the report," Stewart asked pinching the bridge of his nose as he entered into the living room. He frowned at the sound of chirping birds frolicking in the morning dew as an officer handed him a cup of coffee. "Any leads on the whereabouts of Miss. Nicholas?"

"No," Vincent replied in a frustrated manner as he paced back and forth.

It had been twenty-four hours since the attack on the chalet and the disappearance of Cheyenne. The only thing that gave him some sense of connection to her was her locket, which he had nestled in his pant pocket. He had found it on the servant's stairs when he did sweep of the house. It must have been tugged off when she was carried off by the shooter. He rubbed the heart pendant as if was a magical lamp that would tell where she was.

They had no leads on her whereabouts or if she was still alive which, did not sit at all well with him. The idea that she could be dead tore at him.

When he found her shot upstairs the agony, he felt was indescribable. He had come to care for her and that was not a healthy state to be in when you were sworn to up hold the law. She was the suspect, not his ally. Having feelings for the enemy was a sure way to screw yourself and get burned.

If she had snow balled him, and deceived him as he did her...then they would be even, he thought dreadfully. She certainly found his deception cruel and painful. His betrayal had violated every honest, good thing about her. He had violated her trust and hurt her in the worst way a man could hurt a woman. No wonder she hated him.

When he was with her as Vincent Dmitri, he was more himself than he had ever been in on a case. He was more honest and truer to his actions than in the past. However, that was all irrelevant. His personally feelings, the lust he felt for her, could not come into play. He had to look at the facts as a CIA officer, not a man. It was not going to be easy, for their personal relationship was where he derived his ideals about her.

Since day one, she did not fit the profile. She was nothing like he expected. She did not act or come across as a deceptive, manipulate person. She emulated wholesomeness, honesty, and purity. Hell, she embodied all the qualities of a saint. The more he thought about it, she could not even lie convincingly to her merit. Her eyes betrayed her every time. He had known she had been lying when he had asked her about what her attacker wanted the day, she had been taken by gunpoint out of her hotel. If she was not a master of deception that meant she had been telling the truth all along. It would explain why their methods had not been working. She really did not know which made things a lot more complicated. Now that she fled, it was one more thing they had against her.

"If you don't relax, I'm going to have a worn pathway across my wood floors," Merrick said, thinking the next time the CIA wanted to use his house as a base of operations, he would charge a fee. "They'll find her, and the program before it falls into the wrong hands."

"It already has fallen into the wrong hands," he snapped. "Four people have come in contact with it, yet it's whereabouts seem to elude us. The last person who is associated with it, is missing and has no clue about any of it."

"You don't honestly believe that?" Stewart questioned. "Look at the evidence. She's guilty. Secondly if we don't succeed in finding her and getting it back, I can guarantee the agency isn't going to hold up to their end of the deal."

"The success or failure of this operation did not come into play when it was struck, only my reinstatement for this job," he shot back in anger.

"What are you two talking about," Merrick asked, piqued in finding out what was behind the hostility radiating from his friend.

"I guess you didn't read the fine print," Stewart said, as if Merrick had not spoken. "If your new girlfriend has already sold it and is sailing off into the sunset with her millions, or worse yet she's dead, were all screwed including Victoria."

"What was that about Victoria," Juliet said, strolling into the room.

"Hey my sweet," Merrick drawled. "Where have you been keeping yourself?"

"Have you seen our house," she said, "It's a disaster. I have just spent two hours trying to get bloodstains out of my Venetian rugs in the dining room. Not to mention making sure all the glass shattered everywhere was cleaned up. Did you know I found shards in the ceiling?"

"Juliet we'll handle the cleanup and any damages. You just take it easy."

"I second that." Merrick said.

"Fine," she said. "What's this thing with Victoria?"

Vincent let out a heavy sigh. "I made a deal with the agency if they wanted me back, they had to let Victoria out early."

"And they're reneging," she said.

"Not exactly," he answered. "They're just changing the terms."

"That isn't very honorable of them," she said, shooting Stewart a look. "Shame on you."

"Sir!" One of Stewart's officers addressed him. "We've just got report a woman fitting Miss. Nicholas's description was taken to a local hospital then seen early this morning hitching a ride back to Vienna."

"Are we certain of that," Stewart asked, signaling to have his car brought around.

"The witnesses I spoke with made a positive ID."

"All right, Stevenson's contact Vienna International and tell them to be on alert. If they spot her tell them to detain her," Stewart ordered. "West, you're with me."

"Can I tag along?" Merrick asked.

"If you promise to stay out of the way," Stewart said.

"Will do. You won't know I'm there."

"Where are we heading," Vincent asked, grabbing his jacket.

"To her hotel," Stewart said.

"Do you really think she show up there," Merrick asked, as they walked out of the chalet.

"Possibly," Stewart said. "I believe she's a virgin at this and has no idea what she's doing. She is an amateur taking things as they come. She has no idea what she's dealing with. I suspect Lopez inspired her to play in the big leagues and she got more than she bargain for."

"But if that was the case why would he risk sending her in on something this big if she wasn't prepared or had the skills to improvise if things went bad?" Vincent theorized, slipping into an unmarked black sedan.

"Who knows? We are not here to analyze his motives in why he chose to trust his ex-lover for the job. What difference would it make? It's not going to help us."

Knowing it was useless to talk Stewart anymore, Vincent fell into silence. They were going to have a difference of an opinion. Stewart had always been a matter of the fact guy and chose to see things in the same manner. Stewart was not a seeker of the truth. He did not get personal. He stayed neutral, and to the point. The objective was always his focus. He did not care about the history or the evidence the CIA had against the individuals or parties they were after. His job was simple, delegate their capture, and move on to the next mission. What happened to them afterwards was none of his concern. His narrow mindlessness at times disappointed Vincent.

They arrived at her hotel to see police cars and an ambulance parked out front. Their presence did not comfort them to say the least.

They walked into the lobby to see a lot of commotion and concerned guests. A group of hotel staff stood off to the side being questioned by the police while others talked aimlessly.

Vincent approached the check in desk and asked the clerk, whom he knew, what had happened.

"A dead body was found sir in one of the suites on the top floor, Twelve O' five, Miss. Nicholas suite," the young man answered in a low voice, his eyes cautiously surveying the lobby as if they might be being watched. A sense of dread washed over Vincent.

"Was *it*, Miss. Nicolas they found?"

"No sir," he said. "It was a man and from reports I've heard he wasn't a guest here."

"Felix," he said, leaning in. "have you seen Miss. Nicholas at all today?"

"No Mr. Dmitri. I haven't seen her since she left with you yesterday." Felix reported. "Though I just came back on duty an hour ago so I wouldn't know if she returned or not. I could check for you."

"I'd appreciate it, but don't make it apparent that's what you're doing."

"I understand." Felix said.
"Do you know if the body has been taken away?"
"No."
"All right, thanks."

He walked over to Stewart. "What's the report? Did you find out anything?"

"Not really," he said, keeping his voice low. "The clerk said a body was found in her suite, but that's all he knows. As for seeing her, he couldn't comply. He just came on duty."

"I'm sure she'd be long gone by now and not hanging around if she committed murder." Stewart remarked. "Could this get any worse?"

"We don't know for certain she even came back here, let alone kill anyone," he pointed out. "This murder could be non-related."

"The body was found in her *suite* Vincent." Stewart argued. "How could it not be related?"

"He does have a point." Merrick said.

"We aren't going to find any answers by hanging down here." Vincent commented, heading to the elevators. "Let's go check out the crime scene."

Moments later, they stood outside Cheyenne's suite to see the officer in charge giving out orders while another officer spoke with a maid, whom evidently found the body. Others were dusting the room for prints and gathering evidence. A photographer was on the scene taking photos for the crime lab.

Stewart contacted the American embassy and told them about the situation. They contacted the local authorities and as a curtesy let them examine the scene.

While Stewart conversed with the lead officer and Merrick poked around, Vincent made his way over to where the body laid. He took in the position of it and the locations of surrounding objects; the couch, the armoire; the writing desk and coffee table.

As he circled around, he noticed a crumbled manila envelope near the body, under the oblong glass coffee table. He crouched down and picked it up by its edges. He examined it, finding nothing of importance about other than it being there. He found a couple rubber bands inside, which indicated the contents that had been in it, had been bound. More than likely it was money, which gave the authorities an angle for murder. That did not help Cheyenne any.

Setting it aside, he inched over to the body, dreading what he would find. He removed the sheet covering the corpse to see the victim was faced down with a letter opener protruding out of his back.

Taking a deep breath, he placed his hands on the victims' shoulders, and shifted him to his side to get a better look of him. He took in the man's profile, and realized he recognized him from the sketch Cheyenne gave the police of her attacker. He inwardly cursed the heavens and hung his head. This was not good.

He sat back on his haunches and rested his hands on his knees trying to think of plausible reasons why the man suspected of being the second buyer was dead in Cheyenne Suite. The more he theorized there had to be a logical answer that acquitted Cheyenne of any wrongdoing, the more frustrated and aggravated he got. He could not go with the self-defense avenue, for the victim was stabbed from behind. If it had been in self-defense, he would have had to be facing her, not have his back to her. Even if he turned momentary before she attacked, it still would be premeditated for he was defenseless. If he threatened her life where she felt she had no other choice than to kill him, he had to have a weapon - a gun perhaps. From listening to the conversations around him, he had not heard another weapon had been found. That did not leave much room for doubt. Though every fiber in his being knew, she was not a cold-blooded killer. She could possibly be a thief but not a murderer. Obviously, the authorities and his superiors were not going to share the same sediment but he knew something was amiss there. What that was, he did not know, but since day one nothing fitted or made sense. It was too perfect for his liking.

He massaged his head trying to throw off headache that was forming when Stewart came over to him.

"I just finished talking to the officer in charge and found out our dead friend here is the fellow Miss. Nicholas reported attacked her a couple days ago." Stewart said. "It just would be our luck. You know we're screwed, don't you?"

Vincent did not comment, and Stewart continued. "If they find her before we do and arrest her, they have jurisdiction to try her here and insist she stays here until she's tried and sentenced. Do you know what that means?"

"That we're screwed."

"Exactly," Stewart grounded out. "We can't let that happened. We have to find her first and get her out of Austria. We will have a better chance keeping her in our custody if we get her to the US. By the time all the red tape is worked out, she will be serving time for the crimes she committed against us."

"What if she has already left Austria?"

"Then we keep searching." Stewart said. "She's bound to pop up on the radar at some point and when she does, she's going to be glad it was us who found her first."

Coming out of the darkness, Cheyenne eyes fluttered open. She focused in on the bright light streaming in from a small window over to her left that settled on her bed like halo.

She glanced around to see what she could only describe as a mediaeval crypt. The walls were a tarnish color of stone. The floors were wood worn with age. A plain, rickety old wood desk stood on the opposite side of the room. A crucifix was mounted above it. A simple white washed chair stood in a corner and there was a small side table next to the bed with a bible. Lord was she dead? She inched up only to cringe in pain. Apparently not, she thought, as she fell back onto pillows, cradling her side.

Was she a prisoner then? She remembered being shot, then someone climbing into her window, knocking out Vincent and carrying her off. That is all she recalled. She must have passed out and was brought to this...place.

What did they want with her? It was evident they did not want her dead since they patched her up. They must want information from her and plan to torture her until she gave it up. Was this nightmare ever going to end?

What had Gary gotten her into? If she ever saw him again, she would kill him.

Easing up, she dangled her legs off the side of the bed and stood. She steadied herself and made her way over to the small window. Peering out, she could see she was a couple stories up in an old stone building. It towered up like a castle on a crest of a rocky cliff. Her eyes were drawn to a tower where a figure in a brown robe paced. She could hear the low lull of chanting and at the sound of church bells in a distance, substantiating her suspicions that she was in a monastery.

What she did not understand was that if she was residing in a holy place, how could they let-whoever keep her prisoner there? As far as she knew, men of God did not assist criminals nor did they give sanctuary to people who intended to do wrong. It would be hypocritical.

Pinching the bridge of her nose to throw a spasm off, she turned to go back to the bed when she heard the click of the door. She held her breath and froze. The door creaked opened and to her surprise in came Juliet. She blinked and stared at her in confusion. What was she doing there and why did she have her luggage? Did Juliet work with the people who attacked the Chalet or was Cheyenne still in CIA custody? Maybe since the prior location was comprised, they moved her to another location. Then what happened to the man who took her?

Juliet set down Cheyenne's things and said, "You're up and around, that's good. Are you hungry?"

Cheyenne had a sense of déjà vu. This woman was determined to make sure she ate and kept up her strength. Her stomach gurgled at the prospect.

"Yes, I could eat something."

"I'll have the kitchen prepare you something." Juliet smiled. "It wouldn't be fancy mind you, but it will be something to satisfy your cravings. I'll be right back."

Cheyenne not knowing what to make of her or her friendly demeanor, just nodded.

Juliet returned twenty minutes later with a plate of cheese, fruit, and bread. She set it down on the side table and pulled up the rickety old chair for her. Cheyenne eased into it and broke off a piece of bread then cut a slice of cheese. She scoffed it down, giving a little smile of apology for her lack of manners.

"I take it I'm going to be here a while," she said, looking over at the tethered suitcases that held her clothes. "When is the next interrogation session?"

"There isn't going to be one," Juliet said pointedly. "The CIA doesn't know you're here. My husband doesn't even know."

Her eyes widen. She swallowed hard, and her heart began to race. Was her assumption, right? Did Juliet work for the other side? She glanced down at the bread she was about to eat and put it back on the plate.

"You have nothing to fear." Juliet reassured her. "I am not trying to poison you or drug you for information. I am here to help you."

"Help?"

"Yes. I happened to believe you're a victim in all this and are getting a raw deal." Juliet said, taking a bite of cheese.

"You believe I'm innocent?"

She nodded. "Yes, I do."

"But how, I mean everyone else believes I'm guilty. Why not you?"

"Because for one, I'm not them," Juliet said, sitting down on the bed. "Two, I'm an outsider looking in. I have not been taken in by conjecture, personal opinions and by views of others. In a way I have an advantage because I can look at your predicament without bias." She paused and situated herself more comfortably on the bed. "Granted the evidence is pretty damaging but like anything else evidence can be tampered with, manipulated and fabricated. I believe that is the case here. Thirdly being trained to profile people, I can tell easily if that person is capable of the crime he or she accused of."

"You mean can you sense and perceive their moral character just by studying them."

"Precisely," Juliet said. "You can call woman's intuition or instincts but it's a feeling, something you just know. There's no formula or logical reasoning in it."

"But in the realm of things a feeling can't free you from the realities you find yourself in."

"That is true, but a lot times a feeling can lead you to the truth."

"And that's why you're helping me," she said in wonderment.

"Yes."

"But I don't know how you can," she said in despair. "The evidence I'm certain was orchestrated by Gary, not fabricated. If the photos were tampered with, I'm sure the CIA would have discovered that. Secondly, there would be no reason into insert me in a picture of where I live or coming and going from a building they could easily get if they followed me. Plus, I remember them happening. How can I disprove it, since it's evident they did happen, just not how they're depicted."

"Cheyenne," Juliet said resting her hand on hers. "Don't get yourself into a tizzy about it. I know it seems like an impossible task but there's got to be a way to do so. We just have to get the CIA off your back first. And the only way we can do that is by giving them what they want."

"If that was possible don't you think I would have done that already? I mean I don't know where micro-film is, let alone know if I still have it or not?"

"It's just a process of elimination and clever thinking," Juliet said thoughtfully, standing up. "We know the buyers don't have it since they wanted you alive when they attacked the chalet and we also know the man from the ally didn't have it when he was found dead."

"Found dead!" A sense of dread consumed her. "The man who attacked me is dead?"

"Yes, and unfortunately you're the prime suspect since he was found in your suite early this morning," Juliet said, giving her apologetic look.

"*What*!" She bolted off the chair, cringing as a spasm of pain ripped through her.

"Easy, you'll reopen the wound." Juliet admonished helping her sit back down.

"That's the least of my worries," she snapped. "Actually, death would be a comfort."

"Don't say that," Juliet said. "It's just another obstacle to overcome."

"Obstacle!" She shook her head. "That's sure one humdinger of an obstacle." She began to rock feeling as if the world was closing in on her. Her breathing escalated and a horrified thought came to her.

"You didn't kill him, did you?"

"No. He was not there when I cleaned out your place. It happened after I returned to the chalet."

She suddenly felt nauseated and faint. "I'm going to be sent to the gas chamber or worse shipped off to some foreign prison where they torture you like in the '*The Midnight Express*'."

"That is not going to happen." Juliet stressed. "We'll get you out of this mess. We just have to figure out where Lopez put the micro-film."

"You know that is like looking for a needle and hay stack." Cheyenne declared, as she gnawed at her thumb nail. "It could be hidden anywhere. And what if he didn't actually give it to me. What if he just made it look like he did to divert attentions off of himself and to the sell directly himself?"

"Because the FBI would have caught him in the act for, they've been watching him for months." Juliet relayed "If he orchestrated, your involvement for whatever reason, he wouldn't jeopardize the charade by risking getting caught by selling it himself. We have to assume he did plant it on you to sell that you we're involved and we're double crossing him and the buyers. If you were a diversion, he had to give the CIA something good in order for them to get involve and go after you."

"But why me?"

"Are you married?"

"No, what does that…"

"Do you have a big social life, lots of friends?"

"Uh…Oh." She muttered, understanding. "I live alone, don't date much, and don't do much of anything accept work. I'm boring so I'm good candidate to be used. Wonderful."

"That's part of it. You also work and dated the man who's the bad guy so don't beat yourself up."

Easier said than done, she thought. Not wanting to discuss it anymore, she said, "What do we do? Where do we look?"

Juliet dumped her things on the bed. "We start here."

They methodically went through ever item she brought with her; her toiletries; make up; reading material and the lining of her clothes, shoes and other articles of clothing. They came up empty handed.

"This is useless," she said throwing her hands up in frustration. "We'll never find it."

"Don't talk like that. We're just missing something."

"We've gone through everything a zillion time. If it's not in a personal item then where else?"

"If Lopez planted it, he would have put it in something that you always carried close to you or was with you at all times."

"Like a lip stick container," she about laughed out. "Maybe my razor or shaving cream container? Oh, maybe my pain medicine bottle. We didn't look in there. Keys, or credit cards perhaps?"

"They're too small and flat. If we were looking for a micro-dot yes." Juliet conveyed, "But we're not."

They fell silent lost in their own thoughts. Cheyenne reached up along her neck to toy with her necklace, which she had a habit of doing when she was in deep thought, only to realize it was no longer there. She patted her chest and neck area hoping to find it in the folds of her white gown.

"What's wrong?"

"My necklace!" She off handedly said, padded down the bedding, slumping her shoulders in despair to find that it was not lost in the layers of the linens.

"What necklace?" Juliet said. "I thought all your jewelry was accounted for."

"Yes, I know, but this particular necklace I wear more and hardly take off. It was given to me by my mother after my brother died. It's very dear to me and I have to find it."

"I think I remember it. You were wearing it when you arrived at the chalet," Juliet reminisced, bracing her back as she paced. "You also had it on when they did the body cavity search and they didn't bag it, if I remember correctly."

"Excuse me!" She did not like the sound of that. "What's a body cavity search?"

"It's best you don't know." Juliet said.

"What kind of answer is that," she asked. "If you're trying to save me from knowing something unpleasant you shouldn't have said that. I suspect this body cavity search had something to with the fact that I woke up naked. They violated me, didn't they?"

"Not in the way you think."

"But they did violate me?" she insisted.

"We're getting off the subject." Juliet put in. "We need to stay focused."

"Fine," she said.

"With the issue of your necklace..." Juliet suddenly stopped speaking and looked thoughtful. "No, it couldn't be that easy?"

"What?"

"You said you hardly ever took off this necklace, right?"

"Yes."

"And you said it was special to you correct?"

"Yes, that's why I want to find it," she said, wondering where she was going with this until it hit her. "Oh my God, it's in the necklace!"

"Bingo!" Juliet said. "It's the only item we haven't considered or checked."

"But it's missing," she said standing up. "How are we going to be certain it's where Gary hid it if we don't have it to see for ourselves? We could be grasping at straws."

"We could be, but it's all we got. We have to assume it's there because it's the only thing that makes sense."

"True, but it doesn't do us any good if we can't find it."

"As I recall, you didn't have it when you arrived here which means it's either in the vehicle you came in or still at the chalet." Juliet theorized. "We just have to retrace your steps."

"I guess I'll leave that up to you since I can't leave here."

Cheyenne did not like the idea she had to put her life into Juliet's hands. It made her feel she had no control. She was grateful for Juliet's help and didn't know how she ever pay her back, but a side of her felt she should be the one fighting her own battles. She knew if Juliet hadn't interfered, she would either be in the hands of villains who shot her or the hands of the CIA with no hope of proving her innocence. Juliet took a big risk in helping her and could very well go to prison if things do not go the way she planned.

"Listen I need to return to the chalet before my long absence is questioned," Juliet said, breaking into her thoughts. "I'll do what I can in finding your necklace. With any luck we'll be one step closer in unraveling the truth."

CHAPTER 10

Vincent rubbed the back of his neck to massage the kinks out as he watched the tape footage, they took into custody from the Vienna International Airport. He glanced at the clock to see it was half past two in the morning and groaned. He had been at it for over six hours and had not had much luck in locating Cheyenne. There were a dozen cameras in each section of the airport and he looked at about four, the entrance, customs check in; international departure areas and the corridors in between coming up empty handed.

During the process, he theorized the options she might have taken. If she was fleeing because she was scared and did not know what to else to do it was possible, she had flown to Germany, or France, possibly Spain to catch a flight to the U.S. If she were guilty, she would have fled to some remote island or country where she could live quite well and disappear. However, if she were smart, she probably would not have flown but drove, which was an avenue Merrick was checking out.

Merrick had contacted the local authorities to see if any cars were stolen in the last 48 hours and sent the make and models of the vehicles to other law enforcement agencies throughout Austria, Switzerland and France. Merrick also made inquiries at the local car rental agencies giving them Cheyenne's description and instructions to contact them if she rents a car from them. They had scattered reports of her where a bouts from people that were a wild goose chase. They either were convincing themselves they had seen her or falsely passed along information to get attention.

He picked up the file on the report on the murder of the man in her hotel suite. He flipped through it, briefly looking at the pictures of the crime scene and reading over the evidence. He had only glanced at it earlier, not really wanting to know what they had against Cheyenne. He was delaying the inevitable. Stewart had told him he was trying to relive the past in hopes to redeem himself by entertaining that Cheyenne was part of some conspiracy. He could be right for old pains and fears had a habit of blinding you from the truth but he would not truly know that is the case until he found her.

His eyes scanned the report to see the victim was Josef Roth, a drifter and ex-con from Braunschweig, Germany. His rap sheet contained felonies from burglary to assault. There was a restraining order filed against him by his wife four months earlier. It was apparent his was just muscle and did his associates dirty work. He was on the bottom of food chain so his identity or death wouldn't lead him to them to the source. The only explanation why he ended up dead in Cheyenne's suite was to paint a darker picture of her as a murderess.

He sat back in the chairs stretching, letting out a frustrated sigh. He reached for his coffee cup and brought the rim to his lips only to realize it was empty. He pushed away from the desk and stood up.

He headed for the door and creaked it opened not stir anyone. Not that would happen since he had his own wing. How his friend managed to run and live in a house of that magnitude was beyond him. There were only two of them, with the exception with the third on the way. They either entertained a lot or planned to have a dozen children to fill it up. Then again, Juliet grew up in lavish ancestral homes and was accustom to living well for she came from a wealthy family.

He proceeded down the hall towards one of the many staircases in the house and descended down, thinking his friend needed a *YOU ARE HERE* map for guests so they knew where they were going.

He reached the main floor, and flicked the light switch squinting at its brightness. He made his way to the kitchen, which was dimly lit. He went over to the coffee maker, only to sag his shoulders in disappointment for there was not any coffee left. Going over to the cupboard, he rummaged through it for some instant coffee when he heard a thunk noise as if something fell. He leaned back and peered around the cabinet door to see nothing amiss. He rested his hand on his gun but did not withdraw. He heard another thunk noise mixed in with other unfamiliar sounds coming from the direction of the dining room. He slowly went over towards the doorway separating the kitchen to find a warm glow of light coming from the parlor room. He inched forward to see a figure huddling over the table that had the evidence bags from the attack. It appeared the individual was surveying the contents in them.

He stepped further into the parlor, to see it was Juliet. She sensed his presence and turned towards him.

"Hi," she said coolly, taking bite out of a pickle she held in her hand. "Couldn't sleep?"

"No. You either."

"Nope, the baby is restless. I swear he's nocturnal," she said smiling, resting her hand on her abdomen. "He's quiet as a mouse during the day but as soon the sun goes down, he's alive and kicking. Ooh he just moved. Here come and feel."

She grabbed his hand and placed it on her protruding stomach.

"See." She beamed when it kicked. "Doesn't it bring back memories when Victoria was pregnant with Samantha?

"Yes," he said solemnly. "She used to crave pickles too."

"Did she?" she said. "It must be a pregnant thing."

She paused, smiled, and went on. "I guess I'll head off to bed and see if I can lull Junior to sleep with this story I was reading." She grabbed a book from behind her. Yes, an Anne Rice epic about Vampires always puts me out, Vincent thought, catching the title and authors name as she clutched it to her chest. He did not comment but wished her a goodnight.

He reentered the kitchen moments later wondering what the devil she was up to. Why was she poking around in the parlor room like a thief in the night and going through the evidence bags when she had no business going through? What could she possibly find in them that would be any interest to her? Maybe she felt left out and thought going over the evidence would give her some insight into the case so she could be useful. Yet why be sneaky about it? He did not want to think Juliet was up to something deceptive, but this had not been the first time he caught her acting out of character. He spotted her throughout the day doing odd things like lying on floor in laundry room peering under the washer machine. She had told him it was off balance and she was adjusting the levels but for some reason he did not buy it. Merrick could have easily fixed it for her. But then again Juliet was fiercely independent and like handling things herself. Not knowing what to make of her and too tired to question it further, he returned to his room.

Easing back in front of his desk he had been working at, he picked up where he left off. The report mentioned no fingerprints were lifted from the letter opener, which was a good sign. They could not connect Cheyenne with the weapon. He went on to read that clothing and skin fibers were found and being analyzed. They would not know the origin of them for another couple of days.

He breezed along the statements taken by police, hotel management, and the staff. The words were beginning to blur for the lack of sleep was catching up with him. He was about to put it to bed when something caught his eye. He rubbed his tried, strained eyes and brought it closer.

In one of the accounts taken by the staff, a maid commented seeing a pregnant woman on to 12th floor elevator, shortly after eight, carrying luggage. The maid stated she had not remembered seeing the woman prior to that. Vincent wondered if the officer on duty had looked into that or not. The coroner reported Roth's death occurred later that morning indicating this woman's presence would not have pique their interest. He would have to call in the morning to inquire to see if they had checked it out. He had a sneaking suspicion that the pregnant woman had been Juliet on some mission to save the unfortunate. He could be jumping to conclusions, but it was a little too coincidental that a pregnant woman, who had never been seen before, was at Cheyenne's hotel the day after she had disappeared. Then there was Juliet's strange behavior in the parlor, which only added to his suspicions.

Not that it would surprise him that Juliet would aid the enemy for she had a history of pulling the same stunts with operations he collaborated on when she and Merrick were more integrated with INTERPOL as operators in the old days. In most cases, it saved the taxpayers a lot of money because her hunches were right, but there were times she was way off and almost got herself killed for it. However, that did not seem to faze her for she continued to be a torch for those who were accused of wrongdoing. There was certainly something up with her and he was certainly going to find out what that was.

Cheyenne strolled along the hall nodding to the monks as she passed when she saw Juliet coming towards her. She was bracing her back with her left hand and carrying a decorative cloth handbag in her right.

"What are you doing," she said taking the bag, which was lighter than she had thought. "You really need to be taking it easy."

"Cheyenne, you needn't worry about me," Juliet said giving her a smile. "Back pain is a part of the pregnancy."

"That maybe so, but you don't need to be adding more stress to it than need be."

"Lord you sound like my husband." Juliet laughed. "I tell him I'm pregnant, not incapacitated. I do not need my hand held nor do I need to be looked after like a child. I can do things just as well as I could do before. I just happen to be a little slower at it that is all. Besides my son will enjoy hearing he was part of an intrigue."

Cheyenne just smiled and shook her head. Juliet was a stubborn woman and Cheyenne doubted she would get her to see reason. If they were caught or it was revealed Juliet had helped her, her son might not get a chance to hear about his mother's adventure for Juliet would end up in jail along with her. However, there really was not much Cheyenne could do to prevent that. Her involvement was already put into motion.

"Have you had any luck in finding my necklace," she asked as they walked back to her room.

"No, I haven't," Juliet said. "I've turned the house upside down; talked to all the cleaning staff and searched the evidence bags not finding a trace of your necklace. I went to the morgue and searched the personal items and clothes of the dead that were tagged and found nothing. I was almost tempted to check the corpses themselves but since they were already shelved and iced, there was no point in it."

Cheyenne paled a little and felt her stomach turn.

"Creeps you out doesn't it?"

"Just a little," she said smiling wearily.

"Sometimes we have to do things we don't like," Juliet said. "Going to the morgue was my last resort since nothing else panned out."

With her shoulders sagging, Cheyenne said, "I suppose the only thing to do is, is to turn myself in before things get worse."

"If you do that, you'll blow any chance of clearing your name."

"That may be true, but I don't have the resources or the know how to do that," she expressed. "I have no experience, no connections, or abilities to pull off such a task. And without my necklace I have no means of keeping the CIA at bay, not to mention the Austrian police who think I murdered a *man*!"

"Look," Juliet said standing up. "I know it seems the odds are against you and you have zero chance of succeeding but if you give yourself up now the answers you seek will be lost because the trail will dry up. It will be harder to pick up any leads and find those responsible. In cases like yours evidence cease to exist. Witnesses and others involved end up dead. If you don't want to spend the rest of your life in prison, running is your only option."

"But if I run it's just going to make matters worse." She threw her hands up in the air. "They'll be like blood hounds, alerting every law enforcement in a five-mile radius, until they find me. My picture will be posted in every public establishment from here to Talito, which will make it hard to stay low key when I'm trying to clear myself."

"I hear you and I understand." Juliet said. "You're afraid-terrified-at the prospect of it, but you're not going to be doing this alone. I will be helping you through the whole process. Granted I will not initially be with you when you hit the road, but everything will be laid out for you. All you have to do is follow through on my instructions and you'll do fine."

"Instructions?"

"Yes Cheyenne. I have everything routed out for you from how you can get out of Austria undetected to a list of people who will help you when you get to the States." Juliet explained, withdrawing a folder and map out of her colorful bag. She spread it out on the bed and explained that Cheyenne would drive through Austria on back roads, stopping in Szombathely, Hungary to change out cars. Then drive to Graz and take a train to Trieste, Yugoslavia where she would fly to Venice by charter plane. From there she would fly back to the states.

Impressed, Cheyenne said, "I have to hand it to you it seems like a plausible plan but what about my travel papers?"

"Taken care of," Juliet responded, dipping into the folder. "I have a new pass port, birth certificate, and licenses for you. After you land on American soil, you will have to change out those for a different identity. The name you have on those documents will be dead to you once you go through customs. There's a locker that you'll have a key to that will have your new name and instructions on your next move."

"Rochelle Toussaint." The name rolled off her tongue. "I am French?"

"For now," Juliet said. "They'll be looking for American, and the more we de-Americanize you the better."

"I do speak French," she said, taking a closer look at the passport. "Yet I notice my hair is a lot darker, almost black in these pictures, and shorter. And it says I have green eyes."

"Yes. When you get a new name, you get a new look." Juliet said, pulling out a box of hair dye and scissors. She placed a small container on the side table. "Contacts."

"Oh."

The reality of what she was tempting finally set in. It made her feel ill. She could not believe she was contemplating what she was contemplating. She had to be out of her mind. There had to be another way, her mind screamed. Yet deep down she knew there was not.

Juliet handed her the hair die and sent her off to the bathroom.

An hour later her golden blonde locks were a dark chocolate brown, cut into stylish bob.

After several attempts, she put in the contacts and the transformation was complete.

"What do you think?"

"It's going to take some time to get used to." she replied wearily looking at her reflection. "I've never worn contacts before."

"There are going to be a lot of things you're going to have to get used to," Juliet said. "Starting now. You'll be leaving tonight."

"Tonight?"

"Yes. It is too dangerous for you to linger here any longer and it is getting harder to be deceptive around Vincent. He suspects something."

"Great." she muttered slumping on the bed. "This is not going to work. He a CIA agent."

"Officer." Juliet corrected.

"Whatever. Agent, officer, guy with a badge, it does not matter. He will track me down regardless because he relentless. I will never make it out of the country. He'll catch me before I can make the attempt."

"You think it will be him that brings you in?"

"He and the other...officers." she said going over to the window.

"You like him, don't you?"

She snorted. "The man wants to put me in jail Juliet!"

"True, but love has bloomed under stranger circumstances."

"*Love!*" she balked. "I do not love that man. He used me and he lied to me."

"He was only doing his job."

"Precisely." she said heatedly. "He's paid to seduce woman and to lie to people."

"I've had to be deceitful and do things that weren't pleasant. I was paid for it. Are you going to condemn me also?"

"But you're retired from that line work." she insisted.

"Just because I'm married and pregnant now doesn't mean I've hung it up." Juliet said. "Merrick and I still do jobs. Now Vincent did retire. He was only reinstated for this one job." That did not comfort her to say the least. It did not help change her opinion of him.

"Don't stress." Juliet said resting her hand on her shoulder. "There are worse things than loving the man you despise."

Cheyenne did not agree or disagree.

Driving along the long drive, Vincent pulled over to the side and cut the engine. He saw Juliet's car parked in a designated area in front of a grey fortification that had an archway leading into a courtyard. The bulk of the building was situated on a plateau of rocky terrain that tapered off to a valley below. A billow of clouds settled over the highest points, the towers looming skyward as stairways to heaven. It was secluded and isolated, away from the ways of the world where solitude could take up residence. It was a perfect place for a monastery and for the men of God to pray and hide fugitives.

After checking up on the account, the maid had given to the police and speaking to the woman himself, his suspicions about Juliet were verified. When he asked the maid about the luggage the pregnant woman carried, she commented that she had noticed the two large pieces were worn and had seen better days. That could only mean they had to be Cheyenne's. It was very unlikely two woman on the same floor could have tethered suitcases. Vincent then showed the woman Juliet's picture and she identified her as the woman she had seen.

As he looked more into the events of what happened the day Cheyenne was shot, it became known, that Juliet must have been the one who had taken out Cheyenne's captor. She had used one of the fallen officer's gun and replaced it back into their hands after the deed was done to make it look like the officer had gotten a shot off, killing her captor. More than likely Juliet was the one who sent them on wild goose chases too. Stewart and the Agency were not going to be happy about it. Blast that woman, and her instincts!

He stared out the window wondering what course of action to take when he caught a glimpse of Merrick coming up the rear in his side view mirror. He groaned and swore.

"Why are you following my *wife*?"

"Merrick what are you doing here?" he said, causally as Merrick flung open the passenger's side door and slide in. "You here for confession too?"

"Cut the crap Vincent and answer me."

"You're not going to like it?" he said dryly.

"When do I ever?" Merrick said. "But this time I know she's not trying to make me jealous so what's up with you stalking her?"

"I'm not stalking her." Vincent denied. "I'm checking out what she's up to?" He went onto explain his confirmed suspicions and Merrick blankly just stared at him as if he heard wrong.

"I shouldn't be surprised, but I am." Merrick conveyed. "I can't believe after all these years you still presume Juliet is up to her old tricks and hasn't learned from past experiences?"

"Old habits die hard Merrick," he said. "I didn't want to believe it either, but you can't deny the facts."

"The maid could have been mistaken." Merrick countered.

"She ID her and the woman had nothing to gain by lying."

"Lord, why now?" Merrick gritted out. "She's seven months pregnant and about to pop. She's no condition to be taking such risks."

"I agree but you know Juliet. She's always out to fight the good fight regardless of the circumstances or who's involved." he reminded his friend. "She was-is- still one of the best operator's I know, but you know as well as I do, she finds something she's passionate about or determined to carry through she wouldn't back down."

"She lets her emotions rule judgments is what you mean." Merrick put in. "And when that happens, she's risks her life in doing so."

"I don't think she's in any danger, at least not from Cheyenne."

"You seem to forget mate that Ms. Nicholas is wanted for murder," Merrick reminded him. "She's killed a man which says to me she's capable of anything."

"Is that what your guts says or you just basing that feeling on what you've heard and seen," he asked looking at him.

"Both," Merrick said. "It's enough for me."

"Well it's not for me." Vincent argued. "I've always trusted my instincts in the past and they've never failed me. Now I might not be certain on her involvement with the smuggling ring, but I'm damn sure she's not a murderer!"

Merrick did not comment. He knew matter what he said Vincent was not going to agree. When he got something into his head, there was no way of changing it. In many ways, Vincent was just like his wife.

CHAPTER 11

Cheyenne strolled along the garden wall admiring the plant life and surrounding beauty. The sky had turned a gloomy grey, casting a mystical, whimsical feel about the place. One's imagination could go wild under its spell. She wished she could stay there forever getting lost in its peacefulness, but she knew that was impossible. She was terrified what was beyond the walls of the sanctuary. She would be alone, traveling into the unknown with the law not too far behind.

She did not know she was going to pull this off. Juliet might have confidence in her, but she sure did not. The person Juliet felt was inside her did not exist. If she had some inner strength inside her to draw on then it better make itself present because she was on a verge of chickening out.

She did not know what Juliet was thinking. She knew absolutely nothing about being on the run. How was she supposed to act normal without giving herself away? She never had been good at deceiving or lying for that matter. She could not even act that well. The whole thing was doomed to fail. God help her.

Dejected, she slumped onto a bench seat, drowning in self-pity and dread. As if on cue, a stream of sunlight broke through the murky clouds, illuminating the valley below in a soft warm hue. The sight put a smile on her face, chasing the fears and doubt, giving her sense that she might succeed at her endeavors.

She rose and went back over to the garden wall and rested against it, the cool mountain air flowing over her. She sighed in contentment and gazed out on land only to have the moment interrupted by the sound of voices traveling on the wind. She looked in the direction they were coming from and saw two men walking below towards the entrance of the monastery. One of them stopped and gazed up. Cheyenne's heart stopped. It was Vincent. She immediately backed away out of his sight, thinking God must be playing some sick game with her.

Grabbing the hems of the white cotton dress she wore, she broke into a run toward the Abby, dashing passed the monks that prayed, tipping over a sacramental dish as she did so.

"Sorry." she called out as she rushed through the monastery to her room. She flung open the wooden slate door of her quarters and frantically grabbed her suitcases. She began throwing things in them like a mad woman.

Once everything was squired away, she headed out. She dragged opened the heavy old door and almost smacked into Juliet.

Startled, Juliet said, "Whoa there. What...."

"He's here!" She wailed.

"Who?"

"Vincent," she said in a panic state. "He's here with your husband."

Juliet swore. "Go down to the kitchen. There is a door next to the storeroom that leads down to the lower level on the south end of the Monastery. It is where the deliveries are made. There is an old white deliver truck. Take it. The keys are in the glove compartment."

"Okay," she said, hugging her. "I don't know what to...."

"There's nothing to say, just be safe."

"Thank you." With that, she took leave.

"You know we might be too late." Merrick commented as they followed one of the monks down a dimly lit hallway. "Juliet could have already gotten her out of the country."

"That had crossed my mind, but she visited our old friend Valerick early this morning in Vienna to obtain travel papers," he said. "They had to be for Cheyenne. I am certain Juliet is not harboring any other fugitives. Secondly, Juliet would not have sent her out of the country until Cheyenne was well enough to take it on. She was shot if you recall."

"Yes, I know in the side." Merrick said. "That had to hurt like a bitch."

"I'm sure it did." he agreed. "And since she's been under Juliet's watchful eye there's no way, she trekked back to Vienna to kill Roth." he pointed out. "Even if she managed to sneak out with an injury like hers, she would have probably torn the stitches in her side when she stabbed him. The exertion would have weakened her and she would have bled, where at some point she would have transferred it onto Roth or some another surface. From the report the only blood they found was Roth's."

"She could have wiped the place clean before she left." Merrick said.

"Yes, if had been premeditated," he said. "I doubt that she fled back to her to hotel, intent in knocking off Roth. There was no way she could have known he'd be there."

Merrick swore. "The hospital story and false leads were Juliet's doing, weren't they?"

"What do you think? She had to give us something to chase while she set up her deception."

"And this would be a perfect place for her do that," Merrick shook his head. "She comes her all the time to restore their many old manuscripts and books. It's common knowledge and since she's in favor with monks here, she has allies that would help her."

"Exactly."

Sighing heavily, Merrick said, "You better let me handle this mate."

They entered the library to see Juliet sat at a long wooden table, her glasses propped on her nose, examining the binding of one of the many books stacked next to her. She appeared thoroughly engrossed in it.

"Hello my sweet." Merrick called out in a cheery voice. Juliet glanced up. A mixture of surprise and pleasure spread across her face.

"Merrick, Vincent," she drawled pushing away from the table. "What brings you two here? Is everything all right? Has something happened?"

"No not at all love," Merrick responded kissing her affectionately. "We thought we stop by and see if you wanted to go...."

"Where is she Juliet?" Vincent demanded cutting him off.

He had no time for pleasantries or games. He was not going to pussy foot around like Merrick who was glaring at him.

"Where's who," Juliet said taking off her glasses.

"Don't play coy with me." Vincent growled. "I know you helped Cheyenne. Now tell me where she is?"

"I don't know what you're talking about," she stated, eyes narrowing in anger. "I haven't seen nor heard from Ms. Nicholas since she was shot. Now I know you're ticked off because she's the key to this Microfilm you're after, but don't come in here throwing accusations at me as a last resort because you have no leads on her where she is."

"We have a witness who ID you leaving Cheyenne's hotel the day after the attack," he said evenly. "I don't recall me or Stewart giving you the authorization to sweep her room and bag everything. Then there is the matter of you snooping around the evidence bags at two in the morning. As far as I know you're on hiatus from INTERPOL and haven't been recruited into the CIA." She did not comment but glared at him in contempt.

"What were you looking for anyway, something she told you to look for, perhaps the Microfilm," he taunted not fazed by her stony stance. "Did she tell you where to find it? Did she make a deal with you to where you could split the profits?"

"That's enough Vincent." Merrick warned.

"You contacted Valerick," he said pressing on, ignoring his friend. "You went to see him this morning and it wasn't for breakfast or a secret rendezvous. The only thing Valerick is good for is forging documents and unless you're planning on fleeing the country there's no need to look him up."

"Is that your proof?" Juliet placed her hands on her hips and glared at him again. "For your information I visit Valerick quite often. He is an old friend and as I recall it's not against the law to visit a friend."

"Oh, cut the bull." Vincent barked. "He passed you a manila envelope. I doubt it contained a priceless manuscript so cut the crap and tell me where she is?"

"I don't have a clue." she replied.

"*Juliet!*" he bellowed, cocking his gun but not withdrawing. "Don't make me take you into custody because you know I will. Now answer me!"

Merrick stood in front of him. "I said that's enough mate. Back off."

Vincent let out an angry, frustrated yell and swore. He walked out slamming the door. He paused outside counting to ten. He knew ranting and raving was not going to get her to talk even though he knew she was lying. She was being evasive on purpose just to piss him off and it was working. Hopefully Merrick would have a better chance of wearing her down. He figured he use this down time to search the monastery while Merrick put on the charm with his wife. He spotted a monk and asked him to show him all the rooms on that floor. The monk obliged and Vincent went into each one thoroughly checking them. When he stepped into the quarters Cheyenne had previously occupied his cell phone rang.

"What?" he snapped pausing in the doorway.

"Aren't we in a good mood?" Stewart Mathews observed.

"Sorry." he apologized. "Someone just cut me off."

"Where are you?"

"Driving along the countryside checking out leads," he responded his eyes giving the room a once over. "What's up?"

"We just got word Lopez's SUV was found abandon outside of Portland. He was nowhere to be found but there was blood all over the driver's seat." Stewart informed him. "It looks like he was shot somewhere around the chest/shoulder area."

"Did the blood work come back verifying it was his?" he said.

"Yes, it did." Stewart confirmed. "But we won't know how bad his injury is until we find him or his body."

"Then he could be alive, traipsing through the wilds of Maine with a bullet in him or he could be lying in the woods dead with the ravens circling over his remains," he said, walking further into the room. "Lord how could this happen? The FBI had men on him, as did we?"

"Our Guy was called off the detail. As for the FBI I don't know their story."

"Great. Whose brilliant idea was to take our guy off detail?".

"Houser." he muttered.

"The man is an idiot."

"He cut you your deal," Stewart reminded him. "I would watch it."

"Fine, but he's going to set us back if he keeps making stupid decisions like that," he said. "If Lopez is dead, Cheyenne could be next since she's the only one left connected to all this."

"Don't you think I know that?" Stewart said. "This whole operation seems to be fouled up but there's not much we can do about it accept to keep going at it."

"Do they have any leads in how Lopez's car ended up abandoned?"

"No not at present. Other than the indication he might have been car jacked is all they have." Stewart said.

"No prints were lifted?"

"Only his," Stewart answered.

"Did the car have gas?"

"I'm sure it did since it was founded miles outside of Boston."

"That's not what I mean." he said. "Did it have any gas in the tank when they found it?"

"I believe so. I would have to check." Stewart said. "Why?"

"If it had gas, it doesn't make much sense to steal a car, kill it's owner and then abandon it when they went to all the trouble to obtain it in the first place." he pointed out, when something caught his eye. "They had no reason to dump the car for they weren't being chased or hunted down by the local authorities." He leaned down and saw a torn piece of paper by the bedpost. He picked it up to see it was a ticket stub from an airline ticket. He noticed a partial name. It was Cheyenne's.

"I knew it," he bit out. "Damn that woman!"

"What are you talking about," Stewart asked peeved Vincent was not listening but off somewhere else. "Did some woman just flick you off?"

"No. I'm just distracted that's all."

"You can't afford to be distracted right now."

"I know," he muttered. "I have a job to do. You don't have to remind me."

"Just stay focused and find Ms. Nicholas. It's more impertinent than ever we find her if Lopez is dead."

"It seems to me whoever Lopez was taking orders from, did him in," Stewart said as he pulled off the sheets to the bed. There was a bloodstain on the mattress.

"You think he got axed?"

"It's a good possibility," he said, noticing Merrick and Juliet standing outside the door. "He'd become sloppy in his dealings and careless in whom he does business with. That couldn't have made his associate happy."

"If that's the case, Ms. Nicholas's life is in danger. If someone was hired to off Lopez, and possibly Roth, then she's could be their next target." That was not something Vincent wanted to hear. She was already a marked woman by others involved. They wanted either the Microfilm or her dead. He wrapped up the call and faced his two friends.

"I bet if I have this blood," he said referring to the stain on the mattress. "analyzed, it's going to come back as Cheyenne's. Not that I need proof since I have this." He held up the ticket stub. "It has her name on it so that pretty much says it all."

"Wow, I'm so impressed," Juliet, said, in false praise. "What great detective skills you have. I guess you better cuff me." She stretched out her arms and he gave her a look that said he was not amused.

"The gig is up Juliet," he said evenly. "Make it easier on yourself, and give her up."

"I'm her last hope. She's innocent and I'm not about to hand her over to a brute like you whose using her as a bargaining chip so Victoria can get a *get out of jail, free card*."

"I'm not trading Cheyenne's life for my ex-wife's." he argued. "Cheyenne's guilt or innocence has nothing to do with the release of Victoria just her capture."

"Then you're in this for personal gain, not justice, am I correct?" she asked, crossing her arms.

"I wouldn't answer that if I were you." Merrick warned.

"Look, think what you want. I do not really care. My main priority and duty is to find Cheyenne. If you want to stay silent, fine, but if our friends find her before I do, you better pray that the next time you see her, it's not going to be in a body bag." With that, he turned on his heel and headed out.

"She's heading south," Juliet said reluctantly.

"What road?"

"That I don't know," she replied honestly. She had no way of knowing if Cheyenne kept to the route, they discussed but even if Cheyenne did, Juliet wasn't about to give him everything. Just enough to get him started on the right track. The guilt trip would only work so far with her. She was not entirely convinced he had Cheyenne's interests at heart. She sensed Vincent cared for her more than he led on. He had feelings for her, but how deep they ran was another story. His guilt and the passion to right the wrongs of the past could override them.

"What's her new name?" he said.

"You're going to have to track down Valerick if you want that information," Juliet said. "I didn't see the documents. I thought it wise not to just in case I was forced to reveal it."

"She's no dummy my wife." Merrick commented smiling in a proud manner. Vincent gave him a look and rolled his eyes heavenward. Knowing this was as much as he was going to get out of her, he did not comment. He spent too much time as it was grilling her. He suspected that was her agenda, to delay him from getting a better lead on her. She was definitely no dummy.

Cheyenne looked down at the map trying to read it and drive at the same time but was failing miserably at it. She had been on the road for two hours and she was not near where she was supposed to be. She missed the turn off for Graz, and was heading west to God knew where.

She pulled off the road and cut the engine. She spread out the map and tried to figure out where she exactly was. She passed a sign a while back and made a point to remember the town mentioned. She rubbed her arms for there was a chill in the air, realizing she would have to turn back and go about twenty-five miles to the road, that would take her to Murzzuschlag then to Graz.

She folded it back up and tried the starter but it would not kick over. She tried again, but only got a grinding noise. She sat back praying she just flooded the engine. She waited a few minutes before trying it again. It sluggishly roared to life, shuddering and shaking. She put it into drive and started out. She went about five miles when it gave out on her. She rolled to a stop and she hit the steering wheel. She rested her head on it groaning in frustration. She was cursed plain and simple. She glanced at the dashboard to see everything was level accepted for the gas gage. It was on empty. Idiot, she thought. She did not think of checking how much gas she had. All she had cared about was getting as much distance as she could from Vincent. There had been no way in telling when it had been driven last or when gas had been put in it. Lord why had not she been more observant?

Sliding out, she slammed the door shut. What was she supposed to do now? The closest gas station was probably in Graz. She could not call for a tow truck for she did not have a cell phone. Her only option was to walk. Wouldn't that be fun, she thought. What if it rained or got colder? That would not be pleasant. Then there was the chance Vincent could come along and take her into custody. There was nowhere to run or hide if that happened.

Sighing almost in defeat, she began walking, taking in the emerald green rolling pastures with the majestic snowcapped mountains as a back drop, thinking at least she had that to distract her. Time would indeed go faster.

She had gone about two miles when she noticed a drive up a way. As she got closer, she could see it led to a farm. There was a large barn with livestock roaming here and there beyond the fence. Set back in a patch of trees was a two-story house that had the country flare of the old European style. Two foreign cars were parked out front, sedan, and a truck. Maybe she could elicit the owner's help. They had to have a phone. She knocked on the front door and a portly man with a receding hairline answered. "Ja."

"I'm sorry to bother you," she said in German. "My car ran out of gas up the road. I was wondering if it was possible if I could use your phone."

"Yes," he nodded stepping aside. "Where were you headed?"

"Murzzuschlag."

"You'll be needing a ride then?" he said matter of fact. "Murzzuschalg isn't far from here but to walk it would take you some time. I'll be happy to give you a lift."

"That's very kind of you."

"My pleasure," he said. "You are American are you not?"

"Uh....ah....."

"My niece married an American," he said conversationally cutting her off. "Her father is from Virginia."

She just smiled and followed him inside.

After a sip of tea and a few cucumber sandwiches, they headed out to his truck. When they reached it, she noticed a car at the end of the drive. It was driving at a snail's pace as if they were checking the place out. Cheyenne's heart began to race. What if they had found her, her mind screamed, but before she could really panic, the car moved on. She let out a sigh of relief and quickly slid into the truck.

Once on the road she periodically glanced in the side view mirror to see if they were being followed as her chauffeur rattled on about this and that. She ended up knowing his life story by the time they rolled into the outskirts of town. He pulled up to a white building with a low porch that had a sign that read *Danglers's Auto Ausbesserung geschaft'* There was a garage like opening on the side indicating it was a car repair shop, though there were gas pumps out front.

Thanking him, she slid out the truck and he insisted he wait until she got things squared away. She told him she knew someone in town that would help her from there and thanked him again for his kindness. He seemed to buy her story, wished her luck, and drove on. She waited until he was out of sight and headed to other side of the road. She had no inclination of returning to the old beat up truck and filling her up. She was to have already changed out cars anyway and she doubted the tin bucket would make it up through the windy roads in the mountains.

She headed down Main Street in hoping to find a car rental agency when she stumbled on a train depot. She glanced at the train schedule, noting Murzzuschlag seemed to be a major line between there and Vienna. It had an offshoot to Graz. Why go to the hassle of renting a car when she could have someone else do the driving? She had new travels papers, so no one could track her down for they did not know her new identity. She would have to hand over some sort of identification either way. Once she was in Graz, she would get a room and try to figure out her next move.

CHAPTER 12

"Rochelle Toussaint." Vincent muttered massaging his chin as he looked over the copies of the forgeries, he obtained from Valerik. There was a passport, birth certificate, license, and credit cards.

"He sure went all out didn't he," Merrick said peeking over his shoulder, picking up an altered picture of Cheyenne. "I must say she doesn't look half bad as a brunette, though the green eyes don't do it for me. Hiding those beautiful, mystical brown eyes of hers is like covering up a master piece painted by…"

Vincent snatched the picture out of his hands. "Is there something you want?"

"You know there's no reason to bite my head off," Merrick said plopping on the couch behind him. "I was just admiring her qualities like any other man would."

"She's isn't yours to admire." he snapped. "You have a gorgeous wife to lust after."

Merrick laughed. "And you don't."

"What is that supposed to mean?"

"It means I have the better of two worlds and you don't." Merrick replied. "But I can't act on it for I'm spoken for, but there's nothing stopping you. You are free to love her the way you would like to without any hesitation." He paused and took a swig of his drink. "And don't give me that look like I don't know what I'm talking about. You want her. It is plain as day so there's no use denying it."

"You're confusing me with the guy I portrayed to seduce her, the lover." he stated. "I'm no longer him."

"But you're one in the same." Merrick argued. "You just choose to bury that side of yourself because it would complicate things."

"Exactly."

"Then why haven't you told Stewart or the agency that you have a way of finding her, huh?"

"I felt it would better if I find her first myself because if the agency knows how to track her down, they'll notify the local authorities to help in the effort. They will say she is armed and dangerous, putting them on shoot to kill status. It won't take much to provoke them to get their gun off," he explained. "I don't want to have to go down to the morgue and ID her body."

"If you keep them in the dark and they find out you're keeping information from them they'll take you out of the game. Not to mention they will renege on your deal. Do you really want to risk that?"

"The main objective is to get the Microfilm back and bring Cheyenne in," he argued. "When everything is said and done, they're not going to care on how it was achieved as long as they get what they want. And by the time they figure out that I have the heads up on them, she'll be in custody and they'll have the Microfilm in their hands."

"That's if she still has it and you actually do what you say...." Merrick started only to be cut short by Vincent's cell.

Vincent flipped it opened. "West, talk to me."

He listened attentively to what the other person on the other end conveyed.

"Are you sure, when was it used? A half hour ago. Where? Graz? Thanks! I owe you one."

He hung up and turned to Merrick. "Cheyenne used one of the credit cards for a train ride to Graz and a hotel room." He stood up and grabbed his jacket. "We got her."

"I wouldn't be so sure or get ahead of yourself." Merrick said. "She could split before you reach her."

"She got a room," he reminded his friend. "I don't think she's going anywhere anytime soon."

"She could be just freshening up before she continues on her journey." Merrick countered. "There's no guarantee she's in for the night."

"It's the only lead we have on her Merrick," he stressed. "Leave it at that."

"What do you want me to tell Stewart when he asks where you've gone?"

"Make something up but make it believable," he answered, digging into his pocket for his keys, and pulled out Cheyenne's necklace instead.

"Right, that will be easy," Merrick said, taking notice of the necklace. "What's that?"

"Locket," he answered slipping it back and retrieving his keys.

"Apparently," Merrick said. "It is hers, isn't it?"

"So, what if it is."

"Hey, I'm just clarifying a fact." Merrick said, holding up his hands in defense. "Though I am curious in why you're carrying it around in your pocket when it should be tagged along with rest of her things."

"It might get lost," he said flatly.

"And why should that matter to you," Merrick questioned. "If she's just a job to you why protect a trinket of hers?"

"I'll see you in a few days," he said not granting him answer and heading out.

Cheyenne stepped off the train drained and tired. Her wounded side began to hurt and throb in pain. It burned as if it was on fire. She rested against a column and placed her hand protectively over the wound. She cringed when a spasm shot through her. She lifted her blouse to see the wound had not bled through the bandages. She thanked the heavens for that.

Pushing off, she looked around to see if there was a vender and spotted one. She had not eaten since breakfast and she was hungry. She made her way over to it and purchased a few items, scoffing them down even before she got out to the main entrance of the depot. There was a gift shop just inside of it and she picked herself up a guidebook and a map of the city. She flipped through it looking for accommodations.

She found a hotel that would do. A local pointed her in the direction she needed to go and what tram and bus to take which she was grateful for. Graz was a big city and foreign to her. Any help she could enlist was appreciated. She found the people very gracious and helpful.

Standing on the platform of the trolley going down the center of one of the main roads, she admired the architecture and life of the city, wishing she could explore it and take in all the sights. Unfortunately, she was not a tourist on holiday.

She reached the establishment shortly after and checked in. It was very quaint, homey place. It had a beautiful garden and courtyard she knew she would take advantage of that evening.

Once she settled in, she gave herself a sponge bath rinsing off with a quick shower. She felt refreshed and revitalized. She stood in front of the mirror trying not to dwell on the fact she had been shot a couple days prior and began brushing her newly darken locks. The reflection that stared back seemed to be a stranger to her. She did not feel like she knew herself anymore. She was acting and behaving like someone else. How did she get to this point? She never ran away from anything in her life but here she was a fugitive, suspected of murder, running from the law. She felt so alone and confused. God love her, she wished Vincent were there beside her. She missed him. She knew that was ludicrous for he had used her, lied to her, and manipulated her caring for him, but she ironically felt safe with him. How crazy was that? The man who wanted to send her to prison made her feel safe. She should not want anything to do with him.

Everything that he did and said was an act. None of it had been real. He made her think she was worth looking at and being with. He had made her feel wanted and needed. What a fool she had been to believe a man like him would want her. She had been stupid and naive. She must be an easy mark for despicable, good for nothing jerks.

Grumbling, she walked out of the bathroom in a disgusted fashion. As she passed under the doorway, she let out a strangled cry, her towel slipping to the floor.

"*Gary!*" she rasped.

"Hello love," he said, smiling hungrily at her. "I must say I wish you greeted me like this when we were together."

She snatched up the towel and covered herself.

"Don't you touch me!" she warned as he stood up and came towards her. His arm shout out, encasing her by the waist, pulling her roughly up against him. He intertwined his hand into her hair and yanked her head back. He gave her a rough, brutal kiss. She kneed him and smacked him across the face.

"I take it you're not glad to see me," he said laughing off the pain she caused.

"What do you think?" she cried striking out at him. "You set me up!"

"Someone had to be a decoy and unfortunately my love you were a perfect candidate," he said stepping out of her reach. "Secondly you owe me one."

She let out an angry cry. "Why you..."

"Bastard." he finished for her.

"I was thinking along the lines of something more deserving than that," she said. "There actually isn't a good enough word to describe what you are?"

"Why aren't we a little spitfire?" he drawled.

"What are you doing here and more importantly, how did you find me?"

"Quite easily," he answered matter of fact, taking a seat. "I just followed your boyfriend from your hotel to the house in the country which led me to the monastery. I happened to see you overlooking the stonewall. I did not recognize you at first since you reinvented yourself with a new look which I might add looks good on you. I've always loved brunettes." He smiled knowingly and went on. "Figuring monks are of the male sex there was only one conclusion it had to be you. Why else would you be there if you weren't in hiding."

"You then followed me from there."

"Yes, I was lucky enough to see you take off in that old truck you abandoned before hitching a ride to Murzzschlag. I then tailed you from the train station."

"Why? What do you want from me?"

"Do you really have to ask?" He stood. "I mean you might be naive but you're not stupid."

Swallowing hard, she said, "You want the Microfilm."

"Bingo!" He withdrew his gun from the back of his pants and cocked it. "I can't let it fall into anybody else's hands especially the CIA or any other agency. Of course, I knew there could be a chance I was taking a risk by planting it on you, but I had to give them something substantial."

Just as Juliet concluded, she thought miserably. She was a pawn in some sadistic plan of his.

"Let me get this straight, you want the micro-film back to destroy it?" she asked, more confused than ever. "What about the buyers? You're going to let that go and not give them what they paid for. Won't that be bad for business. No one will trust you once it gets out you don't keep your word."

"That's where your wrong love." he drawled, gently caressing her face with the gun. "No one will trust you, because you've been the one, they've been conducting business with, not me. I'm a silent partner." He lowered the gun and placed it back in the crest of his jeans. "See for me, this is not a onetime opportunity to a make a fortune. I have several buyers lined up so I'll be okay, love. You shouldn't worry about me. I'll do all right." He smirked, then put his hand around her throat. "Now enough stalling! Give me the locket?"

"Locket?" she repeated feeling all the blood rush to her head. Their assumptions had been right. He had put the Microfilm in her necklace but she no longer had it. What was she going to do? If she told him she had lost it, he would kill her. He would have no use for her. She had to stall him somehow. She had to get him out of her room and somewhere public where she would have many opportunities to get away from him. She doubted he take her out in front of witnesses. At least she hoped he would not. She had to convince him she had it but not on her, but somewhere safe.

"Well love, where is it?" he demanded as he retrieved his gun and cocked it.

"It's not here."

"What do you mean it's not here?" he growled, pressing the gun into her cheek. "You hardly ever take the damn thing off. It is why I placed the Microfilm in it to begin with. That damn necklace was like a token or memento to a dead lover than a brother. I felt I was competing with it and its memory whenever I was with you."

"You're welcome to look," she offered. "But you won't find it. It's in a safe place."

"Like where, between your legs where's there no access?" he taunted.

Her hand came up with force, smacking him across the face. He smacked her back and shoved her onto to the bed. He crawled over her and straddled her. He grabbed her by the throat with one hand and pointed the gun at her head with the other.

"*Where is it?*"

"I told you it's not here," she gasped, her breath coming short. "But I'll take you to it. It's in the safe downstairs."

He released his hold on her. "You better not be lying because if you are, you're going to wish my associates had done you in when they had the chance."

She sat up gagging, insisting she was not and he threw her some clothes, demanding she get dressed. She slid off the bed, grabbed them and headed to the bathroom.

"I don't think so love," he barked. "You dress here where I can see you."

She did not argue but did what he said.

Once they were on the main floor, Lopez guided her over to the front desk, but no one was managing the post, which she was grateful for. It gave her some time to think of an escape.

"Are you looking for the Wilmot's," a guest asked taking notice of them.

"Yes."

"There in the kitchen."

"Thanks."

Gary pushed her forward almost making her stumble into an umbrella rack.

Straightening up, an idea hit her.

Without thinking twice, she grabbed a wood handled umbrella. She swung her arms out as if she was going to hit a baseball and hit him square in the face, knocking him off balance. The gun clattered to the floor as he yelped out in pain, cursing and yelling. She snatched it up and made a dash for the front entrance. She shouldered a guest coming in as she rushed out.

Once outside she frantically looked both ways trying to decide which way to go when she noticed she had the gun in plain view. She quickly slipped into the front of her pants and began walking.

She wove through the crowded sidewalk, occasionally looking back. She spotted Gary a block down in hot pursuit. She picked up the pace, and tried to figure out how she could lose him. She knew if she darted across the road or even ran down a side road, she would be more exposed. She had to find a place with many people, but there were not many businesses she passed that had large crowds she could get lost in.

She glanced back again to see Gary was gaining on her.

Side stepping in front of pedestrian, she shadowed them for a few blocks when she came upon a bookstore. Panicking, she slipped inside hoping she duped Gary. She made her way over to rows of bookshelves and darted behind one. She peeked around it, her eyes trained on the front of the store. Gary appeared moments later. He paused outside and looked up at the sign. She could see his face had begun to swell and he was cringing in pain. Good, she thought. He deserved everything he got.

He peered into the store and she slowly moved back into the shadows. She heard the chime of the door moments later. Damn it, she thought. She was hoping he would have moved on, but why would her luck change now. She prayed there was a back door.

Vincent stepped out onto the curb a few blocks down from the hotel Cheyenne was staying at. He had hired a chopper to bring him down and had made it there in record time. He locked his rented BMW and made his way up the road to the hotel. He was almost upon it, when he saw a woman jolt out of the entrance. She looked his way and he realized it was Cheyenne. She had something in her hand that she slipped into the front of her pants. It was gun. What was she doing with a gun, he thought?

Before he could react, she took off running. He swore and was just about to go after her when a man charged out, frantically looking up and down the street. He was cradling the left side of his face, spewing and cursing. He took off in the direction of Cheyenne. Vincent followed.

He had gone a few blocks when he spotted the man dip into a store. He figured Cheyenne must of had opted to duck into the place hoping to lose him. Vincent decided to take the side road that crossed the one he was on and cut through the ally. He knew the only exit out of the place was in the back and eventually one of them would come barreling out.

With her heart pounding, Cheyenne inched around the bookcase to see Gary causally dart down one of the isles. She quickly made her way to the back of the store, keeping out of sight as best she could. She paused by a revolving book shelve in the children's book area to see Gary was momentarily detained and made a run for the exit.

She plowed through the door only to be grabbed from behind as soon as she stepped in the ally. A hand clamped over her mouth.

The arm that was free slipped under her shirt and relieved her of the gun. She twisted and squirmed trying to break herself from her captor's grip, but the harder she fought the tighter the hold on her became. She was pulled down the alley a way then dragged into an alcove. The next thing she knew she was pressed up against the wall. She was about to protest and put up a fight when she realized who held her captive.

"Vincent." she breathed, wanting to slump down and cry. How could this be happening? First, Lopez now him. What did she have, a tracking device implanted in her? It was either that or Juliet gave her up.

"Relax." he told her. "I know you're distressed, but things are going to be okay."

She snorted. "How are things going to be okay? *You're here!*"

"Would you rather be in the company of the man chasing you?" he said.

"Not particular but I don't want to be with you either." she said struggling against him. "You're a liar, a deceiver! All I am to you is a job. You do not care if I am innocent or not. *You do not care about me period. I'm......*"

He placed his hand over mouth and "Hush."

She glared at him as he peeked around the corner. He saw the man who was after her bolt out into the ally and look both ways. The man kicked the door in anger and yelled out a curse.

Vincent took a good look at him and thought he looked familiar but he could not place him. Vincent watched him stomp off, swearing and kicking garbage around in the opposite direction. He disappeared around the corner shortly after. He turned his attentions back to Cheyenne, taking his hand off her mouth and replaced it with his. He kissed her deeply and thoroughly.

"That should tell you that you're more than a job to me," he stated, withdrawing. "And for the record I care for you more than you'll ever know."

Taking her hand, he stepped out into the ally.

"Where are we going?"

"Someplace safe."

CHAPTER 13

Checking his rear-view mirror, Vincent drove through the streets of Graz making sure they were not being followed. The sun had gone down and the city was alive and hopping. He had a friend from the old days that would set them up for the night at his hotel. It was on the outskirts of town and would be a good place to regroup.

He glanced over at Cheyenne. She stared out into the night silent as a mouse. She had not spoken since they got in the car. Not that he blamed her but he needed some answers. He needed to know how deep she was in and if she still had the Microfilm. Whether she was guilty or not, he would do what he could to help her.

"What were you doing with this?" he asked straight out, holding up the gun.

"It's Gary's," she said crossing her arms. "He threatened me with it."

"Wait, back up a minute. Gary Lopez is in Austria?"

"Yes. Don't you know your own suspect when you see them?" she said looking at him.

"His face happened to be bashed in so I didn't recognize him." he retorted. "Secondly our Intel said he had been shot during a carjacking outside of Portland. We suspected either he was in hiding, laid up or he was dead. The agency didn't expect he would risk showing his face let alone make a trip over the Atlantic to reconnect with you."

"Apparently you all were wrong," she said touching her bruised neck, remembering his hand digging into her throat and the barrel of the gun pressed to her forehead.

"Did he do that?"

"No. I just inflicted it on myself for the sake of it," she snapped.

"Why did he hurt you? Was it because he thought you double crossed him?"

"No," she barked. "He wanted the Microfilm so he could destroy it."

"Wait, what?" he pulled over.

"Yes, I know. I was as surprised as you." she spat. "Apparently he never planned giving it to the buyers because he never did business with them. This whole time they thought they were directly dealing with me. It was all a rouse to get the *CIA* involved. That's why he risked giving it to me." She hit him. "This is all your fault."

"You're blaming me for this mess." he charged. "I'm not the one who's connected to Lopez."

"So, you're saying I'm naïve and easily duped because I was deceived by Lopez." she spouted. "I suppose it's the truth because I fell for every hook, line and sinker you emulated."

"Look I'm not going get in a fight with you over your insecurities." he barked. "I'm sorry I hurt you but we have more pressing matters to deal with than personal matters."

She didn't respond but stared out the window.

"What happened with Lopez?" he said, moments later. "Did he get the mirco-film?"

"The only thing I gave him was a lot of pain."

"Is that your way of saying no," he said, his patience wearing thin.

"Yes, it is."

"Do you know where it is, where he hid it?"

"Yes and no." she responded, slumping back.

"What does that mean? You either know or you don't Cheyenne. Which is it?"

She didn't directly respond. He wasn't sure she would when she blurted, "I lost it."

"*Lost it,*" he said, turning towards her. "How in god's name did you lose it?"

"It fell off!" she said.

"Fell off?" he repeated as if that was the most ludicrous thing he ever heard. "Off where?"

"My neck," she said angrily. "Gary hid the Microfilm in my locket, the one I showed you that had my brother in it, but I didn't know. Juliet and I did not figure it out until I realized it was gone when she brought me to the monastery. She tried to backtrack my steps from my arrival at the chalet to when she saved me from being kidnapped by the shooters, but came up empty handed. It is as if it disappeared into thin air. It was my only...." Her words faded as she stared dumbfounded at her necklace dangling from Vincent's hand.

"You had *it*," she said not believing her eyes.

"Yes," he said, looking at it. "I found it on one of the steps on the servant stairs. I was keeping it safe until I saw you again. I knew how much it meant to you and thought you would want it back."

That gave her a moment's pause.

She let out a sigh. "You were right, I would have. Can I please have it back now?"

"Not until I have extracted the Microfilm," he said, replacing it back in his pocket and pulled back onto the road. "To think I had it all this time."

"Yes, how ironic." she mumbled starring out into the night, the lights of the city mingling into a blur.

Pulling up to sandstone colored hotel, he cut the engine and stepped out.

Droplets of rain beaded up on the dry, well-used sidewalk as he opened the door for Cheyenne. She mumbled a thank you and followed him into the establishment in stony silence.

Vincent approached the counter, exchanged pleasantries with the owner, and got them a room. She noticed one of the guests, a matron, whom was well dress, wrinkle her nose and give a disapproving look at them as the keys were handed over. She snorted when she caught Cheyenne's gaze and walked out, head held high as if she had the authority on morality. Cheyenne narrowed her eyes and thought, what did she know the old crony. It did not mean that just because they had no luggage, they were renting the room by the hour. Anger consumed her and she wanted to go rant at the old bitty but decided against it. They could not afford for her to make a scene. She knew she must be under a lot of emotional distress to be riled up over that. She had a sudden urge to curl up in a ball and cry. She wanted to be able to blend into her surroundings and disappear. She wanted to go to a place where she could just escape the nightmare she was living and forget something that would not give her a hangover or withdrawals.

She followed Vincent up the winding staircase to the third floor to their room. She was too distracted and upset to take in the classical decor and baroque furnishing. She just plopped on the bed and watched Vincent check things out. She wondered what he planned to do with her. Was he going to bring her back to Vienna and turn her over to the authorities, what?

The idea of going to prison scared the hell out of her. She would never make it through the sentencing. It was bad enough going to jail when you did commit a crime. If you did not make friends fast, you ended up being someone's lackey and punching bag. She would be an easy target. They hurt just because they could.

She covered her face with her hands trying to hold back the nausea threatening to overcome her when she felt Vincent take her hand. She looked up just as he clamped on a handcuff on her right hand. He attached the other half to the bedpost.

"Hey!" she bellowed twisting her hand back and forth as if the motion would break the steel "What is this?"

"I don't want you wondering off."

"Wondering off!" she cried. "Where would I go? I have no money, no passport to flee with. I have no friends. Where could I possibly go?"

"Anywhere you please." he stated, grabbing his keys.

"Where are you going?" she asked as he headed for door.

"Out." he replied.

"Obviously," she retorted. "But why? Are you going to go and get yourself a girl for the night?"

"I already have a girl," he said.

She gave him a look. "Think again."

He just laughed. "What room were you in at the hotel?"

"What room?"

"Yes, room."

"Seven, but....."

"Thanks." he said cutting her off.

"Vincent!" she barked.

"What?" He stopped in mid-stride, and turned towards her.

"You can't leave me like this." she exclaimed in frustration, pulling on her restraints. "What if I need to use the facilities, or there's a fire?

He did not comment but walked into the bathroom. She heard him turn the water on then off. He came back out carrying the ice bucket.

"Here," he said setting it down on the side table. "It has many uses."

She let out an angry cry and sat back down on the bed stewing. He started to head out only to pause as if he had forgotten something. He went to the side table and grabbed the phone. He yanked the cord out of the wall and placed it where she could not reach it.

"I can't believe you," she said glaring at him. "Who do you think I'd call?"

"Your accomplice."

"My accomplice!" she bellowed. "Do you think that I'm that desperate to call Gary for help me when he's the reason I'm in this mess. The man wants to kill me!"

"I'm not talking about your ex-lover." he replied. "I was referring to Juliet."

"He isn't my ex-lover!" she snapped. "I know you find that hard to believe, but it's the truth. Just because society has gone liberal on sex docs not mean I have to. I'm not a conformist."

"I would have never expected you would be." he said. "But regardless of that fact, I don't think you were ever tempted to explore a physical relationship with Gary. He didn't do it for you so it was easy for you to stay chaste with him."

"Really?" she said. "Then that must mean you don't do it for me either since as I recall you hardly got anywhere with me."

"You know as well as I do you would have gone with the moment if the intensity of it hadn't scare the hell out of you," he said, remembering her confession when she was under. "You wanted it to happen. You just hesitated because you were frightened of what I awoke in you and you didn't like it."

"That maybe so but I was in a vulnerable state at the time." she said. "I'd been on a roller coaster of highs and lows that day that I was impressionable to anything. You knew that and took advantage of it."

"That's not true," he said. "When I came to see you later that night, I had no intention of making a move on you. It just happened."

"Yes, because you wanted it to," she said. "It was points in your corner, so don't insult my intelligence by saying it was a product of the moment to where you couldn't help yourself. We might be attracted to each other but what happened between us had been a farce and a product of your perverse training as a CIA officer to extract information. It is no wonder you confuse reality with fiction. My only excuse is I was just plain stupid and naive. You would think I would learn after being with Gary since the two of you are woven from the same cloth, accept you use sex as a weapon to get what you want, where he uses it as a recreational activity."

"Look I don't have time to argue with you over the moral legality of my actions," he said. "When it comes to my job there's a duality in what I do verses' how I conduct myself in my personal life. Unfortunately, I have to do what I have to do to get the job done and if that scars my character, then so be it." With that, he turned on his heel and walked out.

Moments later, he reached the main floor. He nodded to the portly man behind the counter, and dashed out into the rain.

Once he was settled in his car, he made a U-turn and headed back towards the core of Graz. The rain had let up by the time he reached the hotel. He parked a few blocks down and scouted out the area. He knew the local police would have been called to the disturbance involving her earlier that day. A report would have been taken and the identification Cheyenne had handed over to the owners would have been checked by the police. They would have run her name to see if she had any priors or warrants. Since no crime was committed, they might just let it go and file it. However, if they get an itching to pursue it, they might discover Rochelle Toussaint was an alias and their investigation could lead to Cheyenne. Vincent could not let that happen. He had to erase her presence there. Knowing the police would not have dusted her room or removed her things it was safe to say he had a chance of destroying any evidence that would be traced to her.

He jogged across the street and causally turned down a narrow ally. He scanned the side of the building for an open window or stairwell up to the other floors. He noticed there was a metal ladder that led to the roof. He scaled it in no time and climbed into a small window, big enough for him to squeeze through, that he jimmied opened. He glanced around the dark, musty attic and wove his wave through boxes, trunks, and furniture to see if he could spot any of Cheyenne's things. He was hoping the owners stored her stuff up there. It would save him a trip to the basement.

Taking a lighter out of his pocket, he flicked it and a soft warm hue lit the surrounding area. It did not take him long to locate her luggage and belongings. He sifted through it all to see all her identification had been confiscated. Luckily her itinerary Juliet had routed out for her was not taken nor was the plane ticket back to the U.S. They were slipped into lining of her overnight bag. Smart girl!

Leaving them for the moment, he went over to the door. He cracked it opened and listened. The only noise he heard was the muffled sound of a couple bickering from the floor below him.

With the coast clear, he stepped over the threshold and headed to room seven. He found it in order and ready for the next guest. He pulled out a pair of black gloves and went right to work.

An hour and half later, he stood outside a restaurant in Muzzuschlag. He flipped opened his cell phone and dialed a number.

"Stewart, its me." he said when the line was picked up.

"Where the hell have you been?" Stewart demanded.

"I told you I was checking out some leads."

"And you felt there was no need to check in and report?" Stewart asked. "Have you forgotten who you work for? I know you've been out of the field a couple years but it hasn't been that long for you not to remember how things are done."

"Yes, I know and I'm sorry," he said. "I should have told you what I was up to and checked in but at the time I didn't think there would be any harm in checking out some things on my own. You pacifically said to find Cheyenne with any means necessarily."

"And have you found her?"

"Yes and no," he responded.

"What the hell does that mean," Stewart bellowed. "You either found her or you did not. Which is it?"

"I can't answer you with a simple yes or no," he said. "What I can tell you is that I did find her in Murzzuschlag but she's not in my custody."

"And why not?"

"Because she had a run in with an old friend," he said. "Our pal, Lopez."

"Lopez." Stewart ejaculated. "Then he's alive?"

"Yes, and he isn't fairing any better than Cheyenne." he said. "He favors more to one shoulder than the other. I figure he has not fully recovered from the gunshot wound from the carjacking. And one side of his face has swollen up like a balloon." Vincent went on to explain what happened earlier at Cheyenne's hotel altering a few details-like the town. He told Stewart he lost track of them when Cheyenne darted into the train depot, disappearing into the sea of people that herded through.

"Then there's no way of knowing if she's by herself or with Lopez." Stewart said, mumbling a string of profanities. "Did you retrieve the video footage from the depot?"

"Yes, and looks like they both got on a train heading to Budapest." he said. "I already contacted the authorities there to look out for them. Though we do not know if either one of them stayed on the train after they got on, but I am going to catch the next the train shortly. Hopefully they'll pop up on the grid."

"Fine, but keep me posted and stay in contact." Stewart ordered. "I don't want to have to put an APP out on you."

Vincent almost laughed at that. How little did Stewart know he would probably doing just that when it got out Vincent had played them. Stewart was going to be pissed as was the agency but he knew Cheyenne would not get a fair trial if he handed her over. She had too much against her for the jury to suspect doubt. If he could keep them at bay long, enough he might get a head start on clearing her name. It was not going to be easy. He knew that, but if they stayed under the radar, they might have a chance.

Back on the road, he sped through Graz, with Mozart consuming his senses. He stopped off at Café called Promenade and picked something up to eat for them. Whether Cheyenne was up to a late dinner, he was not sure. She probably would rather castrate him than eat.

He pulled up to the curb of the hotel and cut the engine. He grabbed the food and proceeded out, when he felt the hairs on the back of his neck go up. He instinctively went for his gun. He cocked it. It might be the change of weather he was sensing, but one could not be too sure in his line of work.

He took a step forward; eyes peered but did not see anything out of the ordinary. He made his way around the car when something caught his eye. He noticed a blinking red light reflected off a puddle of water under the rear axle. He leaned down to take a better look when he heard someone approach. He jerked up to see the gleam of a blade. It arched toward him, slicing through the air like a guillotine. Vincent felt a searing, stinging sensation his chest. He cursed and bellowed as his attacker tried to stab him again. Vincent dodged its thrust, grabbing his attacker's wrist, and twisting it painful back, pinning it behind him violently shoving him up against the car. The knife clattered to the ground. His dark clothed, masked assailant whipped his head back, butting Vincent in the face. He felt the warmth of blood trail down his face. The attacker spun around and squarely punched him in jaw. Vincent's head snapped back from the blow. He quickly recovered, and charged his attacker. They crushed up against the car. His attacker, not going down easily, kicked him in kneecaps, and then elbowed Vincent in the chest, as he went down.

Breathing hard from exertion, his attacker relieved him of his gun and pointed it at him.

"Good-bye." the man said, in a deadly tone.

"What's going on!" Vincent heard someone bark in German. "What are you doing?"

His attacker redirected his aim at the voice and popped off a round, before turning on his heel, disappearing into the shadows, his pounding footsteps echoing into the night.

CHAPTER 14

Cheyenne, who had fallen in a listless sleep, her face damp with tears, was stirred awake by the thud of the door. She opened her gritty eyes, only to shut them from the brightness radiating from the lamp on the side table. Her body ached and there was a crick in her arm. She turned to her side to see an older gentleman with snow-white hair, helping Vincent sit down in the chair. The man's back was to her and when the man shifted over to make Vincent more comfortable, she gasped. Vincent's face and upper body was covered with blood.

She bolted up, her restraint cutting into her. "What happened?"

"Oh hello Miss." the weathered faced man said, facing her.

He reminded her of the animated father in the Disney movie *Beauty and the Beast.* His white hair was unruly and sticking here and there. He wore these round speckle glasses; one might see on a scientist or professor who headed up the history department in some Ivy League college.

"I'm Aldo. I own this establishment."

"That's all fine and dandy, but that doesn't answer my question," she snapped.

"He was stabbed, ma'am," Aldo said.

"Stabbed," she bellowed, horrified. Whatever animosity and anger she had toward him was replaced with concern and fear.

"And beaten," Aldo added, going to the bathroom.

"By who," she said, pulling her on her restraints, frustrated she could not go to him.

"We don't know miss," Aldo reported. "I'm suspecting it was a mugger, but Vincent here thinks he was some sort of professional killer."

"What!"

"Aldo," Vincent called out in a raspy voice. "Un-cuff her."

"What was that," Aldo said, poking his head out.

"Un-cuff her from the bed."

Aldo took the key from his out stretched hand and went over to her. Once she was free she went to his side and knelt down next to him.

"What can I do?"

"You could assist me by getting him into bed." Aldo suggested.

"I don't need any help." Vincent growled.

"You have a gash in your upper chest seeping enough blood to fill a blood bank." Aldo stated. "I'm surprised you haven't passed out. I don't think your lady friend is going to think your less of a man because you were helped into bed."

Vincent eased forward, braced himself on the armrests, and pushed himself up. He stood and made his way over to the bed. He sat down and collapsed back. He was pleased with himself, even though he was drenched in sweat and gritting his teeth in pain.

"Stubborn fool," Aldo muttered, sitting next to him.

Aldo set a first aid kit on the side table and opened it. He removed Vincent's shirt and examined the wound.

"It looks like the knife only tore the flesh and didn't penetrate into your body which is good." Aldo reported. "Your nose isn't broken. It will be tender and will bruise. This ice pack should help the swelling go down. And I have some medicines that will num the pain."

"Aldo, I appreciate all your ministering, but I need you to do something else for me."

"And what is that?" Aldo questioned, swabbing a cloth with peroxide.

Vincent bellowed an oath when it touched his raw skin.

"What the hell is that, acid," he snarled.

"I have to clean it or an infection will settle in."

"Let Cheyenne do it."

"You need stitches," Aldo stated, gruffly. "Is she a nurse?"

"No, I'm not," she answered before he could.

"You can stitch me up later. There something more important I need you to do."

"More important than this," Aldo inquired, looking like he thought Vincent went daft.

"Yes. Go downstairs and check under the trunk to see if you find a device a size of a key box. It should have a red blinking light," he instructed. "If it's there, destroy it. Then dispose of the car and find us a place we can lay low for a while."

"What's wrong with staying here?" Cheyenne asked.

"It's not safe anymore. Someone has tracked us here."

"Do you think it was the buyers?"

"I don't know. Could be, but I'm not sure," he said.

"But why would they attack you?"

"To get me out of the picture," he answered. "They see me as an obstacle. If they eliminate me, they have a better chance at getting to you."

"That is precisely why I should stitch you up so you don't bleed out before we get you to somewhere safe." Aldo pointed out, pulling out a needle and thread.

"They'll be time for that." Vincent insisted. "It's important you destroy whatever is blinking under my car and ditch it. Cheyenne can look after me until you get back."

Aldo grunted and reluctantly did as Vincent told him to. He left and Cheyenne dressed his wound the best she could. Every time she looked at the nasty gash on his upper chest, she cringed and felt queasy. She would not be any use in the medical field. She could not stomach the visual extent of the injury.

"Were some kind of pair, aren't we?" Vincent said, trying to make light of the situation. "You're shot in the side and I'm slashed in the chest."

"I don't think the prospect of us both having scars is something to boost about," she retorted. "I could have done without it."

"I know but it is ironic we find ourselves in this situation," he said. "We both could be dead."

She did not argue with him there.

"Don't you think we should take you to the hospital?"

"It's too risky. We can't afford to let someone else in the circle," he said. "And if we go to the hospital, the agency will track us down, not mention so will the perk who knifed me."

She stopped what she was doing and looked at him.

"What?"

"You just said the agency will track us down if we take you to a hospital," she said.

"Yes, and they will."

"But they already know where we are," she said. "I'm with you."

"You might be with me, but not the agency."

"What does that mean?"

"It means I'm the only one who knows where we are and I plan on keeping that way until I can prove you were set up."

"You...mean...you believe...I'm ...innocent," she stammered, feeling her heart constrict and tighten.

"Yes," he replied, slipping his hand up the nape of her neck, caressing her cheek. He wiped away a tear as it fell with his thumb before capturing her mouth with his, ignoring the pain it caused.

He kissed her deeply, expressing what he could not with words. He would have encased her and took it to the next level, but neither one of the them was in any condition to do that, not to mention it wasn't the time or place to indulge themselves. However, he seemed to be the only one who realized that for Cheyenne did not appear she wanted to stop any time soon.

"Excuse me." Aldo coughed, ending their intimate embrace.

Embarrassed, Cheyenne withdrew from Vincent turning ever color under the sun. She wanted to cover her face. She felt like her father just walked in catching her make out with her boyfriend in her bedroom. Vincent seemed to get a kick out of her flustered state. He certainly knew how to unsettle her and erect sensations she should not be feeling or wanting. He was still a virtual stranger to her, but he was like a drug, running through her veins. She seemed to lose all restraint when she was with him. It had been that way since the beginning. Why was that? Other men she dated including Gary never had that effect on her. Maybe they were not enough to tempt her or that aspect was not as strong as it should have been as Vincent had said.

With Gary, it was not that she had not been attracted to him. It was just she was a cautious person and did not rush into things. Secondly, she was not like the masses who thought sex was in and all of relationships. There were other aspects in a relationship that could be just as satisfying. Gary never understood that or understood her reasoning behind her taking things slow. Regardless of that though, she did not like the fact that Vincent had this power of her. She wanted to believe there was something else behind it and not just physical attraction but she could not be sure. Anybody could have good chemistry where that is all they had and nothing more. If that were the case, she would have stayed with Gary. Luckily, for her she did not. She could not believe she actually had feelings for the jerk.

"Are you okay?" Vincent asked her, noticing her eyes flare up in anger, hoping it was not he who caused it. In the past, she had always fought against what was brewing between them. She would close herself off and distance herself. At the time, he had not understood her hesitation, but now he understood. Her body was a holy place in her eyes and the only one who could enter it was the one who was worthy enough; a man she truly loved and who loved her. He realized to his surprise, he wanted to be that man, not because he would have access to her most sacred place, but because he wanted to be a part of every aspect of her life.

"I was just remembering something unpleasant." she said, smiling.

Feeling the need to reassure him, she kissed him. He returned the sediment by intensifying it, losing himself once again.

Aldo coughed again, loudly. "I don't mean to interrupt but it's impertinent that you be on your way. A fax just arrived from the local authorities to be on the lookout for Cheyenne. One of my employees has already seen it and it wouldn't take him long to make the connection." Aldo said. "I've made arrangements with my cousin's friend for you to stay at his place. You will be safe there, until morning. It will be tight quarters but it will do." Aldo paused and handed Vincent a set of keys. "I chartered a plane that will take you to Greece tomorrow. I have a place overlooking the sea in Pirgos. Stay there long as you want."

"Thanks Aldo, I owe you one."

"Here," Aldo said, handing him a crushed plastic object. "I thought you would want this."

"What is it?" Cheyenne said, peeking over his shoulder.

"It's an electronic tracker," he replied. "It signals your location to a satellite which then is bounced back to computer it' linked up to it."

"Like LoJack?"

"Yes, but this is a little more sophisticated. This piece of technology tracks your movements where LoJack pinpoints your location."

"I see," she said. "What was it doing on your car?"

"Apparently someone wants to keep tabs on me."

"But why?"

"It could be number of reasons but I think it's because of you," he said. "This puppy is agency issued. They must have known I might not bring you in and decided to make sure that did not happen by planting the tracker. If I hadn't spotted it when I did, they would have been with every step we took."

"I'm sure you would have ditched the car sooner or later," she said.

"But they would have had us in custody long before."

"Well at least we hindered their efforts now," she said.

"Not if you two continue to linger on." Aldo pointed out. "You must leave."

"Yes, you're right." Vincent said. "We just need to wipe everything down first." Nodding, Aldo helped them do just that.

Pulling up to a jazzy club, Aldo informed them that's where they would be crashing before stepping out. It was not exactly what Cheyenne expected they would be hiding out. It was very public and loud.

A stream of people was lined up outside waiting to get in. A bouncer stood by the front door line like a sentry letting in those who made the list and booting the ones who did not. She noticed Aldo wave up to man on the top floor. He had purple spiked hair and was dressed in leather, head to toe. He had one of those spiked dog collars.

He made an appearance shortly after, introducing himself as Blade before showing them around. His pad was upstairs above the club and consisted of two rooms, the bathroom and an open space that sufficed as his living quarters-his bedroom, kitchen and living room. The place was in dire need of a maid and steam shovel. Clothes were spurned all over. The left overs on the coffee table were fermenting into God who knows what. The kitchen was a toxic wasteland. Dirty dishes were piled high. The sink was clogged, reeking of an order that she could not describe.

Blade did not seem too apologetic about his place. He just told them to make themselves at home and help themselves to anything.

As soon as he was out the door, Cheyenne said, "I'm not staying here."

"It's only for one night," he said. "Tomorrow will be in Greece and you'll forget all about this place."

"I'm not going to be able to sleep comfortable here," she said, glancing at the unkempt bed that was under a window that had the outside sign shining through.

"Who says we have to sleep," he drawled.

She gave him a look. "I'm serious."

"So am I."

"I think you should let Aldo look at your wound and stitch it up so he can go home," she said, changing the subject. She did not want to address what he was implicating or entertain the idea while staying there.

"Fine, but he should also look at you," he said. "You haven't had your bandaged changed in a day or two."

She did not argue and he took off his shirt, going over to one of the chairs, surrounding the metal counter. Aldo took off the bandage and went to work.

While he sewed, Vincent took out her locket out of his pants and stared at it. He flinched when Aldo irritated a tender spot and cursed. He set the necklace in his palm and opened it. It began playing *Let Me Call You Sweet Heart*. He noticed Cheyenne stop what she was doing and pause. He hated to think he was destroying a part of her and her family but they needed the Microfilm.

He removed the center, the music slurring and then fading. Underneath was a gold metal plate covering where the musical mechanics rested. He withdrew his pocketknife, getting a displeased look from Aldo, because he was moving too much.

He flipped it open and pricked the edge of the metal plate. It popped off and inside tightly, snuggled in a roll was the Microfilm. He sighed in relief. They now had some advantage to keep the CIA off their back, until they got the evidence, they needed to prove Cheyenne's innocence. It was a task he knew they could not do on their own. He had to recruit some help. There were a few people he felt he could trust that was associated with the operation. Merrick and Juliet were two of them and another fellow officer, Bob Richards. He was an analyst and he could look into the evidence against Cheyenne. If anyone could find discrepancies or the truth, he could.

Trying not to think about the situation, or the memories stirred by the sight of her locket she decided to straighten and clean the loft to keep her busy. She had just started to clean the kitchen, when Aldo told her to sit down so he could check her injury.

"The two of you, I say." Aldo said, shaking his head. He instructed her to remove her top, which she reluctantly did, trying not to look embarrassed that she was half-dressed. Vincent leaned on the counter and watched which made her more uncomfortable.

"It looks like it's healing quite nicely." Aldo informed her. "The entry wound isn't as red or irritated. Though the exit wound is going to continue, be tender. I recommend you take it easy and do not over exert yourself. Your injury is more serious than Vincent's. The outer might be healing but the inside might be a different story. We don't know what's going on in there."

"Should I be worried," she said.

"No but you should be cautious. If you do as I instructed, you'll be fine." Aldo said. "I'll give you some antibiotics." Slipping on her top, she thanked him and he said his farewells.

"We should turn in." Vincent said, once they were alone. "It's late and we have a big day tomorrow."

"But I can't leave this place this way. It has to be sanitized," she said.

"You heard Aldo. He wants you take it easy and that is what you are going to do. No arguments. If Blade wants his place defumigated, he'll have to do it himself."

"Fine, but I'm not sleeping on that bed unless it has clean sheets on it."

He smiled. "That can be arranged."

While Vincent tracked down another suitable set of sheets, Cheyenne went into the bathroom to get ready for bed.

When she came out, Vincent was already making himself comfortable. She was hoping he would have crashed out by the time she was done, but that was wishful thinking. She was surprised she managed to stay on her feet after having the day she had.

She slowly made her way over to the bed, wishing the couch had been more inviting and an option but with Blade needing a place to sleep when he returned; the sleeping arrangements had to be the way they were.

She felt Vincent's eyes on her, as she slipped under the covers. She smiled over at him and said, "Good night."

She turned off the light and settled herself closest to the edge of the bed as possible. Maintaining the position though was another story. The bed sagged in the middle, making the sides bow out, making it difficult to stay put without effort. She knew once she fell asleep, she would gravitate to the middle, finding herself cuddle up against Vincent. Secondly, they did not have much room to begin with for the bed was not any bigger than a standard full-size bed. She might as well accept defeat and try to get some sleep. That is if she could. It was going to take her a while to find some peace while lying next to the man that seemed to consume her whole being. However, she was certain her body would give out at some point and she fall asleep. By the time sun rose, her body was hugged up against his, his arm protectively around her.

CHAPTER 15

Cheyenne gazed out of the window of the Cessna watching the white puffy clouds go by. Below through the patches of blue sky, she could see the coastline of Italy. Like in Graz, she wished she could have seen a little of the country but as soon as they landed in Rome, they were off again. She could not even pick up a few souvenirs at the gift shop because Vincent thought it was too risky to be wondering around the airport, when any camera could pick her up.

However, it did not stop him from going off for a good twenty minutes. Where he went, she had no idea, but when he returned, he had a briefcase, and two large duffle bags that he had not had before. He informed her that the duffle bags contained clothes and other personal items they might need. The briefcase, which looked more like a min-suitcase, had untraceable cell phones, a lab top, other electronic devices she did not recognize and a variety of fake ID's from passports to employee corporation badges. She had looked on with amazement wondering where in the world how he managed to get his hands on it all. She gathered he had to have a contact in Italy that he trusted to obtain what he needed and stashed them in a locker at the airport. Of course, Vincent would not divulge that information. She had to assume that was the case.

She glanced over at him. He was glued to the lab top. His fingers danced over the key board as if he was writing a novel. It appeared he was conversing with someone over the internet in which every message that was sent and received had to be encrypted and decrypted.

Vincent had told her that morning he knew a few contacts he could enlist help find evidence to disprove her involvement. She figured that was who he was corresponding with. She did not know if she should feel hopeful or not. The agency might get whiff they were helping them and blow their chances. Their snooping around would have to send up red flags but Vincent assured her they would be careful and discreet. She wondered how any officer could be cautious and discreet when they worked for the CIA. She was doubtful.

Vincent had already informed her that all the visual evidence was already authenticated and proven they weren't tampered with or fabricated, which she suspected. Secondly Gary had to make sure the evidence against her was legitimate and credible. What infuriated her though was if Gary was involved in this smuggling business, he be in custody and she wouldn't be in this mess but the FBI wanted to use him to get more intel on the organization he was part of, so they could take them down. Bureaucracy.

Vincent explained the FBI had been investigating him originally for a period of two years before the CIA even connected him to the Microfilm. Unfortunately, the FBI did not have any hard-core evidence against him to bring him in. It was not until he got involved with Haden Davis that they got a break in the smuggling business. With the Microfilm in play, the CIA then stepped in to take over. The FBI had not like getting their toes stepped on, but they mutually agreed to share information and continue to follow their own leads into the smuggling ring. Vincent had theorized that her involvement was only a distraction so those involved could clean up Gary's mess. She wished she could turn back time and tell herself not to get involved with the jerk. She had been so blind and stupid. Why couldn't she see him for what he really was? He had to see her coming.

The plane hit some turbulence jolting her out of her musing. Her hands instinctively clutched the armrests. Her drink went everywhere. Her heart began to race and her body stiffen when the plane slightly dipped down and back up again. She did not like small planes. They freaked her out. Vincent rested his hand on hers to calm her and reassured her everything was okay.

They landed in Greece shortly after near Piragos, a seaside town. The caretaker of Aldo's Grecian retreat was waiting for them on the airstrip. The plane shuddered to a stop and the pilot disengaged the door.

Cheyenne stood on the platform and took in the surroundings. The town was nestled along the hills and cliffs that made up the shoreline of Piragos. It had a Caribbean feel, with its blue waters, balmy climate, and pastel painted buildings.

They made their way over to Aldo's caretaker whom appeared to be native of that area for he had olive skin and a dark complexion. They introduce themselves and he said, "I'm Andres. Welcome."

They were on the road shortly after, driving through the quaint town, towards a less populated area. They turned off onto a dirt road that inclined up to a crest. A white, flat roofed house stood against the deep blue sky, that over looked the sea. Cheyenne noticed as they pulled up there were bright colored flowers blooming along the pathway to a courtyard in big sand pots. Inside was open and airy. A balcony was off to the back of the living area with a spectacular view of the Grecian sea. There was a drop-down window from the ceiling that had a ladder resting against its rim, leading to the roof from the only bedroom in the villa. There was a simple bed encased in a wood frame, with a white laced down feather comforter. Translucent curtains adorned the windows. They gently swayed with the breeze. Cheyenne found it peaceful and beautiful. What she would not give to have a place like it as her own to escape to.

Andres brought their luggage in. He showed them where everything was, telling them if there was anything, they needed to let him know.

After unpacking, she changed and went out into the living room. She stopped short, when her eyes rested on Vincent. He was in the kitchen, listening to classically music as he cooked. It took her by surprise for she half expected him to be on the phone, not whipping up dinner. He had been on the balcony since they arrived, pacing, and making a series of calls. Even though he had *untraceable* cell phones, she stilled worried that whoever he spoke with was being monitored by the agency. They might not be able to track his calls but they could listen in on what they were talking about if the people he talked with place was bugged. She knew she was being paranoid but she could not help it. She was international fugitive on the run with a CIA officer who was risking everything to help her. This did not look good and made the situation even more complicated. She had one chance at this. If they were discovered and taken into custody, she was done for, as was Vincent. Even though the thought of going to prison terrified her, she was more worried about Vincent having to pay for his involvement. He had a daughter-a daughter who counted on him to be there and raise her. What would happen to her if Vincent was sent to prison along with her? The idea of it made her sick to her stomach. She just prayed that Vincent knew what he was getting into.

She slumped into a chair and noticed he set the table for two. Two candles were lit and a bottle of wine chilled in an ice bucket.

She realized she never had a man cook for her before. It was nice, though surreal at the same time. Here she was in all this trouble, in this gorgeous Grecian home, about to sit down to dinner with a man she knew she was falling in love with, as it was any other day. Ever since he told her that he believed she was innocent, the anxiety, the stress, the fear of her predicament, did not seem to be as frightening with him by her side. She was not facing it alone now. She had an ally-at least beside Juliet, though she was not too sure about her friend. Juliet ratted her out. But then again if Juliet had not, Vincent would not be there.

"Hungry," he said, setting down a plate of grilled salmon and sautéed vegetables.

"Yes. Starved," she said. "It looks delicious."

She grabbed a piece of bread and buttered it. He poured her a glass of wine as she helped herself to the salmon and sautéed vegetables.

They ate in silence, content to listen to the sound of the ocean. General conversation seemed trivial and unimportant to the calmness of the evening. By the time they finished, the cleaning up and doing the dishes, they sky had turned a burnt orange as the sun dipped in the horizon. They sat out on the balcony and watched it set.

"This has been the best day I've had in a long time," she said, relaxing back in the swing.

"Same here," he commented, smiling over at her.

"Dinner was excellent," she said. "The food was superb. Thank you for putting it together."

"You're welcome."

"Do you cook often at home?"

"Yes, when I have the time," he said. "Most meals in our household usually come out of the freezer or a box. Samantha would like if I cooked more, but most nights I get home late. She usually was starving by that time, so dinner was quick and easy."

"You must miss her?"

"I do. This is the first time in a long while I've had to be apart from her," he said.

"How long have you been away?"

"Six weeks."

"Six weeks," she repeated. "When did you last talk to her?"

"It's more texted her." he clarified. "I haven't really spoken to her since I left."

She rested back, not knowing how he did it. If it was up to her, she would be calling every day, but then again, she was not a CIA officer. He did not have the luxury to keep things normal when he was on a job. In reality, he lived two lives, where the other one did not know about the other. It had to put a lot of strain on his family life when he had to go on long missions.

She remembered Juliet had said he resigned from the CIA. She wondered what made him come back and do this job. He must have known it would take him away from her. Maybe he thought it was going to be an easy, quick mission, though she could not imagine any of the CIA's missions being either. Nothing ever went off without a hitch, regardless of how methodical and organized you were. There was always going to be something that they didn't count on or predict, like what was happening now. They might have suspected he might go rogue but probably never thought he actually would, that his loyalty to them would override his judgment. They apparently underestimated Vincent for it appeared he was making his own calls and rules. He put aside his duty to help her and risked everything in doing so. Now that they were on the run who knew when he might see his daughter again? It could be through a bulletproof Plexiglas partition.

She sudden felt a heavy weight press on her. Guilt consumed her. He was putting her first before his own blood. It was not right, she thought. It angered her that he made her more important. It should not be that way. Suddenly a wave of emotion washed over her. Tears formed and she quickly wiped them away.

"Cheyenne are you okay?"

"Yes, I'm fine," she said, off handily, gazing out, unable to look at him.

"You don't sound fine," he argued. "What's wrong?"

"Nothing," she said her voice catching. "I'm tired, that's all."

"Well you've had a couple of hellish days," he said. "And you're still recovering from a gunshot wound. We should actually check it and change the bandage."

"Yes, I suppose that would be a good idea," she agreed, standing up abruptly, thinking it was good excuse to escape to sanctuary of the bedroom. "But I can do it myself."

Whether he found her behavior odd, she did not know. She just excused herself and walked into the house, trying to shake off the emotional roller coaster she seemed to be careening into. Breathe, she told herself. It will pass. Yet the more she tried to get it under control, the harder it got. She felt her throat constrict as she entered the bedroom. Her chin began trembling. This is ridiculous, she thought. Her sentimental nature was going into overdrive. She knew it had to with the stress of her situation and the strong feelings she had for Vincent that had her emotions in an upheaval. It was bound to come crashing down on her.

She splashed water on her face hoping to cool her flush face when she saw Vincent reflected in the mirror. She lowered her head, trying to hide her distress.

"Cheyenne what's the matter," he said, stepping closer. "Are you in pain? Are you ill?

"No," she said, shaking her head. "I'm not ill."

"Then what it is," he asked, guiding her around.

"It's nothing, really," she stressed, trying to turn from his embrace, but he would not let her.

"Cheyenne," he drawled, giving her look that he was not fooled. "Tell me."

"You shouldn't be here," she said, looking up at him.

"Too bad, I'm not going anywhere until you tell me what's wrong."

"That's not what I meant," she said. "What I mean is you shouldn't be here in Greece taking risks helping me when you have family to consider. You have a daughter that you should be at home with."

"Cheyenne I chose to be here. I was not forced into it. It was my decision. I know the consequences of my actions and the risks. My daughter might not, but what kind of message would I be sending her if I was afraid to do the right thing because of my own selfish needs?"

"*Vincent,* this is more serious than you fulfilling a mission for the CIA," she stressed. "It's gone beyond that. You have gone AWOL and are on the run. I do not see this turning out in our favor, if it goes south. We both could go to prison."

"That is not going to happen."

"How do you know? We could be taken into custody before we can get the proof we need. There is no guarantee we will succeed. We can hope but it is not for certain. You could lose everything, including your daughter, if we fail. Your ex-wife would get full custody of her and you might never see her again."

"That wouldn't happen," he stated evenly. "You needn't worry."

"How can you say that?"

"Because for one I have full custody of Samantha. Victoria lost her rights when she went to prison. Secondly if things go bad my sister will…"

"Wait." She put her hands up, cutting him off. "Your ex-wife is serving time."

"Yes," he said. "She's currently serving fifteen years sentence at Ray Brook Federal Correctional institution for murder."

He went on to tell her Victoria's story and what lead to their divorce, including the deal he made with the CIA. Cheyenne did not know how to respond or even know what to say. The knowledge his wife was in prison came as a bit of a shock and it sure did not put her at ease. It actually escalated her concerns and fears. If he ended up there because of his involvement with her, Samantha would have both of her parents behind bars and with Vincent going against the agency, she doubted they keep their end of the deal of letting his ex-wife out earlier. She would have to serve her remaining sentence. Samantha would be in high school by time she got out. She would have missed out on her daughter growing up as will Vincent. Samantha should have at least one parent be there for her, not that Vincent's sister could not give her what she needs. Love was love, but to have both parents absent in her life at such a young age was not right or fair for that matter. Cheyenne did not want to be part of that, but she had no choice in the matter. Vincent was already into deep for the CIA to look passed his present actions if he turned her in now. It would make no difference. Their fate was already set in motion.

As for the rest she was moved by his admission and touched, he trusted her enough to tell her his inner thoughts, revealing his guilt over his marriage. It angered her he blamed himself for his ex-wife's indiscretions. She was the one who broke their vows by giving herself to another man and to his friend and handler no less whom she was found guilty of killing.

Cheyenne found it ironic how his ex-wife predicament paralleled with hers to where Vincent was determined to free them both from the realities of it. Whether his determination to set things right had to do with guilt or not, Cheyenne had a feeling Vincent was still in love with his ex-wife. He would not be fighting all these years for her if he still did not have any feelings for her. She admired that even though it pierced her heart at the same time.

"What you are thinking," he asked, drawing her out of her musing.

"I was thinking you're too hard on yourself and too forgiving," she said, honestly. "You're also too honorable for your own good. You put others first before your own needs. You let your good deeds interfere with what you really want."

"And what is it I really want?"

"To free your wife from a life she wasn't meant to have and be a family again," she stated,

"You mean ex-wife," he corrected. "And if and when Victoria is released, we might be still a family because we have a daughter, but what we had is long gone. We've both moved on, finding love elsewhere."

"Oh." She coughed. "Right, why wouldn't you." She smiled briefly, feeling like an idiot. She seemed to have forgotten the man she met on her first day Austria was not the same man before her. He had been a carbon copy of the original, who had another life he lived that was contrary to the one he portrayed. She had to face reality, that the real Vincent had roots, and ties to a life she would never know, and could not be a part of it because of that very reason. She had to accept that all she was to him-at least on a personal level- was a damsel in distress and nothing more.

Dejected and feeling a sense of loss, she stood up and started to head back to the bathroom, when Vincent stopped her. He took her hand and drew her to him.

"I don't think you *do* see," he said, caressing her. "When I said I found love elsewhere, I didn't mean it in the past tense as if there is someone at home waiting for me. I was talking about in the present, that it was you I found love with, not someone else."

"But for how long?" she asked, when she found her voice, afraid of what he was feeling was temporary and carnal.

"For as long as you'll have me," he answered, cupping her face. "I love you."

Tears formed at his admission and trailed down her cheeks. He kissed each one away before claiming her mouth. He slid his arms around her, drawing himself more intimately closer to her, deepening the kiss. He hands roamed up her sides, dipping under shirt to caress her. Cheyenne shivered at his touch, even though her body felt like a furnace about to explode. The intensity of the moment and declaration of love only fueled it more, saturating her senses making it hard to think. It was as if they were on a runaway train speeding down a railway track, where the only hope off slowly down was to plunge off the cliff into the icy waters below. Any sense of caution and reason seemed to go out the door when they got to this point. It was a natural thing to occur between two people who loved each other, she knew this, but people have been confusing chemistry with love since the beginning of time. How could she be certain that was not the case here? What was really ruling her, love, lust or both? She was not sure and she did not know if she wanted to. All she knew was that he loved her, and the doubts she had were fading into the darkness of her mind. Her better judgment was being seduced by her needs and desires rioting through her.

When all barriers of clothing were a memory, Vincent scooped her up and carried her to bed. He glided over her like a warm, gentle breeze, taking his time in cherishing her. He loved her slowly and passionately, savoring every detail, moment, like wine. When they came together, their union flowed over them like a surge of water crushing up against a jagged, rocky shore, carrying them to state of euphoria that left them spent.

CHAPTER 16

Vincent stared down at Cheyenne, watching her sleep. He stroked face lovingly, her warm, soft body stirring up against him. He smiled, remembering what they had shared. He had not been this content and sure of his feelings about a woman in a long time, not since Victoria. He had causally dated women over the years, but none of them gravitated towards something permanent. He had shied away of getting too serious.

After Victoria divorced him, getting into another long-term relationship to him was suicide. He did not want to go through another one and have it fail. He could not put his daughter through it either. He might be getting ahead of himself on thinking he and Cheyenne had a future because of the circumstances, but nothing was set. They still had a chance of coming out of this in the clear. The deal he made with agency might even still go through. It just would not happen as soon as he had planned.

Kissing Cheyenne tenderly, he withdrew from her.

He slipped out of bed and threw on a pair of pants. The moon, which was full in all its glory, filtered into the room as he went over to the dresser. He picked up one the untraceable cell phones and flipped it opened. He took note of the time-it was one in the morning- and calculated the time difference in New York. It was eight there, and lights were out at ten so he would get through.

"Ray Brook, Federal Correctional institution, Officer Summer speaking. How may I direct your call?" "A rough, scratchy voice said.

"This is Michael Sutton. May I speak to Victoria West, please," he said, giving Victoria's Lawyer's name. Vincent knew they would be monitor's calls coming and going. They would note who called and for what purpose. He could not take chance of sending out a red flag. The agency more than likely requested the warden to inform them if Vincent called. Hopefully they wouldn't think much of her lawyer calling and not bother to listen in.

"One moment," Officer Summer replied.

Vincent rested his elbows on the railing and stared out into the night, hoping this worked.

"Mr. Sutton." Officer Summer said, coming back on line. "Ms. West is in the infirmary. I'm going to transfer you over there."

"Thanks." There was a click, then a steady ring.

He was worried. Why was Victoria in the infirmary again? This had been the sixth time that year she had been admitted there and they did not know exactly was causing the *Flu* type symptoms she seemed to be experiencing.

"Infirmary, Doctor Helge speaking."

"Hi Doctor. This Michael Sutton, Victoria's Lawyer."

"Oh yes Mr. Sutton. How are you?"

"Fine," he answered. "Why is my client in your care this time?"

"She collapsed out in the yard hitting her head on one of the benches." Doctor Helge explained. "She had a concussion."

"This seems to be a continuing routine for her," he said. "What's going on?"

"If I knew I would tell you, Mr. Sutton." Doctor Helge conveyed. "The symptoms she's been having are getting worse each time but they only last 48 hours. It could be an allergic reaction to something she has had been consuming or has come in contact with. We're looking into it."

"Can I speak with her?"

"Of course. Hold on."

He began to pace as he waited.

"Michael?" Victoria's cultured voice, slurred in surprise.

"Actually, it's Vincent, but don't say my name," he instructed in a rush. "They can't know it's me. Just play it cool and say you're fine."

"Yes, I'm all right, Michael. It is just a little bump. Doctor Helge said I'm in no serious danger."

"Good," he said. "Now is there anyone else in there with you besides Doctor Helge?"

"No," she said, weakly.

"Is he still in ear shot?"

"Yes, I miss you too."

"Listen, when we last talked, I told you I had a plan to get you out earlier, and you told me that would be a mistake. I don't know what that was about, but you might get your wish," he reported. "Things haven't exactly gone the way I wanted to them go. There have been complications."

"With the agency," she said her voice raspy.

"Yes----but how did...."

"I know." she finished for him, able to speak without being over heard. "They came to see me."

"They told you," he said, anger building up inside him.

"Not in so many words." she said. "They basically just asked me if I had spoken to you recently and did, I have any idea where you were?"

"You got that I was working for them out that?" he asked.

"It wasn't exactly the line of questioning that tipped me off. It was how they asked them," she said. "I know the signs on what their after. I used to work for them, remember?"

"Yes, I know." he said.

"Why didn't you do as I asked and drop this crusade, you're on?" she stressed. "If you had left it alone, it would have just ended with me. Now you've risked your life, as well as our daughters."

"What are you talking about? Once I finish this job, everything is going to be okay."

"No, it's not." she insisted. "You don't understand. They do not want me released. They'll kill you before they let that happen."

"But why?"

"Because I know too much."

"Know too much of what?" he asked.

"Of what Kevin was working on before he died," she said, above a whisper. "They believe that I know more than I'm telling, that's why our daughter is danger. If I get out, she is dead. If I talk, she's dead. If I pass go, she's dead."

"Okay back up a moment." he said, pushing off the balcony. "Are you telling me this is rooted to what happened to six years ago when Kevin was murdered?"

"Yes. He was killed because of what he knew, of what he found out."

"And what was it that he found out?"

"I can't tell you."

"Victoria, you can't drop a bomb like that and expect me to let it go." he stressed. "If our daughter is in danger, I've got to know why, so I can protect her."

"It might be too late for that." she said, in despair. "I've already revealed too much."

"Exactly." he agreed. "Your silence isn't going to protect her anymore."

She took a deep breath but did not respond. It was a long while before she spoke that Vincent thought she was not going to answer.

"Kevin found some unsettling information about a few agents in our department. They were dirty and he wanted to expose them. He told me everything for insurance purposes so if anything happened to him, the truth would get out. But when he was killed, I was taken out of the picture to guarantee containment."

"They must have suspected Kevin would have confide in you and set you up to take the fall for his murder." he said, wondering if this had any connection with Cheyenne's predicament. Maybe the same people involved with Kevin's death, had part in setting up Cheyenne.

For all he knew he could have been part of the set up as well. He could not believe this was happening. Someone in the CIA was responsible for his partner death and his ex-wife's imprisonment. He knew he should not be surprised, but he was. He did not know of any law enforcement agency that did not have corrupt people working for them. He just never thought he would find them on his doorstep.

"Vincent, you've got to get her," she pleaded, braking into his troubled thoughts. "If this call is monitored, which it likely is, they might keep their promise."

"Don't worry. I wouldn't let anything happen to her," he stated, with conviction. "And I promise they aren't going to get away with this."

They spoke a few minutes longer and he then ended the call. He turned around only to stop short to see Cheyenne standing in the doorway, wrapped in a sheet looking forlorn. She stepped forward, her eyes pooling in a several of emotions.

"Was that Victoria?" she asked, in a dead tone.

"Yes." he said. "But I explain."

"There's no need." she responded. "I understand."

"What does that mean?"

"That she going to be priority one." she said, hating the feeling that caused. She knew she had no right to demand she be his focus but she could not help it. It hurt she ended up being second rate when it came to his ex-wife. She could understand Victoria was tied to his past, but if he really loved her, why could not for one night only think of her, especially after what just transpired between them. Deep down, she knew, he had not meant to hurt her, but she felt cheap and used. It was her own fault. She let the three little words of *I love you* rule her judgment and actions. She should have thought it through more thoroughly before being carried away with the emotions of it. She should have remained chaste until she was certain he really loved her. Their relationship was far from normal. How could either one of them be certain it was love after knowing each other for such a short time?

"Look at me," he said, bringing her back to reality. "If that were the case, I would not be here, helping you. I could have easily turned you in after I tracked you to Graz and washed my hands of you, but I didn't. I chose to be here, with *you*."

"That maybe so, but a part of you still wants that deal to go through." she said. "You've been at it too long for you just to give up on it just like that. I mean it's had to cross your mind that there's still a chance the agency might honor the deal in the end."

"Whether they do or not, isn't the real issue here. You're afraid I'm still in love with Victoria and that my heart isn't really free, that I've duped myself into believing I'm in love you because I don't want to face the truth. Is that about the size of it?"

"Yes, but can you blame me? Things have happened so fast how could either one of us be sure about anything. I mean I don't even know your real name."

"It's Troy Vincent West, though everyone calls me Vincent."

"Then who's Michael?" she said, recalling his mention the name.

"Victoria's lawyer." he said. "I couldn't risk telling them who I really was so I had to pretend I was him."

"Oh."

"There's something else." he said.

"What?" she said, not liking his dour tone.

"My family and I have become expendable."

"Expendable!"

She suddenly recalled the comments and references he made when he spoke with Victoria. He had been concerned and whatever she had told him he had not been prepared for. There had been a mixture of confusion, anger, and fear in his voice during their phone call but she had not noticed it, until now. She had been too caught up in herself.

He went on to tell her what Victoria revealed to him, tying in the suspicions he had on the attack on his life at Aldo's and threats against his daughter conveying his concerns. He knew it was only time before they would find out that Victoria talked. Since they failed to eliminate him, there was nothing stopping them from using his daughter as bait to draw him out. He could not let that happen. He had to get to his daughter.

Sitting down, Cheyenne stared out into the night as she digested it all with a heavy heart. She knew this changed everything. She could not expect him to ignore the dangers thrust upon his family nor put it aside to help her. He was not going to stand by and not do anything. He had to what he had to do. He had no choice. It was his daughter. She would have to continue on her own without him. As much as she was terrified at the prospect, she had to.

From the beginning, she knew she was going to have to do it alone. All she had to do was make it back to the states and contact the man Juliet told her about. Only problem was she needed new ID and a ticket out of there. She was sure Juliet would come to her aid. She just had to get out of Greece first.

She turned to Vincent. "If we're leaving, we better get started. We don't want to leave any trace of our presence here if our location has been compromised."

"Cheyenne I...."

"Don't." she said, placing her finger on his lips. "You don't have to apologize or try to justify what has happened. It is out of our control. We have to make the best of it and move on." With that, she kissed him and returned into the house.

CHAPTER 17

Cheyenne and Vincent stepped into a hotel set back off a narrow ally, in a quaint neighborhood in Rome. The proprietor, a robust, stout matron with a warm smile, greeted them. She showed them to a small but clean room that overlooked a garden.

Cheyenne dropped her purse on the bed and walked over to the window to look out as Vincent exchanged pedantries with their hostess. She glanced at the simple, but lovely flower arrangement that sat on the circular table. She took a petal of the rose, rubbing its velvety texture between her thumb and forefinger. A pigeon sat outside on the windowsill watching her.

Her mind wonder to the thought, that this creature staring at her could be relaying her image back to a monitor mounted in a van somewhere. She let out a little laugh. The lack of sleep was stimulating her imagination. There was no way the agency could possibly know they have left Greece for Italy. They did not even know they had been in Greece.

They managed to successfully to stay under the radar. She was just being paranoid and antsy because she was about to go out on her own. Vincent would not be too please with idea so she chose not to tell him. She knew she was being a coward but if she tried to convince him face to face it was for the best, they go their separate ways, he would argue the point and seduce her into staying with him. She knew she would not have the strength to say no to him.

At least this way, he could not stop her or change her mind. She would just end up slowing him down and be a distraction he did not need. She would never able to forgive herself if he failed to protect his daughter because of her.

He came over to her and gave her a long, drugging kiss.

"Hungry," he asked, caressing her.

"That would depend on what you mean by hungry," she said.

"I was thinking along the lines of food but if you're hungry for the other, I could certainly oblige you in that area."

"I'm sure you could." She stepped out of his embrace and rested her hands on his chest. "But what I crave is nourishment."

"Then food it is." He grabbed his jacket. "I'll go see if I can find us something to wet our appetite. I believe there is a café not too far from here. I shouldn't be long."

"All, right." She smiled, trying to act as if everything was normal.

Once he was gone, she broke down and cried. She did not know if she was going to pull off this deception.

When he returned, they ate and spent the remainder of the day discussing the details of their next course of action. He had already arranged for them to return to the states. They were going to fly into New York, then rent a car and drive up to Ellsworth, Maine, where he lived with his daughter. Then from there they would find a safe place in Boston to lay low while he looked into her case. It sounded like a sound plan but it did not change her mind. He tried to reassure her could protect both of them and do what needed to be done, but as much as she wanted to believe him and his capabilities, she could not. Like anything else, one of them was going to take precedent over the other.

As the sunset and night settled in over the city, the burning sensation that been slowly growing in her stomach intensified. Her body buzzed as if she had numerous cups of coffee. She could not sit still. She had to move and keep her thoughts occupied elsewhere. Every time she thought about what she was about to do, had her chickening out.

Vincent had noticed her anxiety and took it upon himself to relieve her of it by coaxing her into bed. It was a welcoming distraction, she had not planned on initiating or finding herself caught up in again, but guilt had her giving into the bliss of it. The realities of the world ceased to exist as he cherished and loved her. Everything faded in the background, leaving only a warm glow of contentment. However, like any drug, the euphoria was only temporary.

She lay there, staring at the ceiling, occasionally glancing at the clock. It was just about time. She took a deep breath, said a prayer, and withdrew from him.

She quickly dressed and gathered her luggage. She reapplied her make-up and pinned up her hair. She went over to the chair where his pants were draped and slipped out her locket out of the pocket. She clasped it around her neck and then grabbed her luggage.

She went over to the window and surveyed the area below. All was clear. She hoisted up her bags and dropped them in a bed of shrubbery. She glanced over her shoulder to see if the commotion stirred him but it had not.

She withdrew a letter she wrote and placed it on the side table, with the red rose she had admired earlier. She went over to him and gave him one last kiss before leaving.

Once outside in the hall, she quietly descended the stairs. She made her way out to the garden and retrieved her luggage. She slipped out the door to the back ally, where a cab pulled up shortly after. She got in and told the driver to take her to the airport.

She had called Juliet the day before prior to their leaving to Italy and told her the situation. Juliet told her she would take care of everything that the documents she needed would in a locker at the airport, along with an airline ticket to Chicago. She re-canted the story of losing her key to one of the attendants and obtained another one. Shortly after she found the locker and retrieved what was inside. She flipped opened the passport to see her new name was Stacy Porter from Batavia, Illinois. She wanted to laugh, but the seriousness of her situation prevented her from doing so. What she was doing sounded insane and absurd but it had to be done, if she was going to get her life back. If she had to change her name a dozen times and had to pretend to be someone else, so be it.

She headed towards the area for the international flights to see a line a mile long. She stepped behind a family with three wound up children. The youngest was in her stroller wailing and having a fit. Her father tried to placate to her with no avail. The middle one, who was about three, wove through the partitions, pulling on the tight-knitted straps that went in between each of the circular braces. His mother tried to bribe him with candy. The oldest kept pestering them about when they were leaving. Cheyenne prayed they were not on the same flight as her.

When it was finally her turn, she went up to the counter and placed her luggage on the scale. She handed over her ticket and passport. The airline attendants' fingers danced over the key board as she asked Cheyenne if she left her bags unattended or received any packages from anyone. She answered no and the attendant tagged her bags.

With boarding ticket in hand, she headed for the security checkpoint. She took off anything that would send off the detector including her necklace. If the Microfilm was exposed to any amounts of radiation, the x-ray machines gave off, it might damage it.

She went through and stopped at the end of the conveyor belt. She noticed the individual behind the monitor come in and study the screen closely. They signaled to a guard who stepped up to the area where the flaps hung down. Crap, she thought, what did they find? All she needed was to be detained because she something suspicious metal item that looked like a weapon in her bag.

She recalled an incident involving her father when he was traveling in the states. They had pulled him out of line twice and searched him. They made him dump out his carrying on bag and take his shoes off. When they could not get him on anything, they were actually upset. They thought they had a real winner with him.

As the item in question came into view, the security guard snatched it up and asked whom it belonged to. She sighed in relief to see it was not hers. If she continued to react to each situation in the same manner, they were going to think she was hiding something.

She grabbed her things and continued down the corridor toward her gate. She located it and took an open seat by the window. So far so good, she thought. Once she was in the air, she would be leaving it all behind. At least, she tried to convince herself of that. It was not over until Gary was behind bars and she was pardoned. Perhaps going back to the states would give her some breathing room so she could do what needed to be done. No one there knew she was a wanted woman, unless the CIA alerted them which was a possibility. She did though have more of chance of disappearing into the crevices of society there, than she would in Austria.

A flight attendant came over the central intercom system and announced her flight was about to board. When the called her seat row, she got in line. Her boarding ticket was taken and she headed down to the plane. She found her seat and sat down. Releasing a sigh, she sat back and gazed out the window.

"Leaving without me?"

Cheyenne froze. She felt her heart constrict. She swallowed hard and turned to see Vincent, he steely eyes boring into hers.

"I don't recall mentioning we take different routes." he commented, settling into the seat next to her. "When did that come into play, before or after it was struck? I'm a little fuzzy on the details."

Dumbfounded, she said, "How did you...."

"I know." he finished for her. "I'm trained to know. I have been deceiving people a long time Cheyenne, and I recognize the signs. Even if I did not; I am neither stupid nor blind. Ever since we left Greece you've been different, distant."

"I'm sorry. I thought it would be better this way."

"Better for whom, you or me," he said, forcing her to look at him.

"For both of us," she shot back. "This might have started out as an honorable crusade for you, but that all changed when the safety of your family became threatened. They should be your main priority, period!"

"They always have been." he insisted. "But you are just as important to me as they are. I am not going to sacrifice you for them or vice a verse. We started this together we are going to finish it together. End of story."

"I'm a liability," she stressed, quietly.

"That's not true," he countered. "I know you think that because we've got personal, but believe me, if you weren't with me, you'd be a distraction in thought. I would not be able to focus on my objective because I would be worried about you. Don't you see?"

She did not comment. There was no point in it. They both had their own view of the subject and they would continue to argue over it, thinking their way was better. She had to accept defeat in the matter and let him win. At this point, she did not even know if she could succeed on her own without him.

"I take it you do, for that's why you're not responding."

"Apparently you know best." she relayed, turning from him.

"Come on Cheyenne, that's not fair. This has nothing to do with ego or the fact I am a man and know what is right. It has to do with the fact that it just makes sense that we stick together since both of our situations are intertwined with each other. "

Realizing he had a point, she let it drop even though she still felt it would have been better if they had gone their separate ways, but only because she thought the risks would be less. She feared they were more in danger of being used against each other by staying together, than not. He had to see that but whether he did or not, he was determined to keep them together matter the cost.

Opting to stay on the flight, they arrived in Chicago nine hours later. Cheyenne walked off the plane a walking zombie. She had not been able to sleep much during the course of the trip. The anticipation of being back in the states had her all wound up and on edge.

As they went through customs, and retrieved their luggage, the lack of sleep was creeping up on her. The aroma of coffee was calling out to her as they walked through the airport. She was tempted to down a few cups, but knew if she did, she would be buzzing even more than she was. When the caffeine wore off, she would be useless.

Vincent informed her he was going to try to get them on another flight that was heading to either New York or Boston area for they did not have the time to drive the thousand miles it would take to get there from Chicago. Since their original plan of going to New York from Italy was altered by her rash detour, it put them back a couple hours. They had to make up time because they needed to get to Salem, Massachusetts by a certain time. Apparently, a contact of his requested a meet and needed to see Vincent before they headed to Ellsworth, Maine, where he and his daughter lived. Vincent would not divulge what was so urgent about it but said it was impertinent they get to Salem. He though did not seem too happy about it. He seemed to have mix emotions on the subject, which had her wondering if he regretted his decision of them staying together.

Wanting some time alone, she darted into the ladies' room to freshen up. Staring at her reflection, she had not realized how pale and withdrawn she had become. The stress of everything that had happened had taken its toll. She had dark circles under her eyes and the warm hue that usually gave life to her face was gone. The contour and imperfections of her face were more defined than they had been, not to mention her cheekbones were more prominent. She must have lost some weight due the trauma her body went through when she was shot.

She lifted her shirt and lightly brushing her hand over the small bandaged that covered the entry wound, remembering how tenderly and lovingly Vincent ministered unto it in the early hours of the night before she left him. It put a smile on her face. It was a happy thought she desperately needed to draw her out of the slump she was in. She hoped her concealer and foundation could camouflage on how she felt on the outside.

She walked out the ladies' room, shortly after to see Vincent waiting for her. He had two tickets and told her that they had twenty minutes to make it to the other side of the airport to make their flight to Boston.

Without a moment to spare, they rushed through the terminals and checkpoints without delay. By the time they reached the gate, people were already boarding.

Settled in their seats and in the air once again, Cheyenne was able to relax and drift off the sleep. She was jolted awake two hours later, when the plane touched down on the runway at Logan International. Since it was too late to rent a car once they disembarked, they took one of the shuttles to the airport hotel. They got a room and crashed as soon as their heads hit the pillows.

Early the next morning, they were on the interstate heading north toward Salem. Vincent drove through the quaint seaside town and stopped in front of an old brick building. The sign mounted above the second floor read *Frankfort Antiques*. He stepped out and told her to wait there for him. She did what he asked and waited patiently for his return.

After fiddling with the radio for ten minutes, she noticed Vincent emerge out of the shop carrying a brown leather satchel. He came around the car, got in and placed it between her legs. She eyed it and looked over at him.

"What's this," she asked, as he kicked over the engine.

"Hopefully the evidence needed to clear your name," he said, pulling out onto the road. "There are documents and reports on everything associated with your case, like the murder you're connected with. One of the officers assigned to your case has been helping by researching all the evidence gathered. His conclusions are what are in it."

"He's been the one you've been corresponding with on the computer?"

"Yes. He owed me a favor."

"And he can be trusted?"

"Do you really think I would have gone to him if I didn't think he was?" he inquired, turning to her.

"I guess not. I'm just worried he might have been monitored by your superiors."

"More than likely he was, but you needn't worry. Bob knows how stay under their radar. During the cold war, he worked for the Kremlin in Moscow and one of his jobs was to exposed CIA operatives, so he knows his stuff."

"I see." she said. "How did he come to work for the CIA then? Did he defect?"

"Yes, and when he did, the CIA convinced him to come and work for the agency." he said. "He agreed and became one of our agent's."

"But I thought operatives were considered as Officers, not agents."

"Yes, that's true, but officers are staff employees who are patriots to their own country. Agents are people who are recruited by CIA officers to betray their own countries, like Bob."

"Is that really his name?"

"No, it's Nicolai Dyakonov," he said. "When he came to the states, he changed it to Bob Richards, because he knew of an American by that name that he respected and liked that he had been ordered to kill."

"And did he kill him?"

"Yes."

"Then he took the man's name out of guilt."

"I would say it was more out of honor."

"Oh." she said. "I must say that's a strange way of finding redemption."

"We all deal with our actions in different ways. They might not make sense to those around us but it does to the person who's trying to make amends."

"Do you think that's what Victoria tried to do when she told about the truth behind her imprisonment?"

"I couldn't say," he said. "She's never really apologized for her relationship with Kevin. She went to prison and kept silent because she loved him and wanted to protect our daughter. I don't think she would have ever said anything if I hadn't gone back to work for the CIA."

"This is not your fault." she insisted. "You were in the dark all this time. There was no way you could have predicted what would happen."

"But her hand was still forced nevertheless." he pointed out.

"Yes, indirectly but that doesn't mean you're responsible. Other factors were present that you had no idea about. You can't blame yourself."

He did not respond but gave her a brief smile. He intertwined his hand with hers and raised them to his lips, planting a feather like kiss across the ridge of her knuckles. It sent a surge of heat through her, making her flush. He smiled broadly and let out a short laugh. Her innocent-like responses always surprised and humbled him. Knowing he should focus elsewhere; he turned his attentions back to the road.

Since conversation had melded into silence, she picked up the satchel. She unhooked the flaps and pulled out to the two binders. The first had written transcripts on the investigation and on the photographic evidence against her, which she observed wasn't revisited due since they were proven not to be tampered with and collaborated by her. The second was results on Richards investigating other incriminating evidence against her. She started to read through it to find he didn't seem to uncover anything that could exonerate her until she came to his report on the meeting, she and Lopez supposedly had with the ex-KGB officer, Ian Mekinkov. He had told the CIA he had seen her with Lopez that day but Ian devolved further. He asked Mekinkov if he actually met her and talked to her. Mekinkov answered no, that she never came in, that she was in the hallway but he could see her through the glass window door of his office. Lopez had told him she was an associate and was the look out. Richards then asked if they left together or spoke, and Mekinkov said no, that she left first. The CIA apparently didn't ask the right questions before, Cheyenne theorized, because if they did, they would have seen the discrepancies in her involvement. She was there yes but not with Lopez. He manipulated to make it look like they were to incriminate her more. But the most compelling discovery was, Richards talked with the receptionist at the Lawyers office which was across from Mekinkovs, to collaborate or disprove Cheyenne's story. The receptionist admitted to being paid by Lopez to pretend the paperwork Cheyenne was to deliver was actually scheduled when it wasn't. She didn't know if that was going to be enough to clear her but it did show she was the victim not the culprit.

Finding that hopeful, she moved on to the file marked "*Murder of Joseph Roth.*" In the report, it was stated the authorities had no evidence of yet to tie her or place her at the scene of the crime. She found that news liberating and as she read the next few paragraph's she found herself almost had her crying for joy. A fingerprint had been found on the envelope that had been collected at the crime scene. It was run through AIDS, an automated Identification system developed by the FBI and it came up with a match. It was Lopez's. Cheyenne, suddenly, felt a huge weight lifted off her. She was going to have to give Agent Richards a big fat kiss when this was all over. Thanks to his efforts and Vincent's faith in her innocence, this nightmare she been living might be soon be over.

CHAPTER 18

It was mid-afternoon, when Vincent drove into Ellsworth, Maine. Cheyenne felt like they had stepped back to simpler times. Ellsworth definitely had a New England feel, especially with its old fashion lampposts lighting Main Street. The quaint, quiet community had a Thomas Kincaid feel about it.

Vincent turned onto a country road, where a dense forest loomed on either side, to pull off onto a dirt driveway. It wove up to a small but inviting grey, shingled sided, cape style house. A beat up, baby blue, Chevy pickup was parked out front. Vincent cut the engine and took a deep breath.

"You okay," she said, resting his hand on his shoulder.

"Yeah, I'm just thinking."

"About what?"

"What I'm going to tell my sister."

"How about the truth?"

"It's too complicated and too long to explain. I'll just have to mull through it."

Moments later, they stood on the porch and a woman with long jet-black hair, whom she gathered was his sister, came to the door. She had the same mystical blue eyes as Vincent and the same raw, striking features. The only difference was they were softer in nature. Cheyenne noticed that her eyes were solemn and pooling with emotion. His sister flew open the screen door and encased Vincent in a hug, tears welling.

"I'm so sorry," her muffled voice sobbed out. "I just found out last night. They called me asking me how I could get in touch with you. I told them you were out of town, and gave them your cell number. I guess they reached you."

Cheyenne suddenly felt ill. Were they too late?

"What happened?" Vincent demanded, resting his hands on her shoulders. "Did something happen to Samantha?"

"Samantha," his sister blinked, looking confused.

"Yes, my daughter, your niece."

"No, she's fine. She is at school but she does not know. I thought it would be best if it came from you."

"Kate what are you talking about? What would be best coming from me? You've lost me."

She did not initial respond. She looked at them in a baffled state. Suddenly her eyes went wide and said, "Oh god you don't know, do you?"

"Know what," he said, becoming irritated.

"That Victoria has died," his sister chocked out.

Cheyenne's hand instinctively went up to her mouth in shock, as Vincent stood there in stunned silence. It took a minute for it to register, for when it did, rage hit. He picked up the first thing he saw, a tin pail, and threw it at the windshield of the pick-up, roaring in anger, and then falling apart in anguish. He spewed out angry words and kept repeating, *'They killed her.'*

"What is he talking about," his sister said not understanding his rambling's. "Why is he saying that?"

Not knowing how to answer that, Cheyenne did not respond, but went over to him. He had his arm and head resting on the column, when she came up behind him and slipped her arms around him.

"I don't know what to say other than I'm sorry," she said. "I can't imagine how devastating this must be for you but I'm here for you and I'll try my best to ease the pain any way I can."

He turned in her embrace and kissed her. "I love you; you know that."

"Yes, I know. I love you too." she smiled.

"That's the first time you said that."

"No, it's not," she denied.

"Yes, it is," he argued. "I've said it a couple times but you haven't."

"That can't be true," she said, trying to recall the times she thought she did. Had she not said them aloud?

"I'm sorry you had to find out this way," his sister said, not quite sure what to make of the two of them. "I was certain you knew since you're home earlier."

"My trip had been cut short and I was probably in mid route when they tried to get a hold of me." he theorized.

"I see," his sister said, eyeing them both. "Forgive me, but I don't think we ever met. I am Katherine West. Friends and family call me Kate."

"It's a pleasure to meet you Kate." Cheyenne said, taking her out stretch hand. "I'm Cheyenne Nicholas."

"Are you a new associate of Vincent's?" Kate said, crossing her arms, as she leaned on one of the columns on the porch.

"She's more of a close friend." Vincent responded, before she could.

"I see." Kate did not look like she bought that simple answer. "Why don't you both come inside and I'll get you something to drink."

"Actually, we can't stay," he said, regrettably. "The reason I'm...we're here is to tell you we're taking Samantha on a trip."

Kate's left eyebrow went up as she digested that.

"Like a family vacation?"

"Something like that."

Uh-huh." Kate drawled. "Is there something you want to tell me?"

"Like what?"

"I don't know, maybe that you got a new girlfriend and are running off to Vegas to get married."

"Really Kate, come on." he said. "Does that sound like something I would do?"

"You tell me." Kate crossed her arms and stared inquiringly at him. "It's obviously you two are together and it's pretty serious for I've never heard you tell another woman you loved her since Victoria. Then with you, wanting to rush off with your daughter so soon after you have come home, what else is there to conclude? Are you in that much of a rush for the honeymoon or is she pregnant?"

"Katherine!"

"I'm sorry, but what other explanation is there for you to run off like this?" Kate expressed. "I mean for God sakes Vincent, Victoria just died. You have not even had the chance to morn her let alone tell your daughter, her mother is not coming home. She has a right to say goodbye to her before you bring another woman into her life. No offense, Miss, Nicholas."

"None taken," she said.

"Look Kate its true Cheyenne and I are together, but she's not pregnant and we aren't running off to get married--at least not yet." he clarified, noticing Cheyenne jerked towards him. "The urgency for our departure has nothing to do with our personal relationship. I know it comes at a bad time, but Victoria will get a proper funeral and Samantha will get a chance to say goodbye, just not at this time." He paused and took a deep breath. "We have other pressing matters we have to deal with. I cannot tell what they are, so do not ask. You'll just have to trust me that I know what I'm doing."

Kate shook her head and threw her hands up in the air.

"I'll call you when I get back," he said, kissing her on the cheek." Don't worry."

Kate gave him a look that said other wise and said, "Before you go, I have something for you."

She disappeared into the house and came out with a box full of mail. She took off -what look like a register letter and handed it to him.

"It came for you today. It was over-nighted, so it must be important." Kate relayed.

"Thanks!"

"You will call when you get to where you're going?"

"Yes Kate," he said, kissing her cheek again.

As they headed back to the car, Vincent glanced over the federal express envelope. The postal mark was from the county where Ray Brook Correctional facility was located. It was sent the day of Victoria's death. He figured it had to be an official letter, though it had been addressed to his sister in care of him. Why hadn't they sent it to his address?

Vincent kicked the car over and drove a little way down the drive. He stopped when they were out of sight.

What's wrong?"

"Nothing," he said, grabbing the register letter.

He ripped it open and shook out what was in it. A key slipped out his fingers into his lap. He picked it up and examined the two pieces of paper that came with it. The first was a folded-up sheet of thick paper like an invitation. It was Victoria's death certificate. The other was a plain white business card that had an address and number hand written on it.

"What is it?" Cheyenne asked, leaning forward.

"I'm not sure but I think the key and the card with the address were sent by Victoria or by someone she trusted."

"The key looks like it's to a safety deposit box."

"I would have to agree. I am sure the address will lead us to it. We'll track it down after we get Samantha."

Vincent pulled into the school parking lot of Ellsworth Preparatory and parked. They walked into the building and spoke with one of school's staff. They buzzed Samantha's classroom and asked her teacher to send her to the front. The teacher informed them that Samantha had taken a hall pass to the rest room and she had not returned yet but would send her down when she came back. That was not acceptable to Vincent. He wanted them to present his daughter right then and there, but the woman felt she had authority on the issue, even though he was the father. He demanded she let him go get her or she would have a lawsuit on her hands.

"Mr. West you can't go all over the school searching the girl's bathrooms for your daughter." the woman insisted." Her teacher instructed she would send her when Samantha returns to class. Now please take a seat."

Vincent reluctantly did so, sitting on one the benches provided. He crossed his arms and glared at the woman.

"Stop that." Cheyenne ordered, as she took a seat next him. "She's just doing her job."

"And what job is that, being the school prison warden?" he grumbled. "It seems you need a court order to get your kid out of school these days."

Minutes ticked by with no appearance of Samantha. Cheyenne began nibbling on her thumbnail as Vincent stood up and began pacing. She knew he was worried and becoming impatient. It seemed very unlikely Samantha would take that long to use the facilities. Something was wrong.

"This is ridiculous." Vincent barked. "I'm going to go find her."

He stormed off and Cheyenne bolted after him, with the woman calling after them.

He reached Samantha's classroom and flew the door open. He scanned the startled class to see Samantha was not there. Her teacher addressed him in a calm and cool manner, but Cheyenne could tell she was annoyed. Vincent was short and abrupt with her.

"I'm holding you responsible if something happens to her." he bit out charging out of the room.

Cheyenne followed his lead, wishing he would calm down. He was only going to draw attention to them, attention they did not need. She watched him check every bathroom on the school grounds, but Samantha was nowhere to be found. They checked the playground, the gym, the locker rooms and cafeteria but came empty handed. Vincent sat down on the bleachers and covered his face.

"We'll find her," she said, with confidence.

"I know you're trying to be optimistic but we've been all over this place and she isn't here. They've got her."

"You know as well as I do, they won't do anything to her unless they don't get what they want. She is safe for the moment. Take comfort in that." She squeezed his hand. "Now come on. We don't want to be here when the police arrive."

He nodded and stood up. She started to leave when she stopped her. He pulled her close and kissed her.

"Thank you," he murmured, against her lips.

Knowing what he meant by that, she smiled and said, "You're welcome."

Vincent pulled up to an aging three-story building that housed the local bank of a nearby town thirty miles from Ellsworth.

After flashing, his badge and explaining the reason for being there, one the tellers brought them over to the safety deposit box room.

Leaving them, Vincent located the box and pulled it out. He set it on the table provided and unlocked it to find an envelope in it addressed to him. He pulled it out and read it.

Vincent,

I was hoping this day would never come, but if you're reading this, it must mean my worst fears have come true and I am dead.

Not a pretty way to start a letter, but it is best to get right to the point.

I take it I've revealed some impertinent information to you or I wouldn't have given you the key to the safety box to find this letter.

As you are aware, Kevin was murdered because he was going to expose certain corrupt officers within the agency. He had known there was a chance he would be killed before the truth got out, so, he told me everything in hopes that if something did happen to him, it would still get out.

However, they must have known he'd might do that and devised a plan to silence us both. It is why he is dead and I am being accused of it.

I do not know the circumstances that resulted you into reading this, but the reason, I am writing this letter, is to reveal the location of where I hid the evidence Kevin gathered. Being that we are both dead now, you are the only one who can make sure our efforts were not in vain.

After Kevin died, I bought a strong box-a very large one and placed all documents, surveillance photos and audio documentation Kevin put together in it.

As for the whereabouts of the strong box, it depends on how far in the future you are when reading this. At present it's stashed in my old trunk that use to belong to my grandfather. You know the one, we used to store stuff in our old apartment when we first got married.

Now this is important, the key for the lock on the trunk is taped to the bottom of the first drawer of my dresser. The key for the lock box is hidden in the lining of the memory box I made Samantha.

Do what you have to, to bring these guys down but be careful.

Tell Samantha I love her and will always be with her, matter what happens.

All my love,
Victoria

Setting the letter down, Vincent leaned against counter and dragged his hands over his face.

"Are you all right?" Cheyenne said, resting her hand on his.

"To tell you the truth I don't think I'm ever going to be okay."

"I'm sorry Vincent you have to go through this," she said. "Was the letter from Victoria?"

He nodded.

"What did she say?"

"Why don't you read it for yourself?"

He handed it to her. She took it from him and did just that.

After digesting its contents, she said, "Do you think those involved suspected she would reveal this to us and took Samantha as a bargaining chip?"

"It's a possibility," he said. "They knew she had to know something about what Kevin had been up to for they wouldn't have pinned his murder on her or went to see her in prison after she was convicted. Even though she played it cool, they must have known she been lying. I am sure they did not know to what extent but the little she did know, caused them to threaten our daughter if she talked. They must have known Kevin would have had to have physical evidence of the crimes they committed. Maybe they figured Victoria could give them some clue that would lead them to it and that's why they kept her alive this long."

"I think they forced the situation, Vincent. Whether they were certain or not, she knew about where the evidence was, they took a chance and created a dilemma that gave her no choice but to reveal the location."

"They couldn't have known I would contact her that night."

"Yes, but they knew you would contact her at some point," she said. "But don't beat you up about it. You had no way of knowing what their agenda was."

"Well I do now and they're going to pay for messing with my family," he said. "You can count on it."

Pulling up to an eighteen hundred, farmhouse with evergreen shutters, Vincent cut the engine and got out.

Cheyenne followed suit, pausing to admire his property. The land itself was green and rich in color. There was a large red barn off in a distance. She could imagine horses galloping across the fields, while a woman in an apron stood by the house hanging laundry. Her son would be by the big oak tree, swinging on a tire swing. It left her yearning for the simpler days.

She stepped onto the porch wanting to sit down on the rocking chair and sip lemonade. She took a deep breath, drawing in the crisp fresh air and sighed. She was so grateful for these moments of serenity, though it was all shattered, when she noticed Vincent pull out his gun from the back of his pants. He was suspiciously looking at the front door, checking out the doorknob and inner frame.

"Is there something wrong?"

He placed his finger to his lips. She took that as yes and did not say another word.

He slowly opened the door and stepped in. He panned the area off the foyer and went further into the house. She stayed behind him as he prowled around checking each room. They entered his den and she saw a figure shadowed up against the bookshelves. She almost let out a cry, but caught herself. Vincent had seen it too and swerved into the room, gun drawn.

Vincent stepped in closer. "Move and you're a dead man!"

"Is that how you greet an old mate," the intruder said, dryly, turning towards them.

"Merrick!" He lowered his gun. "What in hell are you doing here?"

"Well, I heard Maine was real nice this time of year so I thought…."

"Merrick," he snapped.

"All right," Merrick raised his hands. "I thought you might need some help."

"I appreciate that, but how did you find us?"

"Guess?"

"Juliet," he said, glancing at Cheyenne.

She gave him a little weary apologetic smile.

"Yes. She spilled everything about Victoria, Kevin and Cheyenne's plan to desert you in Italy." Merrick said, sitting down.

"I wasn't going to desert him," she said, feeling the need to clarify that accusation. "I was just leaving him temporarily so we could individually focus on our situations."

"If you say so," Merrick said. "Though it seems your plans didn't…." Merrick was cut off by the shrill of the phone. Vincent glanced at her before picking it up.

After a brief greeting of hello, he listened intently to what was being said on the other end. From the one-syllable answers,

Cheyenne knew it had to be the individuals who had Samantha. He grabbed a piece of paper and a pen. He jotted down whatever the caller instructed, and then hung up.

"They have your daughter, don't they?" Merrick said, slamming his hand on the desk.

"Yes. They took her from school. I would have told you but…."

"I understand." Merrick said. "What did they say?"

"They want a trade, which was what we expected." He told Merrick about the letter from Victoria.

"When and where do they want to trade Samantha for the evidence?" Merrick asked.

"They didn't. They just instructed that Cheyenne and I take the eight fifteen train to Portland. They would contact me on my cell for further instructions."

"They're either being very cautious, or their planning on knocking you both off." Merrick theorized. "Think about it. With or without obtaining the evidence, they can simply end the threat of being exposed, by getting rid of both you. It's more than likely a trap."

"I'm sure they know we would think that. That is one of the reasons they took my daughter. They knew we would agree to their demands regardless of the implications and risk it."

"Then what do we do," she asked.

"We have to be cleverer than them."

CHAPTER 19

"I found it." Cheyenne announced, lifting off a storage container that was stacked on the green trunk.

When Victoria had gone to prison, Vincent had put all Victoria's things in a storage facility.

Taking the key, they found taped under one of her dresser drawers, Cheyenne unlocked it. She found a layer of towels and sheets on top. She hoisted the strong box out and placed it next to her. Vincent slipped out the key they found in the lining of Samantha's memory box and unlocked it.

Inside were four manila envelopes. They contained files of written reports given by officers on cases they worked on that had gone bad. Each officer who had been there had given their own recount of how things went down. There were bound together with surveillance photos and audio files on flash drives that were labeled and numbered. Kevin gave a brief on each one.

From what Cheyenne could gather Kevin had found out a group of officers were paid to change or manipulate the outcome of operations they worked on. They would falsify their statements, suppress or destroy evidence: leak information to the other side; blow officer's/agents cover, even commit murder to make a profit. Kevin apparently had been investigating them, three years prior to his death, watching their every move, gathering what he could to expose them.

He lost his life trying to do something good. It was a hard price to pay for the truth. The worse part of it, he was not the only one to suffer, she thought. Victoria went to prison and died because of his crusade. Vincent and his daughter had to go through six years of emotional heartache and pain. It did not seem fair.

She picked up one the files. She was about to pass it to Vincent when she noticed the name on the file. It read Stewart Matthews. She knew that name. He was Vincent's handler who had interrogated her at the chalet.

"Oh god," she said.

"What?"

"Kevin has a file on Stewart Matthew's."

"What," he said, in disbelief, taking it from her. He looked it over, shaking his head.

"This can't be. Stewart is one of the most respected men I know. He couldn't be caught up in this."

"Apparently Kevin thought otherwise." Merrick remarked, snatching the pictures that were attached to it.

He breezed through them and made a disappointing sound.

"What?"

"Take a look." Merrick said, handing them to him.

Cheyenne stepped in closer to Vincent to see a glossy eight by ten of a scene in a warehouse, where an exchange was being made, evidently by undercover officers and the individuals they wanted to bring down. One of the men in the photograph was Stewart Matthews.

Vincent flipped through the other pictures that were taken in increments as the events of the meeting unfolded, to see Matthews shoot the leader in cold blood. It led to a shootout where in the end the ones standing were Matthews and the three other officers. The last photo showed them walking off with the merchandise and the money.

"Why did he do that," she said, as he set them down. "Was he ordered to kill them?"

Vincent did not respond, but walked towards the opening and leaned against the door jam. He slid his hands up the side of his face and lowered his head. Cheyenne started go to him, but Merrick stopped her. Merrick shook his head, indicating it was not advisable to do so.

Merrick grabbed the file. "Let's see what Stewart had to say on the subject."

While Merrick read it, she scanned for a place to sit down and found a high back oak chair that had one of the arms broken off. She glanced over, her heart going out to Vincent. It was not every day you find out the person you had trusted lives a sinister life.

It got her thinking, if Officer Matthews manipulated cases to go a certain way like a client trying to buy off a jury, he could have aided in framing her. That meant either he worked directly with Lopez or there was another party involved who was paying him. She could be jumping to conclusions. Stewart might not have had any part in it but it was certain he was involved in Kevin and Victoria's deaths even if it was indirectly. He had to have some say in it for his career and freedom was on the line, if the evidence got out.

Maybe her demise and Vincent's situation were orchestrated from the beginning. It would explain why their situations coincided with each other. Officer Matthews was connected to both affairs. It could be the reason why they wanted both of them at the exchange. They would get the Microfilm and the evidence against them at the same time.

She glanced at Merrick. "Find out anything interesting in Matthew's report?"

"Other than its nice piece of fiction," he said back.

"I guess that means yes."

"It's just like the others. It doesn't correlate with the photos." Merrick said. "It's like a movie with an alternating ending. It's the same story, but some of the key facts have been altered."

"How did they manage to get away with it?"

"They're the CIA." Merrick said. "They're surrounded by lies and secrets. It comes easy to them to deceive since they live it day in and out."

"We need to go." Vincent said, coming over to them. "We have a lot to do before tonight."

He gathered the files and shoved them in the strong box. Without saying another word, he walked out.

Cheyenne stood by the bar, nursing a soda as the train jolted forward. She placed her free hand on the counter to brace herself when she noticed the gentlemen next to her give her the once over. The man was twice her age and a little rough around the edges. He grinned at her and she gave a brief smile out of politeness. She turned from him to see Vincent making his way over to her.

"Any word yet," she said, as he approached.

"No."

"Do you think it will be Matthews who does the trade?"

"Possibly," he said. "I'm hoping it is and that he does something stupid, so I have an excuse to kill him."

"You know that's not going bring back Victoria or Kevin," she pointed out. "It won't turn back time either and fix what has happened."

"I'm aware of that," he said, downing her soda in one gulp. "But it will make me feel better that he paid for his crimes."

"You're an eye for eye kind of guy?"

"I believe in justice and that's what he's going to get."

"Even if it's at your own expense?"

"If it stops the innocent from getting hurt, yes I would."

"But it not going to stop with him. There are others involved. You're going to kill all of them?"

"If comes down to that," he said. "It depends on the outcome of events."

"The evidence Kevin obtained will put them away for good," she said. "That's where the justice lies."

"Listen why don't you go to the cabin," he suggested ending the subject. "I'm going to look around. Check things out."

She reluctantly nodded. "Be careful."

"I will."

She watched him go and disappear into the next car.

She grabbed her purse and made her way to the sleeping cabins. She pulled out the key and unlocked the door. She stepped in only to stop short.

Sitting causally by the picture window with a cigar in one hand and a drink in the other was Rachel Sullivan, her boss.

"Hello, Miss Nicholas."

The door slammed behind Cheyenne. She jumped. She turned to see a tall, bald, stern looking man. She noticed he had a gun nestled in the crest of his pants.

"Don't let Rolph's presence worry you. He's only here for my protection."

Miss Sullivan what are you doing here," she said, her mind trying to grabble with the shock of seeing her.

"I'm here to help you Cheyenne."

"Help me," she questioned, feeling a pit of dread forming in her stomach.

"Yes. I heard you were in some trouble, something to do with snuggling and murder." her boss commented.

She was stomped at that. How did she know about that? Then it hit her. She had to be *the man* the CIA was hoping Lopez would lead them to. Yet she was no man but a sophisticated, successful forty-eight-year-old, cigar-smoking woman. To think she was the core behind the smuggling ring.

Understanding now, Cheyenne said, "You could have saved yourself the trip if you hadn't gotten me into this in the first place."

"That is where you're wrong. Lopez is the one you should give all the credit to. He's the one who picked you and set your fate into motion."

"But he had to get the idea from somewhere." she shot back "I doubt he came up with it on his own. He had to have help and a reason or you wouldn't be here."

"I see nothing gets passed you."

"Just explain why I'm in this mess?"

"You'll have you to ask Lopez."

"I'm asking you," she snapped.

"Why he picked you, I don't know. But the person he chose was meant to be a distraction," her boss conveyed, crossing her legs. "Lopez got greedy and has been doing some freelance work on the side. He was stupid. He had gotten involved with individuals that were on the CIA's radar and they zeroed in on him because of an item that fell into his hands."

"The Microfilm?"

"Yes." Rachel Sullivan took a draw from her cigar. "It made him their number one lead and I couldn't afford that kind of publicity. Eventually his stupidity would have led to me. Something had to be done." She paused, swallowed the remainder of her drink and went on. "It was supposed to be cut and dry. Once they were convinced you were involved and you had it, they would be focused on you, giving us the opportunity to make sure all the leads to him were erased. Initially you were supposed to have been taken into custody after the Microfilm was found in Roderick's possession and thrown into prison. That did not happen that way because Lopez manipulated it to where it would benefit him which is why you're in the state you're in. He used your involvement to shadow his real purpose. He wanted to retrieve the Microfilm and sell it like he originally planned."

"In other words, he took your idea, modified it, and applied it to his own needs to make sure he would come out on top and not you."

"Exactly, it's the reason he's here."

"He's on the train?" Cheyenne half expected him to be behind her, but only Rolph stood there in attention.

"Yes, I've been informed of his presence by associate of mine."

"Stewart Matthews, I presume."

"Aren't you a clever girl?" Rachel drawled, dryly, not surprised, or impressed by her deduction.

"You said you're here to help me," she reminded her. "How do you plan on doing that? Were you planning on turning yourself in?"

"Not likely. What I propose is more of, if you scratch my back, I'll scratch yours."

"What is it that you want from me?"

"Your corporation."

"In what?"

"In making sure Lopez gets what he deserves and that the exchange tonight goes off without a hitch."

"It will." she insisted, evenly. "You have nothing to worry about on that account."

"Then I want to see the files Officer Rogan gathered to make sure you two aren't going to pull a fast one."

"Are you doing the exchange?"

"No. Stewart is."

"Then you have no business seeing them." she retorted. "Those files don't concern you. Even if I agreed to it, I could not give you access to them anyway. They're not here."

"That's too bad." Rachel flipped open a laptop that was resting on the table next to her. "I guess you don't want West to ever see his daughter again."

The screen lip up and a video image appeared. A frighten little girl, Cheyenne recognized as Samantha from pictures Vincent had shown her, sat in a corner of a dingy room with her hands and feet bound. Cheyenne could not tell exactly where she was. It could be motel or the insides of a van for she knew.

"It would be a shame if he lost her too because you wouldn't corporate." Rachel smirked, puffing smoke into the air. "I can't imagine what that would do to his state of mind."

"You wouldn't kill her. She's leverage." she balked, calling her on it. "If anything happens to her, they get nothing."

"Yes, that's true. But we can hurt her."

"You lay one hand on her and Vincent will kill you," she hissed.

"Is he here? I do not see him. He will not know what kind of treatment she would receive until after the exchange. You're the one with the power to make sure she's returned to him in good health."

"You would hurt an innocent child over this?" she exclaimed, appalled.

"Freedom from prosecution has its price. If you want your life back and you don't want West to suffer more than he already has, you'll do as I suggest."

Knowing she had no choice, she reluctantly said, "Fine. I'll take you to where it is."

"Excellent." Rachel smiled. "See how easy that was."

She did not respond but turned from her.

They stepped out into the corridor and she led them to the baggage car.

She unlatched the door and went in. She scanned the shelves and pointed to a trunk.

Rolph rabbed it and placed it on the floor. It had a lock on it.

"Open it." Rachel demanded.

"I don't have the key so you're going to have to figure out another....."

She did not get a chance to finish for Rolph withdrew his gun and shot the lock off.

"That works."

Rachel Sullivan knelt down and lifted the top up. She took out the strong box and opened it. She pulled out the files and looked them over.

As she read them, she made tisk, tisk sounds and shook her head. She seemed impressed with it all and amused. She laughed in wonderment as she breezed through the photos.

"Is this everything?"

"Yes."

"Has any of it been tampered with or copied?"

"No."

"You're lying. A copy has been made for insurance purposes, hasn't it?"

Cheyenne did not admit or deny her assumption. Vincent had known they would have suspected they would. They were not going to go into it not holding any cards.

"Once the deal is done and the trade has been made, you will hand over that copy to me."

"I don't think so."

"We made a deal Miss Nicholas." Rachel reminded her. "You help me out, I help you out."

"Just because you have a government officer in your pocket, doesn't mean you're God." she retorted. "I haven't seen any of this *power* you have, other than threats you've thrown around. Your word does not give me any guarantee you would stick to your end of the deal. Secondly even if I had the authority just hand it over to you, I would not. I am not committing suicide so your associates can sleep at night."

"In that case," Rachel's hand shot up to her throat and clasped onto the chain of her necklace. She yanked it with such force it bit into Cheyenne's skin. Her hand instinctively went up to cradle the scarring. "I'll have to go this route since you refuse to meet me half way, I'll have to take what I want. The Microfilm is really what I need to succeed in all this."

Her boss held up Cheyenne's keepsake necklace. "I guess I'll be taking your place. Won't Lopez be surprised when you don't show up and I do with what he wants most?"

"What makes you think he'll show if I'm not there?"

"Because he's fueled by power and greed. He will not see what is coming until it is too late. Plus, we have a few tricks up our sleeves."

"But the terms of the exchange were specific. Vincent and I are both supposed to be there."

"You seem to forget my dear I have the power to change that. All I have to do is make a call."

Rachel signaled to Rolph, who stepped forward and roughly pinned Cheyenne arms to her side with his. She tried to break free but his hold on her was too strong. His arms were like the jaws of death.

"You know what to do."

Rachel looked at her. "Good-bye Miss Nicholas. It's been a pleasure." With that, she took leave.

CHAPTER 20

Vincent walked through the dining cart meticulously noting each passenger as he passed to see if he could spot Stewart or any other spooks, when his cell phone rang. He flipped it opened and said, "West."

"In twenty minutes, go to the front of the train and go into the first cart behind the engine," a flat, disguised voice said.

"The one that has the sign no admittance," he said, recalling checking out that very one earlier. The window been blacked out and blocked off by a thick heavy chain. He climbed over it and tried the door only to find it locked.

"Yes."

"Is there a password or secret knock to gain entrance?"

"Your humor is not appreciated, West."

"Neither is your tactic's pal." he shot back. "I want to talk to my daughter."

"Bring the documents as arranged and you'll get to see her in person."

"Not good enough," he growled. "I want to speak to her, now!"

"You're in no position to make demands, West."

"And you're in no position to deny me." he threw back. "So, put her on."

The caller did not respond. There was a dead silence on the other end, then a click, followed by a muffled crackling noise.

"Daddy?"

"Samantha?" he drawled, feeling a sense of relief to hear her voice. He could tell she was frightened.

"Daddy!" she said in desperation.

"Yes, baby, it's me."

"I'm scared. I want to go home. When are you coming to get me?" she cried. "I don't like it here. They are mean. Please...."

"Samantha?" he called out in emotion, only to have her voice die off.

"Twenty minutes, West. The hourglass had begun."

He cursed and spewed out an oath. He had to calm himself. He could not let his anger and rage consume him. Vengeance was not the answer even if sounded justifiable. It would not help his daughter. He had to go about this in a rash manner and keep his emotions in check. He could not afford to make any mistakes. He had to have a clear head. Easier said than done, he thought. It was hard not to react when it was so close to home. It was a completely different ball game when a love one was in the heart of danger. It was easier to disassociate one's fears and worries when one's love ones were not involved.

He sighed, slipped his cell phone in his pants, and headed to their sleeping cart. He thrust opened the connecting door and almost walked into a tall red head, dressed in a white pantsuit coming through. He apologized and let her go by. Vincent started to walk down the corridor only to stop. He turned back to see the attractive woman take a seat by the window. A waiter came up to her and took her order. Vincent studied her for a moment, thinking there was something familiar about her as if he had seen her before. His memory was not cooperating. He hated when that happened. The odds of him knowing her from somewhere were slim. The red hair struck him as did her youthful face, even though in appearance she was alluring, mature woman. She must remind him of someone else he knew perhaps an actress or famous socialite.

He pushed it aside, and continued. He came to the cabin Cheyenne and he were staying and knocked, announcing it was he before going in.

He came to a halt when he realized Cheyenne was not there. He checked the one-man bathroom but found it unoccupied. He stood in the middle of the room, with one hand on his hip, wondering where she went off to, when he noticed the ashtray. There was a cigar laying it. She had a visitor. He rested his hand on the butt of his gun. It was more out of habit than feeling the sense of danger. He doubted the cigar-smoking individual was around, lurking in the shadows. It appeared Cheyenne went willingly but that did not mean she had not been threatened.

There was no evidence of forced entry so either she knew the person or her friend had been waiting for her. His first thought was it had to be Lopez but he did not come off as a cigar smoking kind of guy.

He whirled around and charged out. He looked up and down the corridor. He was certain she had not been exhorted in the direction he just came from. He would see her and her newly acquired friend. They had to have gone towards the back of the train where the baggage cart was. He felt anger and rage once again consume him. If those bastards tried to double cross them by forcing Cheyenne to hand over the files before the exchange, there was going to be hell to pay. Then why call him and tell him to meet then in twenty? Perhaps it was a distraction to keep him from catching on their agenda. Yet they wanted both of them there. What was going on?

He made his way through the next four cars and as he approached the door leading out to the platform from the baggage cart, he saw movement. He stepped closer to see Cheyenne struggling with a man that outweighed her in muscle and in height. He did not recognize the barbarian but he knew he was a hired hand. Whether it was Stewart or one of his other cronies that had this guy on their pay roll, he was not certain. What was clear was this hired hand had been ordered to kill her.

He moved into the pocket where the passengers boarded on and off. He withdrew his gun and cocked it. He hugged the wall and peeked into the window. He saw her captor slide open the metal barred door and forcible place Cheyenne in front of the wide opening. Her captor was going to shove her out. Vincent took a deep breath and hunched down. He rested his hand on the door latch and pulled it down as quietly as he could. He inched the door open, shot up, startling her captor, and fired off two shots, crippling him. Cheyenne screamed as the man yelled out in agony as both legs gave way, taking her down with him. The impact of her body slamming into Rolph's knocked the wind out of her. She rolled off him and landed with a thud on the floor. She saw out of the corner of her eye, Vincent approach, and cover Rachel's henchmen. He disarmed Rolph, flipped him on his back, and pinned his bulging arms. Rolph tried to buck him off but Vincent butted him in the head with his gun knocking him out. He tied him up with a bungee cord and threw a tarp over him.

Cheyenne still recovering from the attack and near-death experience, stumbled to her feet, shaking a leaf. She burst into tears, as he gathered her into his embrace.

"I thought I was going to die!" she cried.

"I know." he said, stroking her. "I'm sorry I shouldn't have left you alone."

"Don't blame yourself," she said. "There was no way of knowing this was going to happen."

"That seems to be your famous quote of a late." he commented. "But regardless of that, I should have known Stewart wasn't going to pay fair."

"It wasn't him. It was Rachel Sullivan."

"Your boss?"

"Yes."

She explained what Rachel had told her and Vincent spewed out a string of colorful words. The woman he had almost rammed into had to have been Rachel Sullivan, he thought. No wonder she looked familiar.

"You're not going to like this either," she added. "She has the Microfilm."

"Bloody hell!" he cursed, taking notice of the red, gash marks on her neck.

"What are we going to do?"

He brushed his hands through his hair. "The only thing we can do. Go through with the exchange as planned and get my daughter back. You said she was going to take your place as the exchange because Lopez was going to make an appearance. If we're lucky, it will give us the opportunity to get it back."

Cheyenne felt her pulse race as Vincent tried the door of the blacked-out window. She heard a click that indicated it was unlocked. Vincent went in first with her following.

She stepped under the threshold, her gaze roaming over the luxurious cart with its plush seating and rich, maple tables that were wax to a shine before resting on the men responsible for making her and Vincent's life a living nightmare. She took note that her boss was not present but officer Stewart Matthews attended along with two other CIA officers she recognized from the surveillance photos.

The one on the left, a tall, hefty man with beady eyes and a receding hairline, who looked more like a furniture salesman, had Samantha. His large pudgy hands rested on her shoulders in a firm grip, keeping her immobilized. She looked tired and frightened. Her bottom lip trembled and her eyes watered up. Cheyenne noticed Vincent go rigid and flex his hands. She knew it took every one of his strength to stay put.

The third in the party was average in height, dark skinned, and stocky. He was dressed in all black and he had a gun cupped in his right hand that crossed over his other in a comfortable embrace. He came over to them and padded them down to make sure they were not armed.

"They're clean."

He went back over to his post and Cheyenne's eyes rested on Lopez. He stood off to the side, observing. He grinned lecherously at her.

"Hello love, miss me?" he grinned. "Don't worry. I am next in line. Then it will be our turn."

She could feel the disgust and contempt rise in her but she did not show it. She was not about to give the jerk the satisfaction.

"Since we're all here, let's get this done." Stewart announced, cutting to the chase.

"I second that." Lopez agreed. "Quicker you conduct your business, the faster I can conduct mine."

"Lopez why don't you go make yourself useful and leave." Stewart ordered.

Lopez gave him a cold stare and gave him look the defined he did not appreciate being told what to do before compiling. He made himself a drink, lit a cigarette, and went out on the platform that separated the cart they were in from the engine.

"Do you have the files?"

"You know we do. You made sure of it," Vincent replied, his eyes shifting to his daughter.

"Drastic measures had to be taken, Vincent. Your ex gave us no choice. We we're back into the corner," Stewart shrugged helplessly. "It was just business, nothing personal."

"It's always personal Stewart "he ejaculated." You and your associates manipulate and take lives for a profit. You targeted my family for god sakes. You ruined four lives. Victoria's; my daughter's; my partner's and mine, not to mention Cheyenne's. You, Rachel Sullivan--yes we know about her, Lopez and whoever else you have in your pocket, orchestrated the whole mess she's in. You'll do anything to cover your ass's and stay in business."

"Bravo. You have us all figured out." Samantha's captor drawled out in false praise. "We aren't here to justify or explain our actions or what we do. There are no stories to tell that would satisfy you and answer your questions. The fact is we are wired differently, plain and simple."

"I couldn't have put it better myself," said the other one.

"Enough." Stewart ordered. "Let's get on with it."

"Fine, you let go of my daughter and I'll give you what you want."

"Destroy the copy of the files and I will."

"Can't do that," he said. "You have your insurance policy; I have mine so if you want the copies then you better guarantee that my daughter, Cheyenne and myself walk out of here alive because having the originals aren't going to protect you and your associates from spending your remaining days behind bars."

"Fine," Stewart bit out his eyes narrowing coldly. "But I'm not letting your precious daughter go until we have the originals in our hands first."

Vincent did not comment, but slid over the strong box, tossing the key at Stewart. It landed on the floor, next to the officer who stood guard. He picked it up and gave Vincent a contorted smirk. Stewart placed the strong box on one of the tables and instructed his friend to open it. He scanned the contents, and then shut it. He signaled to the officer who held Samantha captive and he let her go. She ran to Vincent and threw her arms around him. He picked her up and hugged her tightly, murmuring nurturing words.

Cheyenne felt tears form. The return of his daughter was just as potent to her as it was to him, even though she had no connection to the little girl. The thought of any child being taken and treated the way she had been would have been distressing to anyone.

The conductor came over the central intercom system to announce they were stopping at the next depot. She noticed the CIA officer who had Samantha grab the strong box. The other one nodded to Stewart and slipped his gun into the back of his pants.

When the train came to a halt, they departed, leaving Stewart in their company. Lopez strolled in, stubbing out his cigarette before addressing them.

"You two seem to be very popular today. I had to take a number." he commented, leaning up against one of the windows. "I didn't like that very much but that was the deal if I wanted to get my ten minutes with you." He paused and lit another cigarette.

"Our friend here," His gaze shifting to Stewart for a moment, "saved me a lot of time by including me in this meeting and delivering you to me." He stared knowingly at Cheyenne as he stepped closer to her. He stopped when he felt the cold steel against his temple.

"You touch her or move any closer to her and I'll blow your head off." Vincent warned in a deadly voice.

"I thought you had checked him for weapons." Lopez bit out.

"We did but apparently he had one stashed elsewhere." Stewart answered. "I told you having him here was going to be detrimental to your health. You threatened the woman he loves and he almost lost his daughter. He isn't in a good place right now, so I wouldn't piss him off."

Lopez stepped back. "You have nothing to worry about lover boy. You have already corrupted and spoiled her. She is tarnished goods and unworthy for the taking. She's....."

He did not get a chance to finish. Vincent punched him squarely in the face, snapping his head back causing him to stumble. He cursed but did not react.

Instead of looking angry, he appeared pleased as if he got off on provoking him.

"What a good example you're setting for your daughter." Lopez taunted, as he cleaned the blood off his lip that had trailed down from his nose. "The big bully picking on the defenseless one. You might as well take pleasure in that assault because that's the last one you'll ever inflict on yours truly."

"I doubt that very much but if believing that brings you comfort by all means entertain the idea."

Lopez just smiled as if he was amused by the notion than threatened by it.

"I know love, you were looking forward to clearing your name and living happily ever after without me in the picture but unfortunately it isn't going to happen. Your destiny lies elsewhere. Now hand over the Microfilm or Officer Mathews is going to be forced to do something very unpleasant." Stewart held up a small box with a blinking red light. It was a hand held remote.

"You rigged the train to a bomb?" Vincent said, not believing the lengths they would go to add to their bank accounts and to stay out of prison.

"You have your insurance, I have mine." Stewart said, throwing Vincent words back in his face.

"If you hurt anyone of us, the copy of those files ends up on the CIA's front door." Vincent reminded him.

"Relax Vincent. We're not threatening your lives but the two hundred and sixty-three people on board." Stewart said. "We wouldn't be breaking any of the terms you requested. You, Ms. Nicholas and your daughter will still walk off this train alive. It's the passengers who might not."

"And I suppose in order to prevent that you want a gassed jet plane for you, your stooges, and pretty boy over there?"

"Something like that?" Stewart said. "Though does it really matter? I would think saving two hundred and sixty-three lives would be more important."

"How do we know you'll keep up your end of the deal and won't blow us to kingdom come once you set foot off the train?"

"Because you made sure if we kill you, we get exposed." Stewart said. "We're not stupid nor are you, so we'll take our chances by keeping you alive."

"You didn't with my ex-wife. She could have exposed you too, but you still killed her."

"She broke her promise and in doing so she opened a Pandora's box. If she had kept quiet and heeded our warning it would have ended with her, but she had to involve you and Miss Nicholas forcing us to take action." Stewart said.

"That's a bunch of crap and you know it. You were slowly killing her with small doses of poison no doubt administered by the good old doctor in the infirmary even before she talked. That is why you put a hit on me. You knew if she was released, that would come out and an investigation would have been put into motion. If I were dead, her earlier release would have been tabled. But that didn't happen, so you just moved up the time frame and did her in because you knew she would tell me everything."

"You're right. I would not deny any of it, but our plans blew up in our faces, Vincent. You saw to that, so now we have to do what is best to our advantage. If letting you live is loss we have taken, then we will."

"Look," Lopez cut in. "You two might find this display of sharing enlightening, maybe even cleansing, but can you do it on someone else time? Because I seem to recall you have already had your moment. Now if more has to be said then swap cell phone numbers. I hear you can talk free on the weekends."

"You sure seem to be in quite a rush for someone who thinks he has it made."

"Just give me the necklace or would you rather I take it by force?" Lopez bit out his focus zooming in on Cheyenne.

"I'm afraid someone has already done that?" she replied, revealing the abrasions on her neck.

Lopez's eyes clouded over and said, "Who?"

"Me."

CHAPTER 21

Rachel Sullivan stepped forward, looking quite pleased as she viewed her audience until her eyes rested on Cheyenne. She gave her a deadly cold stare. She clenched her manicure nails wanting to wring that delicate bruised neck of hers. She should be dead but West prevented her from that fate. If Matthews had done his job of eliminating him in the first place, her mangled body would be rotting in the wilderness. But no, lover boy escaped death to save her from it. Rolph had taken Cheyenne's place leaving her one man short. Even though the odds were in her favor, not having Rolph was like losing an appendage. She would not let this set back keep her from doing what she came to do.

She withdrew Cheyenne's necklace from inside her pant pocket and dangled it out in front of her.

"It amazes me how this piece of jewelry has gotten around," she mused. "It's hidden treasure has become one man's obsession: another's freedom from injustice and to many others a threat to national security." She paused and came further into the car. "The item in questioned had one goal, one task, and that was to be a diversion, a means to an end, yet its path was altered by greed and power."

"You're Saelec," Lopez gave a short laugh. "I must say I was expecting the man behind the scene to be more of an independent entrepreneur who had connections and the capitol to run an operation of this proportion. Not a company man, who turns out to be a red headed, corporate bitch in high heels that is limited by her status."

"That was the idea," she smiled. "As for being a woman that was just the cherry on the top."

"What do you mean?" Cheyenne said.

"It means my position in the company was a ruse to protect my interests and keep the authorities guessing."

"In other words, by shadowing her identity and her sex gave her more freedom to be involved with the organization without threat of exposure." Vincent clarified. "But Lopez franchised out, weakening that safe haven she had created. She was not going to let his carelessness and unorthodox business practices fracture what she worked so hard preserve."

"But if she is like the mob boss of the smuggling ring, how do Royden and Alder fit into it?" Cheyenne wondered. "I.C.S has been in the Royden family for over a century. It's an established company who's had other people in their employment longer than she has been Vice president."

"Yes, that's true, Miss Nicholas, but the Royden family was fabricated by my grandfather when he took over the family business over a hundred years ago," Rachel explained. "Actually, it has had many different names tied to it over the years, the purpose being to secure its origin."

"I don't understand. If you and your family were that cautious and would go to such lengths to protect its legacy, then why risk exposure by revealing your identity?"

"Because I turned out to be someone who could rival her own ambitions." Lopez answered. "I surpassed her expectations and that scared and angered her. She didn't feel in control and the preservation to stay in control is a strong motivator that makes the most distrustful person put aside their fears."

"And greed curses and condemns men, as it will you."

"That's where you're wrong."

With a slip of his hand, Lopez revealed a gun and discharged it. An echo of screams from Samantha and Cheyenne followed.

Stricken in shock, Rachel Sullivan clutched her chest, blood staining her pristine white suite as she fell to her knees.

"Didn't see that coming, did you?" Lopez sneered, snatching Cheyenne's necklace out of her blood-soaked hand. "Do you actually believe I went to all this trouble just to screw you over and take home the prize?"

"Stewart," she rasped, not understanding why he just stood there watching and not taking action,

"Sorry, my loyalty lays with one who pays me more for my allegiance and that's him."

"What is it you want? If isn't the Microfilm and riches it will bring then what?"

"Your organization?"

"My organization."

"Yes. If you're to be greedy, then why not go to for gusto."

"You mean to say you manipulated and orchestrated everything to get her out in the open so you could step into her shoes." Cheyenne said, disgusted that she actually found that impressive.

"Pretty ingenious, isn't it?" Lopez smirked. "But in order for it to come full circle she's got to die. Stewart."

Before anyone could react, Stewart fired off a shot ending her life. Cheyenne shut her eyes and covered her mouth to hold down the nausea. Vincent embraced her wishing he could have prevented them from the horrors they have been subjected to. His daughter was already traumatized by the events that had unfolded and she would be for a long time to come.

"Look at this way she had to die at some point." Stewart commented. "I just helped her get there a little sooner. Secondly, we do not want to coddle our children from the realities of the world. People die and the more they understand that, the better they'll be."

"Maybe in your sadistic, twisted mind you might think taking a life before it's time is the natural process of life but in the real world it's not. It is called murder. There's nothing justifiable in it where you're concerned."

"You could say the same thing about the almighty." Stewart shot back. "If it's such an issue with you can bring it up when you see him."

"*NO!*" Cheyenne cried stepping in front of Vincent, as Stewart drew up his gun. Just as he was going to shoot, there was a loud screeching noise, followed by an abrupt jerky motion. His hand shout upward, firing off a round towards the ceiling as everyone was forced forward, then back as the train came to a halt..

Recovering first, Vincent took the opportunity and charged Stewart, knocking him clean off his feet. His gun clattered to the floor, skidding into the wall. Cheyenne started for it, when Lopez prevented her from reaching out to it by grabbing a hand full of her hair. He yanked her back and roughly shoved her forward. She tumbled into the tables and fell onto the ground with a thud. Lopez snatched up Stewart's gun and proceeded to fire on Vincent as he struggled with Stewart, when Merrick appeared tackling him to the floor. The gun discharged, the bullet ricocheting off steel pole holding up one of the bar stools, hitting Stewart in the thigh. He buckled under the pain giving Vincent the advantage. Lopez and Merrick fought for the gun, grunting and swearing as they wrestled on the floor.

Grabbing the gun, Merrick barked, "Didn't your mum tell you, you shouldn't play with guns? They're a hazard to your health."

"As are knives," Lopez growled, catching him off guard, plunging his pocketknife into Merrick's side. Merrick cried out in pain as Lopez twisted it before pulling it out. Merrick's hand instinctively went to the wound as Lopez tried to plunge the knife into him again. Merrick arched his arm, preventing him from striking and wedged his leg into his chest, shoving out. Lopez stumbled backwards into the stools. Merrick made it to his feet, and hoisted Lopez up. He laid hard punch on him. Lopez's head snapped back and crumbled to the floor. With his breath labored and his side, burning Merrick bent down and padded Lopez down. He found Cheyenne's necklace and pocketed it. Knowing Vincent could handle Stewart, he went over to Cheyenne and Samantha.

"Are you two, all right," he asked, kneeling next to both of them.

"That should be something we should be asking you." Cheyenne said, looking at his knife wound. "What are you doing here anyway? You are supposed to be in Washington handing over the files to the CIA."

"Mission already completed." he said, raggedly. "It's over for them. We nabbed Stewart's men at the last stop by pure chance when the CIA dropped me off."

"Dropped you off?"

"Yes, they've been following the train from the air in a chopper. They had decided to fly ahead to the next town that had been on the schedule and wait for the train so I could come aboard. "he explained, handing her the necklace. "Now enough of the chitchatting. Take Samantha and find your way to the roof. We'll meet you there soon enough."

"I'm not leaving you here wounded and bleeding."

"I'll be fine," he reassured her. "GO!"

She took Samantha's hand and made a dash for the door. Lopez came to, to see them disappear over the threshold.

Fueled by rage, he inched up not to spook Merrick, and grabbed a bottle of wine that had been dislodge when the train came to an abrupt halt. He swung it up and bashed Merrick in the head with it. He went down like a ton of bricks. Relieving him of his gun, Lopez went after Cheyenne.

By this time, Vincent had subdued Stewart. He lay crumbled on the floor unconscious.

It took every ounce of strength not to retrieve his gun and shoot him. Vincent knew just because he deserved to die did not mean he had the right to take it.

Vincent tied his arms behind his back with his belt. He then padded him down and found the remote. He saw Merrick brace himself up and groaned in pain. Standing up, he went over to him.

"Are you okay," Vincent asked, as he helped him up.

I think so," Merrick said, toughing the soreness on the back of his head. He felt a sticky substance. He lowered his hand to see blood.

"You better get that checked out," he suggested. "Here"

"What is it?"

"A remote. The train is wired to a bomb," he said, heading for the door. "That's the trigger."

"What?"

"Just keep it safe and don't push the red button," he said, heading out.

"Oh right." Merrick muttered. "Thanks for the heads up."

With Samantha in tow, Cheyenne wove through the passengers who crowded around talking aimlessly as the conductor tried to calm them down. People were shouting out questions and scenarios. It was either that an animal found its way in the track, or a passenger had a medical emergency or there was a train wreck. A few thought the train was being taken over by terrorists, which they assumed from the spotlight of helicopter as it circled.

She was just about to reach the end of the dining cart, when she heard shots ring out. Lopez had entered the car, shooting wildly, yelling to everyone to get down. She pulled Samantha into her embrace and covered her as she crouched down. The sound of wood splitting and glass shattering co-mingled with screams permeated the air. When it died down, she reached for the lever of the door and shoved it opened. She crawled through guiding Samantha, before scrambling up. She heard Lopez yell out it rage.

They broke into a run and charged through the next car with him in hot pursuit. They reached the baggage car and passed through the thorough way. She instructed Samantha to climb up the metal stairs to the roof. She soon followed when Lopez burst through the door. He grabbed her ankle and tried to pull her down. She slipped and lost her footing. Samantha screamed, and then shouted at Lopez to leave Cheyenne alone.

"I'll leave her alone when she's dead," he snarled. "And when I'm through with her, I'm coming after you little girl."

"Not if I can help it." Cheyenne bellowed, kicking him in the face, then shoulder. His grip loosened and she twisted her leg free.

She scrambled up the stairs and joined Samantha. They scuffled over the top of car only to stop when it ended. She realized they were going to have to jump across the breezeway below in order to get away from Lopez and wave down the helicopter.

Without a moment to lose, they leaped across. The chopper spotted them and veered over to them when Cheyenne was tackled from behind. She went crashing down on the roof. Pain ricocheted through her. She glanced up to see Samantha had stopped.

"Go!" she screamed. "Run!"

Lopez flipped her on her back and pinned her arms. She squirmed under him, bucking, and kicking but it didn't have any effect. Lopez just got angrier and meaner.

"I'm going to enjoy this." he smiled.

"Not as much as I am." Vincent barked, as he hauled him off Cheyenne, his gun jerking into the air and disappearing into the darkness of the night. "This will be the last time you mess with her or me."

He punched him square in the face before hurling him off the roof. Lopez landed in a shallow ravine battered and bruised. The chopper flew over them lightening the spot, as officers converging on the area. Lopez was scrapped off the ground and taken in custody.

Cheyenne stood starring out the window of a hospital room in Boston. She had fractured her ribs when Lopez had tackled her on the roof, but she had not known it until she tried to reach up to get onto the chopper. The next thing she they were on their way to the hospital and she placed on a gurney. They kept her overnight and now she was back for a checkup.

It now had been forty-eight hours since her nightmare ended. Her named had been cleared, thanks to the Microfilm and evidence gathered in her defense. Matthew's and Lopez were arrested and were awaiting a sentence hearing. Rachel Sullivan was pronounced dead on sight, her body taken to the morgue.

Merrick had his side patched up and his head stitched up. He had to stay a night to make sure he did not have a concussion in which had Juliet on the plane over. Merrick was not too pleased she was making the trip. She was a month for her due date and he stressing that something might happened to the baby or her if she over did it. Vincent who had minor cuts and bruises had been tended to and sent home.

At the particular moment, he and Samantha were in the garden outside waiting for her. They were laughing and enjoying each other's company as a father and daughter should. They looked happy but she knew under the smiles there was still a lot of pain and loss. Granted they were working through it but it was going to take some time before the emotional scars would heal. It made her wonder if accepting Vincent's marriage proposal was the right thing to do. Samantha just lost her mother and went through a horrific experience of being taken from her father. To enter her life as a mother figure might hinder the healing process and make matters worse for her.

She knew Vincent was still coming to terms with the issues of his marriage to Victoria. Even though she fell out of love with him and ran to his partner, a part of him still loved her. Not that she expected him not to, but he had not had time to bury the past. He had been too caught up in trying to fix it and figure out what went wrong, then deal with it on an emotional level.

Secondly, their romance was a product of the intense rather dangerous situation impressed on them by outside forces. She doubted if they had met through work or a mutual friend, it would have progressed as fast as it did. She had to be sure that was not the case and the only way to do that was to test it. She knew Vincent and Samantha had to have some quality time together, regardless. Maybe being apart for an awhile will do them some good. She just had to have the guts to set it in motion.

She walked out the entrance to see them sitting on a bench eating ice cream. She sat down, exchanged pleasantries.

Vincent smiled. "I have something for you."

He dug into his pocket and withdrew her locket. He placed it in her hand. "It's been restored back to its original state."

She opened it and *Let me call you sweet heart* crooned out. She flipped it over to see an engraving. *In memory of a brother whose spirit never left us, but remained to inspire.*

Cheyenne felt tears form but quickly wiped them away. She could not get emotional.

"It's beautiful," she said, kissing him.

"There's one more thing," he said, digging into his pocket, withdrawing a ring.

He took her hand and slipped the diamond on her left middle finger. "I thought we make it official. It was my mothers."

"Oh Vincent." she sighed, with emotion. "You're making this very hard."

"What do you mean?" he asked.

"Vincent, we need to talk."

"I don't think I like the sound of that."

She stood up and went over to a shaded spot under an oak tree. He followed.

"What's wrong?"

She took a deep breath and told him. He exploded.

"You don't want to marry me because you think Samantha and I have issues?"

"I didn't say that."

"But that's what you're implying."

"No, it's not," she stressed. "I'm just stating you two need time without me in the picture."

"I know making this commitment is scary but running away isn't the answer."

"I'm not running, Vincent!" she said. "I'm giving you space to heal and a chance to find some peace."

"I already found peace with you," he said, stepping closer to her.

She backed up. "No, you haven't, not really."

"How can you say that?"

"Because I look in your eyes and I see the turmoil," she said. "I look in Samantha's eyes I see pain and anguish. The only way it is going to be replaced with joy and happiness is if I am not around. She needs you right now, not a substitute mother."

"I would never ever consider you as a substitute mother or wife?" he said, angrily. "How could you think that?"

"Because that's how it will be if you shove your past under the rug and not deal with it." she said. "I'm sorry, but rushing into this would be a mistake."

"And your answer to this is *to leave* us?"

"Vincent it's not like I'm walking out of your life forever." she insisted.

"Well its sure hell feels that way." he snapped. "I mean how long are we talking here? Six months, a year?"

"I don't know, maybe. You really can't put a time limit on it."

"Are you sure this about us and not you?"

"Don't do this," she said.

"No really. You think I am rushing into things asking you to marry me. Your reasoning's being that we have baggage, which I might add most couples have entering a relationship but you wish us to unload it before I commit to you. But I believe you're just using that as an excuse because of insecurities you have that you don't want to deal with." he said. "You're so damn afraid that what I feel for you can't be real that you convince yourself of it and duped yourself into believing that my heart isn't fully yours because of the loyalty had to my ex-wife. You would think after all that we've been through and shared should prove that I love you, but apparently you still don't trust me."

"That's not true and you know it." she shot back. "If I didn't trust you or love you, I wouldn't have given myself to you that night in Greece."

"Then I guess it's our love that isn't enough for you to stick it out." he said.

"Vincent...."

"I can't do this right now. If you think this is for the best, then so be it."

He turned on his heel and left her standing there.

CHAPTER 22

Cheyenne strolled along the Boston Common stopping on the bridge, overlooking the waterway. A couple, snuggled together in a swan boat, meandered along the water. She felt a piercing longing, as she watched them. There seemed to be love everywhere she looked. If she did not know any better she would think the Boston Common was *Lover's Lane*. Every time she turned around, couples were walking down the paths hand in hand; enjoying each other's company on the lawn; riding bikes together; or just being a couple period. Romance and marriage had been thrown in her face ever since the day she told Vincent they needed some time away from each other. She did not regret it because it needed to be done but in the same breath, she hoped she had not made a mistake.

The first couple of weeks had been torture because he would not return her calls or speak to her. He even made sure their hearings were not on the same day so he did not have to see her. She had known he would be angry but not that angry to shut her off completely. He wanted to hurt her she realized as she had hurt him. She did not blame him. Her rejection-as he saw it- was what broke the camel's back. Instead of helping, she apparently made it worse by stepping away. She did not know. It had been eleven months since she had seen him and he had not made any contact. She tried to but always got his machine and when she went to see him in Ellsworth, he had not been home. Though it was possible, he was and just refused to answer his door. She should have tried harder. She had given up too easily.

She sat down on a bench, and looked down at the engagement ring that Vincent had given her hanging off the chain that rested against her chest. She thought it was appropriate to wear it around her neck in honor of him and their love even though it was a constant reminder of heartbreak.

Sighing, she took a sip of her bottle water, when she was distracted by a wail. She glanced over at the stroller parked next to her and rested her hand on small, rosy, unhappy infant's tummy.

"Are you hungry," she asked, picking him up.

She cradled him in her arms and grabbed a baby's blanket. She draped it over and proceeded to breast feed him.

A month after her fall out with Vincent, she found out she was pregnant. She had been overfilled with joy but also dread. Here she had pushed him away to test their love and heal, to find out they created a life together. That definitely complicated things. She knew he had a right to know but how would she know he would not come to her out of obligation. He might have wanted to marry her before but knowing he had a child might have more precedence over how he felt about her. For all she knew he could have realized she was right and decided to sever all ties. There had to be doubt or he would not have ignored her this long.

But then again, he could say the same thing about her. She did not exactly go pound on his door and force herself back into this life. Ringing him up a couple times was not much of an effort on her part. She had let her uncertainties and fear get the best of her. It kept her from doing what was right.

Maybe she had been stupid for thinking she knew everything and had authority on how the relationship should go or not go.

She had been reacting to what her gut had told her and her heart. If she had been wrong, she was paying for it a hundred-fold.

She was alone, deprived of Vincent's company and love. She was unwed with a baby in tow. Even though having her son was the best thing that ever happened to her, she felt like God was looking down at her wagging his finger at her for listening to her body, and not her head.

Granted it was not as if it was some one nightstand she had with some guy she met in bar but she was brought in a very moralistic home. You did not go around giving yourself to man because you believed the love you shared was enough of a justification to act on it. The physicality of love was a temptation that was hard resist, she knew this, but once the deed was done you cannot take it back, nor could send back the gift that came with it.

Cheyenne spent the majority of her pregnancy out west in Arizona with her family. She knew they were disappointed in her. They had supported her and understood but she could tell they would have preferred she had been married before baring any children.

She contacted Juliet, who had been compassionate and helpful during the transition. Juliet had promised she would not tell Vincent until she did.

When she returned to Boston, she was determined to introduce her son to his father. The coming weekend, she planned to drive up to Ellsworth and camp out on his doorstep, until he showed up, if that turned out to be the case.

She gazed down on her son and gently stroked his head. Sighing with contentment, she looked out onto the park to see a bunch of college guys play football when her eyes rested on a man a short distance away. It was Vincent. Her stomach did somersaults and her heart began to race. She could feel the blood rushing to her head. What was he doing there, her mind raced? How did he know she be there? Had she summoned him with her thoughts? No that was impossible. It was just coincidental he happened to be on her mind when he decided to show up out of nowhere. She was not prepared, at least not fully. She had planned a speech but that was for when she found herself on his front porch. It would be just like him to ruin her plans.

She stood up as he approached, the blanket slipping off her shoulder. He stopped a couple feet from her. His gaze fell to the baby, who was still nursing. She felt the heat rise in her cheeks as she adjusted the blanket to cover herself.

He looked at her with a mixture of pain and confusion. "You had a baby?"

"Yes." she said, smiling briefly. "This is Michael, your son."

"My son," he said, his voice cracking with emotion. "I have a son?"

"Yes. He's three months old."

"I can't believe this," he said, stepping closer. "When were you going to get around in telling me about him after he graduated out high school?"

"No. I was going to come up to your place this weekend and tell you."

"This weekend!" he ejaculated. "How about eleven months ago?"

"I tried to tell you when I first found out but all I got was the cold shoulder."

"So, you gave up?"

"Vincent it's a two-way street. You could have made an effort to contact me."

"I was trying to abide by your wishes."

"I suggested we take a step back not for you to alienate me."

"I had been angry and hurt Cheyenne. I know that is no excuse but hearing your voice brought pain and seeing you would have been agony that I could not bear. Even when I came to understand and accept your decision, I couldn't bring myself to see you." he shot back. "I'm not trying to make excuses or say it wasn't hard on you too but God Cheyenne we had a child together, a son. His presence should have been enough for you to put aside your fears to tell me. We could have been together and been a family like we intended to be."

"I'm sorry, I didn't mean to keep this from you this long, but I was afraid that our child would bring us together for the wrong reasons."

"Cheyenne I knew I wanted to be with you the rest of my life the day I realized I loved you," he said, stepping closer. "The fact we created a life doesn't change that fact or influence what was already deeply rooted. I get you were scared. You had your doubts that what we had between us was fleeting and temporary. I do not blame you. I started doubting it myself but I am here to tell you it was not. Being away from you these eleven months has only intensified the longing to have you in my life. As for my past, it is always going to be there whether you are with us or not. It is a work in progress and I do not want to spend another day without you because of it. I want us to be together, Cheyenne. I want to create more Michael's with you. I want...."

"You want more children," she said, in surprise.

"Yes, with you I do."

Her eyes filled with tears. "Then we better go find a priest because I'm not conceiving another one unless I have a ring on my finger."

"Then you'll marry me."

"Yes. Didn't I say as..."

He did not let her finish. He reached for her, cocooning their son and kissed her like a man who just came home from a long stay at sea. When he withdrew, he took Michael from her and rested him in the stroller. He returned to her side and slid his hands alongside her neck. He unclasped her dainty silver necklace and took off the ring. He raised her right hand and slid the diamond ring once again on her finger. He kissed it and she said, "This is not what I meant when I said I have to have a ring...."

"I know." he said, smiling. "I'm just putting it back where it belongs. I know I still have to ask your father for your hand in marriage. Then we have to find a church, you a gown, and myself tux, a photographer, a florist, a reception hall, a...."

"Vincent," she said, hooking her arms around him. "Why don't we just go find a church and get married."

"And forget about all the little details?" he said, kissing her.

"We already have the little details, you, Samantha, me and Michael." she said. "That's all we need."

Printed in the USA
CPSIA information can be obtained
at www.ICGtesting.com
BVHW051432270723
667886BV00012B/148